# K-9

## Navigating the Journey

## By Sharolyn L. Sievert

### Illustrated by Emily B. Boote

Trust the true Navigator!

Sharolyn L Sievert
2014

# K-9 Search:
## Navigating the Journey

## By Sharolyn L. Sievert
### Illustrated by Emily B. Boote

ISBN-13: 978-1497391888
ISBN-10: 1497391881

1. Search and Rescue operations – fiction
2. Search dogs – fiction

**Published by: K9 Search Books**

*www.K9SearchBooks.com*

Printed in the United States of America.

# In Honor of K-9 Ariel

*Ariel – Hebrew for "Lion of God"*

*MN Veterinary Medical Association's*
*2013 Professional Animal of the Year*

# And special thanks to

*Renae for her knowledge on the making of maple syrup*

*and*

*Justin for his fascinating information on forestry*

# The Lord will perfect

*that which concerns me. Your mercy, oh Lord, endures forever; do not forsake the works of your own hand.*

*Psalms 138:8*

# *Prologue*

The impact knocked me flat on my face, my nose buried in wet decomposing leaves and pine needles. I had not expected the blow or I might have prevented using my stubby nose as a brake. Landing, the air knocked completely out of my lungs, I couldn't speak and wondered if I had actually broken a rib or two as a searing pain shot through my mid-section.

Lying there, the weight of another human being pinning me down, I considered, not for the first time, why I placed myself in these situations. I had never been exceptionally adventurous or brave. My life has been lived calculating the benefit of the action versus the risk it entailed. Staying safe usually won out. Of course, my rational thought reminded me that no matter what had brought me to this point, the fact remained that I was here.

Shifting, hoping to relieve the pain, I finally managed to pull in enough oxygen to whisper "Get off of me."

"Hold on, don't move." The voice in my ear was familiar and sounded calm, but underlying the calm was a steely order.

Ignoring the order, I arched my back up, hoping to stop the pain. I had figured out it wasn't a broken rib, but a rock the size of Gibraltar that I had landed on. I wanted off that rock.

Even as my body managed to make some headway on getting the two hundred plus pound man off my back, I was suddenly reminded why we were lying there. The silence of the woods was shattered by the report of a rifle. The bullet wasn't far off target, hitting the tree just above our heads and showering us with bark and needles.

Even as I instinctively flattened once again on the horrible rock, I realized I had no idea where my dog was. He had been ranging ahead of us, his blaze orange vest making him an easy target for the crazed rifleman, whoever he was.

"Where is my dog?" I tried to lift my head to look, only to hear another rifle shot, and a new covering of bark clearly reflected it was aimed at us.

"Stop moving. Your dog is over to our right and so far, whoever it is, hasn't shot at him."

"I'm having a hard time breathing. Seriously; I landed on a big rock that is nearly going through me. It hurts – can you try to slide off?" With incrementally slow movements, the officer who only came along for the walk, moved.

Taking a deep and sweet breath of air, I tried to move off the rock without incurring another shot in my direction. I've never been shot at before; I never wanted it to happen again. Part of me wanted to just get up and run as fast and as far as I could. Part of me wanted to remain exactly where I was until it was all over with, and it was safe to move again.

Finding someplace in the middle, I was able to lift my head without moving much. I was looking for my dog. Ariel, seemingly unaware that our lives were in danger, was still working. Doing the job he was trained to do. Doing the job I had trained him to do, placing us both in this position.

It was my fault I had agreed to go out on this search. It was my decision and no one else's. The others from Elk Ridge Search and Rescue who were out here in the woods had agreed to follow my lead. They were also my responsibility. If any of them were injured or killed, I don't know if I could live with myself.

Shifting my rapidly cooling body, I drew more fire in our direction and a harsh word from the man who had just saved my life.

It had started so simply. Could we come? A man went out to gather maple syrup and didn't come home. As far as they knew, he wasn't armed or dangerous.

Either our missing person had more firepower than anyone realized, or there was someone else out here in the middle of the woods who didn't want us there.

# Chapter 1

*Oh Lord, you have searched me, and know me.*

Some mornings are harder to get through than others. This morning was one of them. I had gotten up on time, but discovered that someone had thrown up during the night. I stepped in it with my bare foot, which is how I found out.

Washing my foot was easy; cleaning the carpet they chose to use was another story altogether. Why is that dogs, if given a choice, will always pick carpeting and not hard flooring to have their accidents on?

Neither dog laid claim to the mess, but as Ari walked by it to leave the room and Jael went clearly out of her way to avoid the area, I had my suspicions it was the latter that was responsible. Unlike humans, my dogs didn't usually return to the scene of the crime for fear of being blamed for it.

I managed to get my shower only fifteen minutes late, and made up part of the time by not caring what I grabbed from the closet. It ended up being a pair of jeans and a green wind shirt over a white polo. I had three white polo shirts hanging in my closet. Each had a different logo; one was for the Minnesota Vikings, one for a national K-9 organization, and one simply had "K-9 SAR" embroidered on it. I had no idea which one was under the wind shirt, but rather hoped it wasn't the Vikings as it would seem odd to wear green over the purple and gold.

I started my coffee and grabbed a fig bar that had become a recent addiction to go with my morning cup of Joe. I used the excuse it was all natural so, therefore, healthy. Of course, my mom still claimed the coffee was black poison that would eventually kill me, so I guess the coffee cancelled out the fig benefits.

Taking the dogs outside to our fenced backyard, I rushed them along in their normal morning business. Returning to the house, tripping over the dogs as we hurried, I put together their breakfast.

We had recently changed our dog feeding plans. Jael, my beautiful but crazy search and rescue K-9 partner, had developed what appeared to be grain allergies. Taking the advice of my best friend and K-9 mentor, Bev, I had switched them to a raw food diet.

The biggest difference we noticed immediately was my mom no longer liked to feed my dogs. She never has appreciated the finer points of feeding them; handling raw meat on their behalf only increased her distaste for the job.

Putting a raw chicken wing in each bowl, I added some chunks of beef heart and pureed vegetables. I knew Jael would eat anything; and had, just about. Ari, on the other hand, was much pickier about what went into his mouth. At ten years of age, I gave him credit for knowing his own mind. After all, I hate broccoli and while I had to eat it as a child, as an adult, I no longer felt I had to.

Putting the dish down, Ari immediately sniffed each item and then looked up at me with a baleful expression that clearly said "do you really expect me to eat this?"

In the time he made his non-verbal assessment, Jael had inhaled the entire contents of her dish and was heading straight for his. Mom and I had learned to stand guard over Ari and his food dishes. Jael was reaping the rewards of living with a picky eater; she was getting plump stealing his food.

Nudging my older dog, I reminded him Jael would be perfectly happy to eat his food if he didn't. And I was perfectly willing to let her do it if he didn't hurry up.

Is it wrong to lie to a dog? Yes, it actually is. I recanted and simply said he'd regret not eating his breakfast in about two hours. As if understanding me, he began eating one small bite at a time. The wing was carefully lifted out of his dish and dropped, his lips slightly pulled back as if it might contaminate his mouth. Yes, dropped on the carpeting near his food dish, not on the linoleum.

As if on cue, Jael slid past my leg like a small tiger shark and snatched a mouthful of beef heart before retreating to her designated wait corner. I had no way to get the meat out of her mouth; she swallowed it whole within a millisecond of grabbing it.

Ari, now looking aggrieved at the theft, gobbled the chicken wing he had planned to abandon moments before. He finished what was left in the bowl, licking it clean as if to tell me it was quite a tasty breakfast after all and not nearly enough.

Struggling between impatience, anger and frustration, I picked up the bowls, rinsed them and dropped them to drain in the sink. Pouring myself a well-earned cup of coffee, lots of sugar and cream, I headed for the door. Even as my hand connected with the knob, I heard my mom.

"Rebekkah, did you forget?"

I stood there, trying to remember if I had forgotten something. And if so, what it was I had forgotten. I had fed the dogs, yes. I had my coffee and fig bar. I had the mail that needed to go out. What was it I had forgotten this time?

"I don't know Mom, did I forget something?" I hated it when I forgot things. I had too much on my mind lately.

"You were going to bring me into town today. I need to do some shopping."

I had forgotten. Since we had moved out here to no man's land, mom had to plan her shopping. Once to twice a month was shopping day, and usually on the second or fourth Tuesday because that is when Martha and Margaret made walleye for lunch.

Waiting, now very impatiently, for my mom, I contemplated my day. I was nearly twenty minutes late for work. Granted, I was one of the owners, but that didn't give me any license to be late. McCaffrey House worked on a slender staff of dedicated employees, and I was one of them.

Mom finally came out and I watched as she made her way across the icy path to the circle of bricked driveway. When we first arrived, weeds grew and thrived from between the bricks. The entire summer we fought skirmishes with those weeds. Sometimes it appeared we were winning, but then they'd reappear. Winter won the battle by covering the weeds with snow. I knew, however, the war wasn't over. Come spring, they'd be back.

Arriving at McCaffrey House, I acknowledged the gardens with a smile. They were now shrouded in burlap and snow for the winter, but they were cared for with love by our maintenance man, Harold. In the spring, they would bud, blossom and bloom with color and beauty. Harold didn't appear to have to wage war on weeds. I think they simply acknowledged his superiority and died a swift death.

I remembered the first time I saw this place; the gardens that begged for attention and the wood logs that made up the exterior walls glowing warm in the sun. I still loved the view, with the house framed by the amazingly large trees that lined the drive.

Entering in through the garage, I trotted up the stairs that brought me into the back hall that, if I turned right, would lead to

4

the apartment that ran over the length of the garage. If I turned left, it would bring me to the main part of the house. I used to live in that apartment and muscle memory, trained to go right, had to be retrained to go left.

I went left and quickly assessed that in my absence, my staff of five had already set up the breakfast buffet for our guests and I was definitely late.

Swinging through the floor-length café doors, I greeted our cooks, Margaret and Martha. They were really chefs in their own right; however they never went to school to get a title. They put out food that made people want to eat and ask for the recipe later. We even had guests who recommended McCaffrey House simply because of the food.

The caramel rolls were coming out of the oven as I walked in, Margaret flipping the pan over to release them and let the sugary goodness melt down into the rolls. It made me hungry just watching her.

As I watched, I saw the beautiful little diamond on her left ring finger. It still startled me, that shiny bit of metal on that frail, blue-veined hand. It was a strong hand, but clearly one that belonged to an elderly woman. The ring, winking at me in the light, was a constant reminder that she no longer lived in the apartment over the garage with her sister Martha. She now lived with her new husband just a mile away.

Martha, as if following my train of thought, touched me with her own aging hand, giving my arm a gentle squeeze. It was a silent reassurance she was still alright with her sister's decision to marry.

They had been spinsters, the two of them living together, cooking in their own cafe for many years. In their eighties, they looked as different as night and day. Martha, short and round, was opinionated and had nearly driven her sister away rather than accept the marriage.

Margaret, when I met her years ago, was thin and serious. Now, she glowed from within and, amazingly, had even put on a pound or two since her marriage to Jack Hedstrom.

Smiling back at Martha, I went about my tasks for the morning, which was to help move the food from the kitchen to the buffet area. Someone had once asked me if we purposely vented the baking smells into the rooms. My response was we didn't need to. People would find the food no matter what, and sure enough, many of our guests were already waiting.

McCaffrey House was my idea, not that I did it all myself. My mom would be the first to tell people that Rebekkah comes up with some good ideas, but executing them isn't in her repertoire. She was right. In this case, I had the idea, but it took help to get McCaffrey House up and running.

Pop McCaffrey, the original owner, had gone along with my idea of turning his amazing lodge-like home into a Bed and Breakfast for people with disabilities. A place where people could come and be treated to the beauty of the north woods of Minnesota, and even enjoy the activities we do here, such as snowshoeing, ice fishing, hiking, and canoeing.

Pop was gone now, but he left McCaffrey House as a legacy to his wife Virginia, whom he lost many years previously. Virginia had been wheelchair-bound much of her life, and it had pleased him to see others like her enjoying his home.

He willed the ownership of the business to five people, three of whom worked here fulltime; Martha, Margaret and me. In addition to us, there was Margaret's husband Jack and the man who had introduced me to Pop, Adam Drahota.

With the buffet up and running, my job changed from delivery to service. If someone wasn't able to serve themselves from the buffet, I'd do it for them; or I'd take their empty plates away as they went for seconds, or refilled their cups as they chatted with the other guests. We had found by serving the meals at a communal table, our guests became family. It was a good feeling that made the B&B not just survive, but thrive.

Breakfast over, I made the normal announcements about things to do and places to visit. It was March, so there was still plenty of snow on the ground for people to enjoy a snowshoe, or a dog-sled trip, or just a visit around the town.

Elk Ridge had been a slowly dying community when McCaffrey House opened. The young families were moving away, leaving only the elderly. That had changed in the past few years. Several small storefronts had opened and prospered, among them an exclusive little candy shop as well as a gift shop, both that focused on Minnesota products. I heard that the hand-harvested wild rice and maple sugar candy were the most popular items sold.

As the guests departed, the real work began for my staff. Martha and Margaret were done for the moment, but that left the clean-up to Agnes, Bella, Megan and me. Agnes and Bella disappeared to tackle making up the rooms clean and fresh while Megan and I handled the remains of the breakfast buffet.

As we worked, I saw Connie emerge from the apartment she shared with Martha. A longtime friend and one of my search and rescue mentors many years ago, Connie had fallen on some rough times recently. It dawned on me that she likely had been prompted to get up by The Sisters, who retired to the apartment after mealtime was over.

Connie's story, like so many, started when she lost her job. Without income, she then lost her home to foreclosure. The downward spiral continued as she had to find a place to live for herself and her two children.

To be honest, I had expected her long before now to show up in Elk Ridge. She had, or at least I had believed she had, developed a relationship with our local pastor. Instead, she moved in with another man, and at that point, we sort of lost touch.

I didn't know what happened after that; nor had I asked. I was uncomfortable with the decisions she had made, and wishing them unmade did no good. However, when Pastor Dave Michaels approached me a few months ago with her situation, I had done what I could to help; partly, because of our long-time friendship; partly because of guilt.

Connie arrived at Elk Ridge just before Margaret's wedding. Needing a place to heal and recuperate from life in general, we made the agreement she could stay in Margaret's old room in exchange for helping out around McCaffrey.

I had hoped she'd settle down in Elk, get a job, possibly even join our K-9 SAR unit, and make a life for herself here. That hadn't happened quite yet. I hoped in time, however, it would happen.

"Connie, how are you doing today? I sort of expected to see you this morning in the kitchen with The Sisters." We had taken to calling Martha and Margaret "The Sisters", likely because they tended to call each other "Sister". It had the downside of causing those that didn't know them to assume they were Catholic nuns.

8

It wouldn't have been a downside, except Margaret had startled some people by kissing her husband when he picked her up one night. And it wasn't a brotherly kiss either.

Connie glanced up at me, and I wondered if I detected a glint of something unknown, unreadable in her eyes as she responded.

"I'm sorry Rebekkah; I wasn't feeling all that great this morning. I only just woke up and was coming to find out if I can help." She did look tough this morning, with bags under her eyes. Perhaps I was only imagining the strange look.

"If you're not feeling well, maybe you'd prefer to stay in the apartment? Don't want to spread germs around here!" Megan offered it lightly, but I glanced at her as it didn't sound like Megan to be negative, even in a light way.

"Oh, I don't think I'm sick. I just didn't sleep well last night. I'll be alright. What can I do to help?"

Tasks were given, and just as we started, my cell phone rang. It only rang for two things. My mom calling to tell me my dog, namely Jael, had done something wrong. The other reason was there was a search for a missing person. I rarely got calls for anything else. Mom was out shopping and Jael was at home. It had to be a search call.

"Elk Ridge Search and Rescue, how can we help you?" I kept my voice business-like as I also didn't recognize the number that came up.

"Rebekkah? This is Sam at the market. Your mom just collapsed. We called an ambulance, she seems really dizzy and isn't able to stand up or anything."

"What? Is the ambulance there yet? Should I come there or go to the hospital? What happened?" I was heading for the door when I realized that my mom, while handicapped, could still drive and had my truck with her.

"Megan – do you have your car here?" She rode with Agnes to work whenever she could to save money, but today I prayed she had her car with her.

"Sure, what happened? What's wrong?" Megan rummaged through her purse as I listened to Sam explaining that my mom had gone in as normal, was shopping using the little motorized cart they had, when she suddenly said she didn't feel very good. A moment later, she said she was very dizzy and had fallen out of the seat. Thankfully she hadn't hit her head or anything; she just slid to the floor.

Megan was just handing me her keys when a hand pushed them away. I don't know how he had done it, but our sheriff had come into the kitchen without making a sound.

"Rebekkah, I was driving by when I heard the dispatch. I'll drive you to the hospital. Don't worry; I'm sure she'll be fine."

Connie suddenly came to life, putting her hand on Sheriff Rafael's arm as she said to me, "I'll help Megan – you go ahead Rebekkah. She maybe just ate something or, well, I don't know, but we'll be fine here."

As I followed Sheriff Benjamin Rafael out the door, I could see her taking charge. I only hoped Megan would accept it for the time being, because in reality, Megan should be the person in charge when I left.

# Chapter 2

*You know my sitting down and my rising up;*

We rode quietly, Benjamin and me. Years of friendship had created a bond that didn't require conversation. The only show of emotion he had was when he took my hand as we drove. I was grateful for the company and that I didn't have to drive. My hands were actually shaking and I hadn't realized it until I felt his hand, steady and strong, on mine.

The trip to the hospital took nearly an hour. I hadn't been to Mercy Hospital in a very long time, and then it was for a friend's heart attack. Now I had my mom here and no idea why.

"Benjamin, my truck is likely still at Sam's. Do you think well, maybe Pastor Dave or Adam might be willing to help get it here for me?" He simply nodded, and I had a suspicion he was already figuring out the logistics.

Entering the emergency room doors, I found the desk and explained who I was. Sit and wait was the response. I sat. I waited. The television was tuned to the endless talk shows people watch now, and there wasn't a single interesting or current magazine to be found. Feeling somewhat helpless, I slipped out the door and called my siblings to let them know. I forgot it was during normal working hours until I reached voice mail after voice mail. They may live hours and states away, but their work hours weren't much different than mine. I simply left messages.

When I returned, I found a nurse waiting for me and I was escorted into a small curtained enclosure where my mom sat on the edge of the bed.

"I'm alright Rebekkah, honestly. I don't know what happened, I just got really dizzy. I still am, but it is getting better. They said my blood pressure was really high. It's always been

11

low, you know that." She sounded defensive, so I wondered if the doctor was after her about her health.

"Yes, mom, I know. You pride yourself on it. Probably had escalated due to the stress of all this." I nodded around the ER room.

"No, it was much too high to write it off to that. I'm Dr. Hansen, and her blood pressure was 175 over 90. That is up into the hypertension range." I turned to meet a very petite woman with blonde hair pulled up onto her head where it splayed out like a water fountain.

"What happened? What's wrong?" I had been trained as a medical first responder, and I knew the normal blood pressure for adults. My mom's was perilously close to stroke range.

"Well, the dizziness could be caused by Meniere's Disease. That is simply an issue with the inner ear that can cause spontaneous episodes of vertigo. Such as your mom just experienced. The only problem is we don't usually see such high blood pressure too. But what we may be seeing are symptoms of two different things."

"What do we do?" I had never heard of this disease, and I could tell by mom's face, she hadn't either. The good doctor wasn't offering any help either.

"She's only had one episode; usually we don't test or treat until there are more definitive symptoms or more episodes. For now, go home, see how things go. If it recurs, contact your local physician."

"I can go home?" Mom's voice still sounded stressed, but I guess that would be normal under the circumstances.

"You can sit here if you need to for a bit, but yes, you can go home." With that, the fountain head of blonde hair on the tiny body left the room.

"Mom, I don't know if we have a way to get home yet. I asked Benjamin to see if they could get the truck driven over here, but not sure there has been enough time."

"That's fine. I'll take my time getting ready to leave. I'm much better, but I still feel very odd."

As I left the room, a nurse caught my attention and said I needed to stop up at the front desk. There, I found the keys to my truck. To my amazement, not only had my truck arrived, but it had been topped off with fuel, and our groceries were in the back.

Mom slept most of the way home, and by the time we arrived, she felt nearly back to normal. It was only mid-afternoon, but too late to drive back to McCaffrey to be of much help. Calling, I told Megan that I'd be back in the morning, only to be reminded that it was my day off; nothing like a crisis to make one lose one's bearings. I followed up my previous voice messages to my siblings, explaining not to worry, everything seemed fine for now.

Taking the dogs out, we went for a long snowshoe, something we didn't get to do very often anymore with my work schedule.

I loved watching my dogs as they raced through the snow. No matter what happened in my own life, the dogs took things in stride. They maintained a steady course through life. Eat, sleep, work, and play, that's the life. And for these two, work was play. They didn't understand that in looking for missing people, they were doing a very serious task.

Returning home, we played in the yard with their favorite toys, two very large and very purple balls designed for horses. Ari, as if inspired by playing with a horse toy, suddenly reared and stomped his front feet on the ground, giving his ball a good

shake. Laughing, I informed them it was time to go in, and monitored them as they each carried their respective balls into the small garage.

I fixed dinner for the dogs and for my mom and myself that night. I didn't cook often, but I could cook. Tonight it was pancakes and eggs. As we ate, I could see that my mom, while tired, was perfectly fine. If anything, she was simply embarrassed about the whole thing. Still, it worried me. Should she even be driving?

"Your sister and brothers called while you were out with the dogs. I told them I was fine, it was just an odd episode and the doctor sent me home; nothing to worry about." She looked steadily at me, as if waiting for me to confirm what she had told the others.

"That's what the doctor said I guess. If it happens again, this dizziness, we just go in to Dr. Sheffield." Gary Sheffield was the local doctor and we all liked him very much. He was nearing retirement himself, so the town of Elk Ridge was a good fit for him as well as for the community. We didn't require a great deal of care out here, and what we did, he could generally handle.

That night, as my dogs tried to take over my bed, my phone went off. Flipping it open, I responded sleepily, "Elk Ridge Search and Rescue, how can we help?"

"This the K-9 group? We have a missing guy that wandered away from a drug rehab home. He's vulnerable, and while he was wearing a coat and boots, it is getting cold out. Can you come?"

Flipping on a light, I grabbed my reading glasses and the pad of paper that was always at my bedside.

"Sure; can we get some information from you first?" At the grunted assent, I asked the first major question that normally I didn't need to ask, "What agency are you calling from?"

"Oh, it is my cousin's friend. I mean, I'm not connected with an agency or whatever. Billy, well, he was doing meth there for a while, but he's off the stuff and wants to get clean. The only thing is he hates this place they put him, and he left last night. They told my cousin's family, and the police are out looking, but we want to bring the dogs too."

"Okay; sure I understand. What you need to do is have your law enforcement agency call us. We can't deploy without their request. You see, they generally have a search strategy and plan, and often have their own resources, or know if the situation would warrant using a search and rescue K-9."

It wasn't often we got calls from families, but it did happen. Often it was simply because Law Enforcement didn't know that K-9 resources were available, and once the family notified them of the options, they did call. Just as often, however, they didn't want to use them because of previous bad experiences. Or, Law Enforcement knows something the family doesn't which would prevent using civilian resources. It was still hard to explain all that in a midnight phone call to a stressed out family.

It took a few minutes of further explaining, but in doing so, I learned the location and situation. Knowing it was unlikely we'd be called, I still started our unit's calling tree. If Law Enforcement wanted us, we needed to be prepared to go.

No follow-up call was received, although I was awake most of the night, just waiting. Had I fallen asleep, I'm sure they would have called. In the morning, I checked the internet for any news. One always worried about the missing people that we don't get called to help.

It was a small blurb in that community's news site that I finally found that William "Billy" Chester had driven away in a stolen vehicle from the drug rehabilitation facility and was caught in the wee hours, two counties away, and charged with grand theft as well as driving while under the influence.

I sent the link to my unit members so they would know what happened. While dogs have been known to track a missing person in a moving vehicle, it wasn't something that comes under normal SAR response. This is especially true if the missing person also stole the vehicle and was drinking at the time.

That resolved, I continued my morning routine and was glad to hear my mom moving around. They were good sounds, normal sounds. Perhaps yesterday really had been a fluke, but I wasn't convinced. I had noticed in the last few months she had been

16

more tired than usual; that she had become more forgetful and seemed to stress out much faster than normal. I attributed it to her aging, but maybe it was this Meniere's thing.

Today was a training day however, and I was looking forward to it. I hated to admit that I wanted to put mom's problems out of my mind; she did seem alright this morning. Besides, we had been so busy with Margaret's wedding last month; training had taken a back seat.

Pulling together my gear, my dogs followed me around as close as they could. Too close, as twice I stepped on Jael's feet and another time one of them tripped me. All it took was grabbing my boots and they knew.

Finally geared up, I loaded the dogs into the truck and started the ninety minute drive to the training area. It was a state park that allowed us to train off-leash, and was large enough to actually challenge the teams. This week was Al Cook's turn to set up our training.

Arriving at the park entrance, I took advantage of arriving early to renew my annual park pass. As I was leaning through the open passenger door of my Yukon, peeling the old sticker off, someone slapped me from behind.

Glancing over my shoulder, I thanked Marge for the greeting and told her to hand me the new sticker. Marge didn't work a dog, but was a terrific asset to our unit.

"Can I ride with you to the area? Al said there isn't a lot of parking down there." Marge carefully peeled part of the backing off the sticker and handed it to me.

"Sure, you can throw your gear in beside Jael. She'll bark..."

"Yes, I know, I just ignore her. If she's polite, I'll give her a snack."

I knew as soon as Marge opened the back door because Jael lit off in a fit of barking. Just as suddenly it went silent and I smiled as I heard Marge praise Jael for being quiet. We'd been working on this problem for quite some time but had made little progress so far, and it was very frustrating to me.

Pulling off the park's main road, we drove down ever smaller roads until we were on the final minimum maintenance road that was covered in slushy wet snow. The truck bucked from one side to the other on ruts left by the previous vehicles. We finally arrived at our destination, which was normally off-limits during the winter months. Al had gotten permission, somehow, to let us train in there.

Crawling out, Marge and I stopped and stretched out our backs. One thing I'd learned in doing SAR, either you threw your back into whack on some of the drives we made, or you threw it out. Mine was out.

We checked in and I counted heads as people arrived. Everyone from the unit had shown up; Al Cook, Amos Taylor, Marge Lee, Karen Poling, Chris Kohlstadt, and Al's wife Paula. Paula wasn't technically a member, but she usually attended trainings and helped out when we needed hiders or someone to tag along with a K-9 team. There were also two people I didn't recognize. One was clearly paying attention, one wasn't. Yet, they appeared to have come to the training together.

Al took control of the briefing and introduced the new people as Craig and Peggy Lundquist. Further introductions would wait until after training when we sat down to coffee someplace to warm up.

18

Assignments were given out based on Al's made-up scenario. A couple had gone hiking and camping in the park; however they didn't return as planned. Their vehicle was still in the lot where they parked it, and the park rangers had done a hasty search of the campsite. To add authenticity to his briefing, Al motioned to someone who I hadn't noticed, and realized it was, actually, a park ranger.

"Hello folks, glad you're here today. I'm Erick Vanderwal with the Park Service. We did locate the couple's campsite, and did a hasty around it," the man hesitated, a half-smile crossing his face, and I knew he felt rather silly doing the play-acting. Still, he pulled it together and continued, "We located numerous snowshoe tracks around the site, and did attempt to follow them. However, they were very confusing and we weren't able to find out where they actually went."

His job done, the ranger smiled and as quickly as he could, fled the scene. Al waited until the ranger had pulled away in his truck before adding, "Obviously Park Rangers don't have lawful jurisdiction, the county sheriff does, but his information is important to our search. He or other rangers here today may stop and watch and talk to people about the dogs and SAR. Don't be nervous, they really are just curious."

Turning, Al pulled a clipboard off the hood of his truck and flipped a page on it. Glancing around, he finally made eye contact with Amos.

"Amos, we want you and Powder to attempt a track from the campsite. You'll need to drive over there, is that alright? We didn't want everyone to park on top of the place we know our missing persons last were," as an aside, he said to Craig, "We call it the point last scene," before proceeding, "So we staged here. Craig, you expressed an interest in seeing the bloodhound work, here is your opportunity. Be aware that it is snowy out there, so

19

use your snowshoes. If you need a pair, Rebekkah usually has a spare she can lend you." He pointed toward me, so I raised my hand to help locate where I was.

"Rebekkah, do you mind running tech behind Amos? Then Karen, I'd like you and Chief to work an area north of the campsite, and Chris, you and Onyx to work an area to the west. The areas to the east would be swamp and water. Open water due to the natural springs, guys, so if we have to go in there, wear appropriate gear. To the south is the main road which seems a lower probability as they could find their way back if they went that way."

We organized ourselves into groups, and I tossed my snowshoes and pack into Amos's truck next to a snoring and drooling Bloodhound. Craig had brought his own snowshoes, but I could see they were the inexpensive plastic type for play, not wilderness, so I added my second pair to the pile.

At the campsite, we sorted out the equipment. Craig decided to stay with his own shoes as he was used to them. Amos, a gentle kind soul if there ever was one, told him to take five steps off trail and come back and then decide for sure. We watched as he took first one, then a second step off the beaten path by the campsite.

The small plastic snowshoes creaked as they were put under pressure of his weight against the soft snow. A moment later, Craig was stuck and unable to pull the shoes up out of the deep snow. I was glad to see him smile instead of get angry. Good attitudes in adverse or embarrassing situations are imperative in SAR.

Helping him out, we switched him over to my spare shoes and within minutes, he was easily maneuvering around as Amos geared up Powder.

The big girl huffed the air as the harness was being strapped on. Turning, she studied a direction to the north and huffed again. Then, with great energy, she swung her giant head back and forth, nearly shaking herself off her feet. Drool, previously hanging harmlessly from her jowls, was sent flying some twenty feet to either side of her. I had learned to stand directly in front of or directly behind a bloodhound. We forgot to warn Craig as a string of sticky drool landed across his chest.

"Craig, let it dry, then it will peel right off. Seriously, don't try to wipe it off!" It was too late. The drool was now smeared across his very nice coat.

Amos didn't bother to apologize. Bloodhounds drool; it is a fact of nature. If you're around them, you will get it on you. They also stink. They are, however, amazing trackers, and any good Bloodhound handler will tell you that the tracking makes up for the drool and smell.

The scent article of one of the camping party was presented to Powder, and she huffed again. With no hesitation, she turned and snuffed the ground around the campsite. Her long ears dragged along the ground and her eyes were completely shrouded by the wrinkles of skin. She didn't care. Her whole focus was now on the odors coming into her muzzle.

Realizing that the maze of tracks was also a maze of odor for his dog, Amos took her thirty feet further out from the campsite and let her cast out again. I knew his goal was to sign-cut the most recent trail, and took the time to explain it to Craig.

"Close by the campsite, the odor is all over and leads everywhere and nowhere. So, Amos has taken Powder away from the heavy concentration of odor to see if she can locate the most recent trail leading away by crossing her over the top of it. We walk perpendicular to the trails leading away. Watch her head."

21

It was the trail that went north, the one she had huffed and stared at before even being given the scent article. Dogs, as they gain experience, learn to hunt for the missing man odor before they're even presented an article to sniff. In this case, my only and best guess is that Powder, smelling the overpowering odor of the campsite and its occupants, was searching for the hottest trail out. She ignored the smell of the rangers because their scent wasn't as strong. Theory only, and I knew a younger, less experienced dog, would likely not have made that connection.

When a Bloodhound goes, they go full-steam. Powder was no exception as she yanked Amos forward, her head low and steady on a snowshoe trail. If you've never run in snowshoes, it's an experience. I usually end up with bruises on my shins as the toe of the shoes comes up out of the snow and slaps my leg. Craig, not used to the shoes, or in running in them, went down quickly.

"AMOS! Slow your dog down if you can!" I turned and helped Craig up. The other downside of snowshoes is, if you do go down, the shoes can tangle you up and make it even harder to regain your standing position.

Back on our feet, I gave him some tips for moving faster, and turned to catch up with the dog team I was supposed to be supporting. Grabbing the radio I had been issued by Paula, I let base know that we were heading on a track to the north.

There was a pause at the other end, a long pause, which made me wonder what was going on. There was no other radio traffic to explain it. Finally, I heard Paula's voice come back, "Are you sure you mean the north trail?"

"Yes, north trail. We are definitely going north." I was now starting to pant a bit. Snowshoeing is an excellent cardio-vascular workout, so trying to talk at the same time can be more difficult.

"Please check with your handler if he's sure his dog is on trail."

At that moment, I knew that the scenario was blown. Something had gone wrong. Base knew which trail the person was supposed to have left from the campsite. And apparently it wasn't supposed to be the north trail.

"Amos, did you hear that?" I called forward to the man behind the dog that was throwing herself head-long into her harness.

"Yes, and tell them I'm going with my dog on this one."

"Base, this is K-9 Alpha. Handler will continue this trail at this time. If that changes, we will let you know." Craig had caught up and, amazingly, was keeping up with us.

"What's wrong?"

"Base knows how they set this training up. It sounds to me like perhaps either the dog is off trail, or the person they have hiding took the wrong trail out of the campsite. Not sure which yet, but I trust Powder's nose. Too often the human in the equation doesn't always follow directions."

"Okay. I understand. I think…so the person who laid the trail might have taken the wrong one?" I nodded, glad he understood quickly.

We went another hundred yards when suddenly Powder stopped and circled back. Backing up in snowshoes is nearly impossible as the tail of the shoes generally gets caught in snow clumps or anything under the snow, like brush or rocks. Turns are accomplished by navigating a small pirouette in one spot without stepping on your own snowshoes, or walking in a large circle, depending on space and conditions. I waited to see what would happen before making the effort to turn around.

Powder huffed in every direction, studied Craig and me as if she realized we were there for the first time; and likely, for her, we were. Still she hesitated.

"Did the trail run out Amos?" It was hard for me to see, but it looked like the snowshoe tracks continued on.

"Yes for the dog, but there are still tracks going north. About ten yards back, there was a split in the trail. I'm going to take her back there."

We turned around, with me explaining to Craig the best way to do so. Arriving back at the split, we could see there were snowshoe marks heading the other way as well. They went to the west, and Powder, with only a minimal huff, took off down the new trail. She had simply missed the turn in her haste.

"K9 Alpha to base." I paused and waited for the response. Even as I released the mic key, I heard K9 Charlie radio in. They had found a potential clue. I had no idea which area Charlie was in, but had to wait patiently for base to get their information recorded before they responded back to my call.

"Base, we have a change of direction to the west. K-9 is working well and we are all in good shape here." Figured I might as well update them on our situation and our health and wellness check at the same time.

"Received K9 Alpha. You are now heading west. Can you provide the coordinates for our map?" I did so, using my GPS to give them the information.

"Craig, can you see Powder?" Amos called over his shoulder and both Craig and I looked forward. I recognized what I was seeing because I had worked with this team often. Craig only looked quizzically at me.

"That is known as a proximity alert. See her front feet? We call it Powder's happy dance. She's getting very close to a strong source of the odor she's trying to locate." We watched as Powder's front feet danced up and down as she moved forward.

"You mean the missing person?"

"It could be the missing person. It could be clothes or gear if they happened to take them off. It could be a place where the person hunkered down for a long period of time and left a pool of their smell there."

In this case, it was our missing person. I didn't recognize the face, but realized by his uniform, that he was a member of the Civil Air Patrol. Powder was clearly proud of herself as she carefully and gently pawed at the young man. He was comfortably snuggled in a warm sleeping bag in a small windfall of tree branches and from all appearances, was playing on his smart phone at the time of the find.

"K9 Alpha to Base, we'd like to notify you that team Zulu has joined our group." Zulu was our new code word that the subject has been located alive and well, and able to move on their own.

"Affirmative K9 Alpha; is Zulu able to offer any information that we could use at this time?" Smiling back at Craig, I interpreted for him.

"Base wants to make sure we interview our hider here. In the real world, he wouldn't be a hider, he'd be a possible missing subject, a potential witness, or even someone totally unrelated to our search. No matter what, we should ask questions and find out what they might know."

"Hello there, my name is Amos with Elk Ridge Search and Rescue. The dog there is Powder. She'd love it if you would give her this toy to play with," Amos handed the CAP cadet a small stuffed bunny.

"Did she find me?" He asked, almost in wonder. He held out the smelly little toy and then patted Powder's giant head.

"Yes, it appears she did. Can you tell me your name?" Amos asked it casually, but he was still interviewing and needed the information.

"Oh, yes, I'm Jerry and my friend – no, my girlfriend and I were camping. We decided to go snowshoeing, but she got mad at me and took off. I guess she knows the area, but I got lost." He smiled up at Amos, and I knew he had relayed the information he was supposed to for Al's scenario.

"K9 Alpha to Base," I paused and listened to the response to go ahead before continuing, "Zulu has provided us with additional information. Do you want me to call it in or relay via radio?"

Again, Craig's eyebrows went up. I whispered, "Sometimes on a real search the family or media may be sitting right next to the radio, and we don't want to give them sensitive information. Sometimes, like today, it doesn't really matter. We still need to train for the reality though."

"Go ahead with the information Alpha."

"Zulu has changed call sign to Jerry at this time."

I waited as Amos asked Jerry if he remembered where his girlfriend had split off with him, or what direction she had taken. She had gone north, but he didn't really remember where it was.

Amos nodded at me and I relayed the information to base that another person had likely gone to the northeast of our current location. We had gone north and split off to the west. Based on the direction of travel at the split, we believe Jerry's supposed-girlfriend Sheila had continued north.

With that information given, we helped Jerry pick up his things and made our way back to the campsite. Powder carried her stuffed bunny the entire way back, and I knew she'd fall asleep in the truck with it between her front paws and under her wet muzzle. Amos periodically washed it, but the bunny was permanently stained and smelly. It was also completely intact; Powder never chewed or tugged with her toy, it was merely to carry and hold gently.

As we drove back to base, Jerry wedged in beside us, we listened to the radio traffic from K-9 Charlie and K-9 Bravo, otherwise known to us as Karen with K-9 Chief and Chris with K-9 Onyx. Bravo / Onyx had gone to the north - that much I remembered. A moment later, Amos said something about Bravo being to the west.

"No, Amos, I think Onyx is working the north, isn't she?" I'm nothing, if not stubborn. Amos, knowing it, just said, "Possibly," and fell silent.

I couldn't let it drop that easily however. I knew he was humoring me. "Really Amos, I'm sure that Al said he was sending Onyx to the north side. Chief was going to work to the west." I had my steam up and to be honest, I'm not sure why it was so important to me to be correct. Perhaps it was because I was worried about my own memory lately.

Craig, glancing between us, simply said, "Not sure who is who, but whoever it is, sounds like the team going north has a better chance of finding the other hider."

Jerry, as if suddenly waking up, said, "You just never know."

All three of us looked at him, and I realized Al had likely created yet another twist in his search scenario for us. After all, the cadaver dogs hadn't worked yet.

# Chapter 3

*You understand my thoughts from afar off.*

Base appeared to be in complete control of the search, although I could see that Al was off to one side with the park ranger, who had returned in our absence.

Taking advantage of the lull in the action for myself, I called home to check on my mom. All was well; she was busy working on the budget. Feeling more and more that the episode was a chance occurrence, I returned my attention to the mock search.

"Everyone, please gather around; we have new information coming in that will perhaps alter our priority areas." Al waved his long arms and soon everyone at our incident command post was circled around him, "First, K-9 Chief located an article north of the campsite which appears to belong to our second missing person." He indicated a point on the map for everyone's benefit. The only thing I noticed was Al's glance my way. He had been correct on which dog went where. Sending an apologetic look his way, I returned my attention to Al as he continued.

"Erick has come back to let us know a group of cross country skiers were on the trail going past the swamp and they noticed some snowshoe marks going into an area that is considered unsafe. They used their cell phone to call into the rangers to let them know the location. At this time, we have two area search dogs working live find scent; however we have the possibility of a person having gone into the swamp. Rebekkah, it is unlikely they would have survived the overnight temperatures last night. That being the case, can you take K-9 Ari over there? He does both area and cadaver, so this would be a good time to utilize him."

Nodding, I glanced again at Amos. He would return the favor of providing field support for me. Craig, standing nearby, asked if he could tag along as well.

We were soon loaded in my truck, with K-9 Jael barking fervently at the strangers who had joined us. She finally quieted down when she realized they were ignoring her. With an indignant sniff, she laid down in her crate with her back to us.

Ari, on the other hand, was schmoozing with Amos. He knew Amos, but being a proper gentleman, he waited until being formally introduced to greet Craig.

"Craig, Ari is our senior citizen of the unit. He's about ten years old, and is currently certified for live find area search as well as human remains detection, which we also call HRD or cadaver. And he loves most everyone."

I could see in my rear view mirror the beautiful black and tan dog, classic in his looks and regal in his demeanor. He offered his head to Craig for a scratch and found a new friend.

Parking beside a small trailhead, I unloaded my dog. I knew that the rangers would frown heavily on us if we tromped on top of their beautifully groomed cross country ski trail, so our snowshoes came out once again. While I wouldn't inhibit my dog from running on the trail, the humans in the party would be walking beside it in the deeper, soft snow.

Offering Ari the scent article that I was provided for our hider, Sheila, I watched his black nose sniff deeply the scent, then told him to find.

We didn't have a point last scene for Sheila except the trail back at the campsite. Here, we had to work Ari into the wind, which could skip over tall trees, pool in protected areas, and even swirl in lowlands. My dog would sniff and determine if he detected the odor of Sheila in that wind, and if he did, where it was coming from.

I trusted this old dog, although like every good handler, I knew he wasn't infallible. Often the dog can only get us into an area, where ground teams or posse would finish the work of finding the person. Other times, the dog can help us to eliminate an area as low probability because they don't detect odor in it. And still other times, the terrain and conditions make it nearly impossible to work a dog effectively.

Today was a beautiful scent day. The wind was light, but steady. It wasn't blowing this way and then switching back again. It was strong enough to filter through the trees, but not so strong as to skip completely over them.

Ari, his blaze orange vest making him visible through the trees and looking bright against the white snow, started off in his normal fashion. He tried to find a walking trail of his missing person first. If you can find a trail, it's that much easier, and he knows it.

Finding no trail, he quickly turned down the cross country trail and began his methodical search pattern. It was self-taught from a night certification test that we had failed. He learned from that failure far faster than I did. Trotting down the trail, he'd periodically dash into the woods on one side, then cross back out, and then do the same on the other side of the trail. We call it quartering, although I'm sure Ari didn't worry about what the humans called it. He simply knew that if he didn't break the plane of air between the trail and the woods, he might miss something.

That plane of air is a hard concept for humans to understand, although I'd seen many dogs figure it out themselves. It is like a brick wall, stopping the movement of air from a cooler area,

31

generally the woods, and the warmer area; the trail. By passing through the invisible wall, the dog can check both the cooler and the warmer areas for odor, and actually help it move a bit.

Ari, while he didn't move fast, wasted very little energy as he worked. We often frustrated evaluators during our certification testing because so many wanted to see a dog run out at top speed and search fast. Ari had learned long ago that it isn't always the rabbit that wins the race. Keeping a steady pace, he saved his own energy, covered as much ground as the faster dogs, and still managed to do the job in about the same amount of time.

It was subtle, the behavior change, but I saw it. I had worked with this dog his entire life, and it was simply watching his left ear suddenly flip to the side which caught my attention. I lifted a hand to my field tech, Amos, as he walked slightly to my right and behind. He knew from years of working with me what it meant. I had seen something from my dog.

We slowed as Ari slowed. With his head up, then lowered, he stepped off the trail and went into the snow on the side of the trail. It was then I realized we were in swamp land as my dog simply disappeared into the snow. Moving fast, I caught up to him as he struggled to free himself from the soft, quick-sand like snow. Pulling him up by his vest, I looked over the terrain that lay in front of us.

For about twenty feet, there was nothing but crisp, white, virgin snow. Then we could see the swamp reeds, the de-tufted old cottontails sticking up, barely showing. The snow had to be close to three or four feet deep there and the consistency of sugary sand from the recent melting temperatures. Yet I knew my dog had caught the odor of his target, Sheila, across that white gap. Where was it coming from?

Standing back, I took out a small bottle of carpenter's chalk with a bit of baby talcum mixed in to keep it from clumping. Giving it a squeeze, blue chalk puffed out. I carefully puffed it again, changing the level to where Ari's nose was. Then I went up on the trail and puffed it again, to see if the direction changed.

The wind caught the powder and by the drift of blue, I knew that the wind was coming to us from across the swamp area. Pulling out the trail maps Ranger Vanderwal had given us, I could see the trail we were on would take us around that swamp to the other side.

Patting Ari, I encouraged him to keep working and explained to Amos and Craig my plan was to take the dog around to the other side via the trail, versus trying to cross the swamp, which could be open in places, and therefore unsafe.

Ari wasn't as easy to convince, but eventually came with us. I had Amos mark on the GPS both where Ari had picked up odor and where I could see he lost it as we continued down the trail. This information, when relayed to base, could help triangulate, based on the wind, where the odor might be coming from. That is, if our trip around the swamp turned up nothing else.

It wasn't much longer, however, when my dog again had the classic ear turn, followed by a slowing of motion. He also added what I knew to be his proximity alert; his tail began a very slow and steady wag.

He turned back toward the swamp and I could see this time he was on a snowshoe trail. The person had come through the woods and crossed the cross country ski trail we were paralleling and walked straight into the swamp reeds.

Ari, excitement building, actually took a few bounding leaps before he realized the snow wasn't packed and he still sank in.

Catching up once more, I went ahead of him and stamped the snow down as I followed the snowshoe track. Ari, experience again kicking into gear for him, let me take the lead. He knew it would be easier walking for him.

About one hundred feet into the snow, and deep into the swamp grasses, we started finding clothing articles. I could hear Amos reporting each article as we found it, and as Ari came across each one, he'd stop and paw at it to show me. The trail, however, came to a stop as the grasses stopped and I was facing open water. Al had warned us of the natural springs in this area that kept the water from freezing solid in the winter.

Ari, however, had pushed past me and was intent on sniffing toward the water. Calling him back, I secured him with a long line that I had clipped to my belt and let him out again.

Within a few moments, I saw yet another behavioral change in my dog. He went from happy leaping toward the odor of Sheila and joyfully pawing at the articles to a different movement altogether. His motion had changed to almost slow motion, and his head was carried very low, swinging slowly back and forth like the head of a snake.

Amos, watching from behind us, simply whispered "HRD?"

I nodded and waited as Ari carefully made a slow check along the edge of the open water. Amos likely knew as soon as I did that Ari had found where Al and his devious crew had hidden a cadaver training aid. Ari, lowering his chest, gave the approximation of a play bow. It was his final trained response to finding the strongest point of odor of human remains.

Amos radioed in, but I didn't truly listen as I rewarded my dog for the find. As I gave Ari his favorite treats, I was wondering how on earth they managed to get someone to snowshoe to open water, drop a training aid into the water, secure it who knows how, and then simply disappear without leaving a trail back out.

I didn't have long to wait, as Amos tapped me on the shoulder with a question.

"Did you hear that? Do you want to attempt it?"

"What? Sorry, I was trying to work out how they did this." I pointed to the open water and back at the trail.

"You weren't listening. Okay, pay attention this time. They have a boat standing by at a bay just over there. They brought your truck over and want to know if you'd like to work Jael on this problem from the boat."

"Seriously? They have a boat out today?" I hoped someone had a camera; it would be worth the photo, "Sure, I have PFD's for both the dogs and myself in the truck." Personal flotation devices, or what we old timers called life vests, were almost always in my truck. In Minnesota, you just never know when you'll need them, even in the winter.

Praising Ari as we walked back to the trail, we answered questions from Craig about what the dog had done, and explained, as best we could work out, how Al had managed to accomplish such a terrific training problem for us.

"I wouldn't have guessed they'd bring a boat in today, but if they have one, what they must have done was had our hider walk in, leaving articles along the way..." I paused and glanced back, wondering suddenly if we had picked them up or not. Reading my mind, Amos simply nodded and held up a handful of things we had found.

"Anyway, so when Sheila reached the water's edge, they picked her up in a boat and brought her back to the dock after they put a training aid in the water to mimic a person who drowned."

Craig was silent for a moment, probably thinking that we were completely insane to go through all this effort, but he surprised me with his question, "What would he have put into the water for your dog to find?"

It shouldn't have surprised me. People are generally fascinated with the idea that we somehow have a human body we keep someplace and take out just for training events. We don't, but what we do have has to be carefully tracked and maintained. They also have to be legally obtained, with documentation to go along with it.

"I'm not sure what they put in, but usually we use bone or teeth for water training as they are stable and don't wash away."

"Human? Where do you get human bone? I mean, I know that people have teeth pulled all the time, but bone?" I wasn't sure if Craig was grossed out or simply curious.

"Well, we have purchased bleached and cleaned human bones legally via the internet. But our unit also is able to obtain fresh bone from people who undergo joint replacement surgery. They fill out a form, it is witnessed, signed and all that. Then during the surgery, when the surgeon removes the chips of bone that will be replaced by artificial parts, they retain it and provide it to us for training. We have to maintain the documentation, keep good records, and when the time comes, dispose of them by acceptable bio-hazard method, which is basically incineration."

We had arrived at the dock area, and I could see a small canoe sitting in the water, waiting for us. My truck was parked nearby, and I loaded Ari, putting on his warming jacket so he didn't cool too quickly after working so hard.

Changing our gear from wilderness to water, I pulled K-9 Jael out of the truck and strapped on her own PFD. Many handlers don't use them on their dogs, but I once saw a dog dive overboard during a training run and if we hadn't had divers in the water at the time, the dog might not have made it home.

The water was cold that day, as it often is in Northern Minnesota. The handler couldn't lift the dog into the boat because there wasn't anything to grab but slippery wet dog fur. Assuming the dog could swim back to the dock, they simply held his collar and started back. Within minutes, it was obvious the dog was tiring and lethargic. A rescue diver, there for the training, had to carry the dog back. The dog was hypothermic and nearly unconscious by the time they reached shore. I never wanted that to happen to my dog.

Jael, a petite sable colored Shepherd, never ceased to engender the question, "What breed is she?" Craig was no exception. As we walked toward the dock, he asked.

"She's a purebred German Shepherd that was donated to me by a breeder in Connecticut to do SAR work. She suffers from Attention Deficit Hyperactivity Disorder, or ADHD. At least, I think she does, as she can't seem to slow down!" I was kidding, or at least sort of kidding. Jael really was a dog that required full-time attention and training to keep her mind and body engaged. This made her a terrific search dog, but also a pain to live with.

As we approached the canoe, Jael displayed, to all who wanted to watch, her best imitation of an impatient kindergartner. Her whining increased as we got closer to the water, her excitement overflowing her ability to remain a calm professional.

Loading her into the canoe, I watched my paddlers, two nice young Park Rangers, looking suddenly far more concerned than they were moments before. I didn't blame them. The water wasn't frozen, but it was incredibly cold, nonetheless. An out of control dog could flip the canoe faster than a person can blink.

"Jael. Calm. We're here to work," I patted her side and finished with, "Load, gentle."

With amazing calm, Jael carefully stepped into the canoe, one foot at time. It looked very impressive, the control I had over my dog. The Rangers in the boat relaxed, and only I needed to know that I was as surprised as they were. Jael had ridden in a canoe before, more than once. But she rarely entered so carefully. I often had to hold her with a death grip to keep her from leaping off the dock.

We paddled away from the dock, and Jael, head up, nostrils sniffing, began whining. She wasn't in odor; I knew that. She was simply excited. She'd been stuck in the truck for hours; she wanted to do something, anything!

I directed the paddlers to paddle a grid pattern toward the area where we knew the source was located. I had always loved canoes, but like the paddlers, I wasn't sure I liked being in one, in March, with snow and ice all around us.

It wasn't long before Jael suddenly and in dramatic fashion hit the odor. The whining stopped completely; her concentration was on her job, and not on her excitement or the humans in the boat.

Her focus became incredibly intense as she filtered through all the scents and odors floating around us, from above the water, on the water, and most especially, below the water. I watched, waiting for the body language I wanted to see.

Jael, when she encountered HRD odor on a boat, would lean way over the side and try to literally taste the water, or look deep into its depths as if she could see what she was seeking. As we paddled between an old tree stump coming out of the water and the land where the snowshoe trail had ended, Jael nearly tipped us over as she threw her head and upper body over the side of the canoe.

Pushing my weight to the opposite side, I was able to counterbalance her lunge, but I didn't get a chance to drop the buoy or mark my GPS as planned. Jael, in the meantime, was scrambling over me to get to the back of the canoe as it slid silently away from where she knew the odor was strongest.

"Turn it around; go back over there, I need to drop a buoy!" I was smothered in my dog's chest, fur filling my nose and mouth as I tried to give the paddlers direction. I could feel the canoe turning and Jael promptly got off me to turn and face the direction of the odor again. Holding on tight to the dog with one hand, I held the buoy at the ready with my other.

Jael threw herself again, succeeding in actually dunking her head under the water as I dropped the buoy over the other side, while trying to be ballast for her weight at the same time. As I dropped, I started praising her, and with much more skill than I thought I possessed, I managed to pull her reward toy from under my own PFD and clip it to her collar.

The paddlers watched, amazed I'm sure, as my dog merrily grabbed the tennis ball dangling from her collar and attempted to throw it over the side of the canoe. It flipped out, curved down, slapped the water and then flipped back up where Jael caught it in mid-air.

"We can head back now. She'll play with it all the way back." I periodically swung the ball so she could grab it again. I knew that Jael loved to give her toy to whatever she found, even if it was a deceased person. We quickly discovered doing water work, this wasn't the best thing, as we lost several balls that way. Jael, being very dedicated to her reward toy, didn't like to leave them behind, either. She was willing to do almost anything to go back and get it.

Using it in my favor, I attached a tennis ball to a braided leather handle with a carabineer. By hooking it to her collar, she could toss the ball overboard as often as she wanted, but we never lost a toy, and she entertained herself all the way back to the dock.

Unloading, I thanked our paddlers profusely for risking their lives, and promised if they'd be willing to do it again some other day, they could ride with my other dog instead. He was a gentleman. They did the only thing they could, they smiled and nodded.

"Nearly lost her there, didn't you?" Amos was smiling as he said it, and I noticed that both he and Craig were holding binoculars. They had watched our antics out there, and likely enjoyed the spectacle.

"Yes; well, she found it. I dropped a buoy, so someone will have to go after it and pull the source. Is Al coming over?"

"Yep, they just radioed they'll all head over this way. All the dogs worked really well it looks like, but we'll get a debrief over coffee."

"Craig, how did you enjoy your day?" His wife, Peggy, had obviously driven over on her own, and I could tell simply by looking at her that she had spent the entire time in her or someone else's vehicle. She was clean, dry, and no flushed cheeks from being out in the wind.

I glanced back at Amos and Craig as I put my gear away. I was interested in Craig's answer as well.

"More than I expected. Do you train like this every week?"

"No, Al did a terrific job this week. Often we simply train on fundamentals, such as obedience, or reinforcement training of our own skills, like navigation. Often it's rather boring!"

I nodded as Craig glanced at me for confirmation. I had to agree. For most of the handlers I knew, obedience was the most boring thing to train for, although some did enjoy it. It was, however, critical to the safety of our dogs.

# Chapter 4

Spring was welcomed by everyone as temperatures began their slow daytime rise. As if it didn't want to relinquish its hold on the land, the drifts and banks of snow diminished at a much slower rate relative to the warmth of the days.

The delay in snow melt was largely due to the nighttime temperatures which were still dropping below freezing. This created a rise and fall of temperatures, which, while sometimes irritating to the humans, actually made the perfect conditions for a very special harvest.

Like any crop, much depended on the weather, not on the calendar. However as March approached, the equipment came out, and hopes would rise for another good yield. March, with its cold nights and warming days, started the sap running in the maple trees. I'm sure the sap ran in other trees as well, but somehow they paled in comparison to what the maples produced.

What I had not known until I moved north was that Minnesota actually produced maple syrup. Good syrup that even won national competitions. While we likely would never be able to challenge Vermont for the quantity produced, apparently we could in the flavor department.

To be honest, I was raised on the fake stuff, and even after being exposed to the real deal, had only enjoyed pure maple syrup mass-manufactured and purchased at the store. Arriving in Elk Ridge however, I learned the importance of the amber liquid. The state park nearby held maple syrup classes and demonstrations every year, and it was part of McCaffrey House's challenge to monitor their website to verify when they were held so we could notify our guests.

We didn't need to encourage our guests to attend the local syruping classes. It was something of a rite of passage for the families that stayed with us during the critical month of sap running. And in fact, McCaffrey celebrated that special time of year by putting small maple sugar candies on people's pillows instead of our usual chocolate.

While we supported the local industry, I had never actually participated in the gathering and making of the syrup. Each year I promised myself I would. But each year, something came up; or I made excuses as I was too tired, or too busy. This year, however, I finally had a good reason to go. I was asked.

The phone rang as I was updating my training logs for the dogs. This part of being a K-9 handler for search and rescue I really disliked. That first year, so many years ago, I was given an incredibly confusing form that was full of things to check, circle and fill in. It was so full, in fact, that some of the words were actually turned sideways and almost unreadable. I wasn't trained how to fill it in, just told to get it done.

Over the years, I modified, cleaned up, and simplified the form I used. In fact, I had converted it to a small database program I wrote all for myself. It was into this that I was typing when my home phone went off.

"James," I gave only my last name, as I had heard my parents do ever since I was old enough to understand the English language. I also tended to spell my name by using the military phonetic alphabet. It was a carry-over from being raised by a twenty year veteran of the United States Air Force.

"Rebekkah, what are you doing on Saturday?" The voice belonged to Amy Drahota, a friend and supporter since I came to Elk Ridge. She had battled cancer for many years, and over the last year, her dream to bear a child of her own was taken away from her. While the entire community mourned for her, she continued to keep her faith that God would grant her the desire of her heart.

To answer her question to me, I had to stop and think. Was I scheduled for anything? Training was postponed this weekend as so many of our members were busy or out of town. Shaking my head, I couldn't come up with anything.

"I'm free, I think. What's up?" I continued typing as I spoke, the phone pinned between my shoulder and my ear. I hated being behind on my training logs, and I was very behind.

"Surprise! Girls' day out; my treat. Will you come?" Amy sounded buoyant and happy. She often sounded that way, even with the disappointments she'd experienced.

"Sure; when and where?" I put the last notation into the log and sent the pages to the printer. My true training logs were actually two ring binders, each about four inches thick, one for each dog. I had another binder tucked away for Gus-Gus, my dearly missed SAR K-9 partner that I had lost the previous year. Just like my current dogs, if any of the searches he participated in went to court, it was possible I could still be called to testify. The logs were critical.

"We'll meet at the church at eight. Dress for being outdoors in the woods – your favorite place to be!"

Saturday had dawned bright and clear, and because it was clear, the temperature was lower than normal at just about 15 degrees. I knew the sun would warm it up quickly, but I still dressed with long underwear under my jeans and layered like a good Minnesotan. First a T-shirt, then a hoodie sweatshirt, over which I put my three-season coat with its zip-out fleece liner. The last thing I put on was my winter hiking boots. This time of year could bring cold feet, wet feet, or even hot sweaty feet. I chose waterproof hikers and hoped for the best.

Checking on my mom, I could see she was tired already, but seemed alert and I decided that the event that landed us in the emergency room was a one-time thing, as the doctor had indicated it might be.

Pulling into the parking lot of the church, I could see Amy waiting beside her car, chatting with our pastor. Dave, tall and blonde, was much too good looking to be a pastor. Or at least, I thought so. He was a good man, however, and a good friend too.

"Well Amy, here I am. Who else is coming?" I gave both Amy and Dave a hug. I had been raised by parents who weren't much into hugging, so I'm not sure where I inherited the hugging gene, but apparently I did.

"Morning to you too, Rebekkah!" Dave laughed as he said it, pointing out that I hadn't greeted him.

"Sorry Dave, no reflection on you, I'm just curious to know what Amy has planned for us today." Dave patted my shoulder, gave Amy a hug and with a wave, went to the small parsonage behind the church.

Amy, looking petite and beautiful, smiled what can only be described as a devious smile. I was simply glad that she only looked petite and not frail, as she had looked for so many years.

"I invited the gals from your SAR unit, Chris, Marge, and Karen. I've also invited Megan, Connie and some ladies from church as well."

"Are they all coming? Connie said she hasn't been feeling so hot lately."

"No, she said she had plans. But it sounds like everyone else is coming except Chris."

"So that is why we had to cancel training. Very funny. And where are you taking us? Is it so mysterious?" I liked to plan for things; I wasn't spontaneous at all.

I didn't have long to wait. As soon as everyone had arrived, Amy finally spilled that we were going out to the park and learn to make maple syrup.

We drove to the park in the church van, thanks to Pastor Dave. Checking in, we jelled as a group, just out to have fun together. The fact we were doing something that I had wanted to do for some time only made it even more special.

With gusto, we split into smaller groups and went with our instructors, carrying our buckets and old-fashioned hand-drills. We were looking, as directed, for maples that had a diameter of at least ten inches. Almost immediately, I realized that it was rather difficult to tell trees apart without their leaves.

"The Sugar Maples make the best syrup as they have much higher sugar content, whereas the Red and Silver have higher water content and it takes more sap to make syrup." Ted, our guide, began the task of teaching us how to identify the different trees by the bark, the color of the twigs and even the buds, which were visible at this time of the year.

"If the tree is less than ten inches in circumference, we could stress and even cause the tree to split, so we want to avoid that. Here you go; here is a good solid tree, about twenty inches." He patted a tree and as he helped us set the angle of the drill bit for optimum sap run, he continued, "You don't want to tap too close to an old tap, either above, below, or to the side."

I pushed hard as I carefully drilled the first tap hole. I didn't tell Ted I was normally inept around any kind of tools. Reaching the two inch mark, I carefully removed the bit and watched, amazed, as what looked like water bead up and begin to drip out of the wound in the tree.

"Here, put the spile in. You'll want it tight enough you can't pull it out, but not so far you'll split the wood." He watched as I gently tapped at the cone-shaped metal piece. With it firmly set, I carefully hung my bucket, making sure the plastic cover to keep out foreign objects was in place. Looking up proudly, I realized I was on my own, the others had moved on to their own trees.

As I stood there, I wondered how often people got lost tapping maple trees. Glancing around, I recognized that, of course, they could simply follow the taps and buckets back to safety.

"What are you thinking about, Rebekkah?" Amy had come up behind me and slid her arm around my waist.

"How often people lose their way in the woods. Look, Amy, my bucket has sap!" I watched in wonder as what looked exactly like water dripped rapidly into my bucket.

Soon, Ted had us gathering buckets and toting them back to the sugar shack, a building set up simply to boil down the sap. I carried Amy's bucket, explaining it was easier to carry both as it balanced me out.

"Pour the sap directly into the kettle there. We'll keep this boiling until the sugar content is at least sixty-seven percent; any lower and the syrup could sour."

We all watched and then were sent out to get more sap, bringing it back to add to the kettle.

"How much sap does it take to make syrup?" Megan asked the instructor. I realized that she had been in a different group of sap collectors than mine.

"The ratio is forty to one, or forty gallons of sap to make a single gallon of syrup. Some years, it is easy to get that much, others, not so much. Sap gathered earlier in the day is generally sweeter than later in the day. Anyone else have any questions?" Ted paused, and then pointed to the visitor center and explained samples of syrup would be found there.

I had to admit that knowing we had helped make syrup today made the tasting even better. Or maybe it was the friendship of the women around me. Either way, it was a wonderful day.

It didn't stay that way. Returning home, a jar of maple syrup and some maple sugar candy for my mom, I found her in another spell of extreme vertigo. Calling Dr. Sheffield, I explained what was going on, and was soon on the road to his small clinic.

Two days later, it happened again, this time after I had gone to bed for the night. Dr. Sheffield, realizing that this time my mom's blood pressure was actually exceeding stroke range, finally made the decision to put her on blood pressure medicine. Meniere's disease had been eliminated as a cause; high blood pressure appeared to have taken its place.

No explainable cause except old age; it made my mom frustrated and angry. She had taken pride in having low blood pressure her entire life. Now it was spiking simply because she was aging? It didn't make sense to either of us, but as I was often told in the SAR world; it is what it is. Learn from it and move on.

Hoping that the medication would take care of it, I went to training the following weekend. I was looking forward to enjoying a terrific time of running a navigation course set up by

Chris. Our dogs remained home, and we spent the day tightening up and challenging our orienteering skills.

Chris handed out sheets of paper with ten compass points written on it, followed by two blank lines. Each list, while starting at the same point, was different from the others. This prevented anyone from simply following the previous team. She did allow us the luxury of going in teams of two, but then told us it was for safety, not cheating.

Karen and I stepped up to the first flag, clearly labeled with a big "A" on it. Standing over the top of it, Karen lined her compass up based on the first bearing written on our paper. I watched as she used her sighting mirror to find a point in the distance to navigate to. Then it was my turn. I too, lined up over the flag, and with care, saw that to follow a bearing of one hundred forty five degrees, I should aim for a fence post. It was falling down but still clearly visible and not likely to move.

Our goal, as explained by Chris, was to follow each compass bearing until we reached another flag. We were then to write down how far, in meters, it was from the previous flag. The second blank line was so we could enter the letter of the new flag. No flag was more than five hundred meters from each other, so if we went that far, we missed the flag. To entice us further, she informed us that there would be a prize to the winning team.

As there were ten bearings listed, we had to find nine more flags after "A". And they weren't the size of a flag that hangs on a flag pole; no, they were about ten inches square and at most, three feet off the ground.

Karen started the first leg, and I could see we both were lining up to the same fence post. As we walked, I carefully counted paces, using my right hand to lightly slap my right leg each time I took a stride with it.

It was a tip taught to me by my first search management instructor, who believed that search managers should know what the people in the field had to do. And one of them was navigation. Too many times people assumed a pace was every footstep when in reality, it was every time the same foot hit the ground, a full two-step stride.

I knew my pace count was seventeen paces for every hundred feet. That worked out to fifty one paces for one hundred meters. At ninety-three paces, we reached our next flag, labeled "D". If my math worked out, we had walked approximately one hundred and eighty two meters. Give or take. I wrote it down and lined up to take our next bearing.

Lining up over flag "D", I sighted to what appeared to be a unique rock formation. Karen lined up second and, for me, it appeared she lined up to the same formation I had. Fifty meters later, it was obvious we both were going at a different bearing.

"Karen, do we go back and recheck, or just keep going our own way and hope for the best?" She wasn't too far from me, but at our present course, we'd be close to one hundred feet apart at three hundred meters. Further if we kept going at the same angles. If we entered trees, which were likely as we could see them ahead of us, we could easily lose sight of each other.

"I lined up to that stand of birches. What did you use?" I looked where her finger was pointing, and tried to relocate my rock formation. They suddenly all looked alike. There was a formation to the left of the birches. There was another one to the right, and even one directly in front of them.

"Karen, I've lost my bearing. I have to go back. We're supposed to stay together for safety. Do you want to wait here while I recheck? We'll be in line of sight to each other."

With her agreement, I carefully lined up to a back azimuth from where I was standing. It is a fancy orienteering way of saying, "turn around one hundred eighty degrees and go back where you came from". That meant retracing my steps and relocating that last flag.

We were not allowed to bring our GPS with us, which was yet another way to keep us from cheating. The global positioning system would help us with distances, direction and even recording our position at any given time – such as where that last flag was at. This exercise was completely about using our compass.

As I walked, I remembered the first time I held this compass in my hands. It scared and fascinated me at the same time. When asked what we should carry into the woods, a compass was the obvious answer. It was a good answer too, but with it came the realization that while it told me which way was north, unless I knew where I was and where I had to go, the compass was useless.

Walking alone in the woods often makes a person a philosopher. You think deep thoughts and, as I walked, I thought about how in life we need a compass to help us find our way. However, if we have a compass but aren't using it, or don't know how to use it; it's useless.

I found flag "D" and carefully lined up again to our next bearing of two hundred seventy degrees. Imagine my surprise to find Karen directly in line with my sighting mirror. More for curiosity, I looked for that rock formation. It had a funny pink stripe running almost straight up, and yes, there it was, on the other side of Karen.

With a wiggle of my nose, I realized that while I had started down the right bearing, somehow I had mistaken one rock formation for another and veered off course. So easy to do, we always tell new members not to use a tree unless it is so unique it can't be mistaken for another tree. Simply put, as you get closer and closer, all trees look alike. You need to site to an object that won't move, that is truly unique and never changes.

While my rock formation seemed perfect for taking a bearing on, in reality, as I marked my bearing and started toward Karen, I realized that with the changing angles and changing light, what had looked unchanging, wasn't. The pink stripe slowly disappeared and the formation to the right appeared to grow a stripe.

By the end of our navigation course, I was tired. The pack on my back felt at least ten pounds heavier than when I started, but the finish line looked so incredibly good. It was a relief as Chris helped peel the weight off my back and shoulders and congratulated Karen and me on a successful journey.

We weren't the first team in, but it felt like it as everyone cheered. And when Amos and Marge came in shortly after us, we joined in the cheering.

Al came in last with Craig Lundquist, who had decided to join as a probationary member. It made sense they were the last in, as Al would have been mentoring Craig on the use of a compass. They received cheers too; and congratulations to Craig on taking on his first navigation challenge.

A quick check of our papers revealed that everyone had come within the margin of error on our distances, and everyone found their correct flags.

Chris then held up a hand and as we quieted down, she asked "did anyone see anything besides the flags out there?"

I could see the looks on everyone's faces. Chris had done something to challenge us, and it was looking very much like we didn't measure up.

"Well, I can tell you that one team did, specifically one person in that team did. At flag "H", they found a person about ten feet away from the flag."

I knew in a flash who found the person; Al, who came in last, wouldn't have been worrying about winning the prize, he would have taken the time to train Craig and mentor him. In slowing it down, he would have had time to observe.

"Al and Craig, you win the prize for finding our missing person. Craig noticed something in the brush and went to investigate, where he found our hider, Marvin." Each man received a bag of chocolates, and the rest of us learned a lesson. We get so focused on our destination, we sometimes lose track of what is around us, or someone who might need help along the way.

# Chapter 5

*You are acquainted with all my ways.*

My mom, hating medication, decided that if her blood pressure was the problem, she'd change her life style. In typical James fashion, decided she wasn't taking any more of the medication. Instead, she changed her diet, removing most of the salt. This of course meant most of my salt too. I liked salt.

I was willing to sacrifice however, because it was quickly obvious that it was working. There weren't any more episodes of vertigo, she could think again, and communicate without the pauses. She also lost a little weight as well, which was good. I only wondered if her tiredness and forgetfulness would ever get better, or if it was something we'd have to live with now.

It worried me as I'd come home from McCaffrey, or walking the dogs, or a search training, and find she had forgotten to turn off the oven or left a burner on. I'd find her asleep in bed with her computer and all the lights still on. Realizing your parent is aging is difficult. I had to remind myself she wasn't fifty or even sixty anymore. She was in her seventies, and likely it was just catching up to her.

Into this, came a search call. I debated if I should go, but mom wouldn't hear of me staying home. I had trained for this; I had to go when someone needed us. I called Gary, asking if he'd stop and check on her after his clinic closed if I didn't make it home for the night. I didn't tell my mom that it was because I was worried she'd leave a burner on and I'd come home to a house fire.

We were given little information about our missing person over the phone, but upon arriving, I found it incredibly odd that something I had just wondered about had occurred. It was almost as if I had a premonition or something.

Our missing person had gone out to gather the sap buckets and not returned. The briefing provided the information that the family had checked all around their grove of maples and not found him. Which also meant the area was trampled.

"Folks, Don Wussow is fifty-eight, in good health, no known medical issues. He checks his buckets twice a day, usually. The family noticed he was missing when they smelled the kettle had burned out – they smelled the charred sugar." The deputy glanced around before continuing, "We know he walked out this way, however the tracks have pretty much been obliterated. We have a number of resources here today, included mounted posse, firemen for line searches, and K-9 teams. Any questions before we give out assignments?" A few were asked, one of which was critical for the dogs.

"Are there any tree planters out where we'll be searching?" I blinked, and glanced over at Amos who stood nearby. He put up a hand to indicate he'd explain later.

A moment later, the officer giving the briefing mentioned there was a ravine nearby that the family was concerned about. Ravines are a safety hazard for any K-9 handler whose dog works loose like mine did. It concerned me as well and my attention was back with the briefing.

As I waited to get my assignment, Amos filled me in on what the person had meant by tree planters. I had lived in Minnesota for more than two decades, and his information made me wondered what else I didn't know about my state.

I had always assumed that the family owned farms were self-sustaining; or, even if they were larger farms, the locals did the work. What I learned from Amos was that in this area that didn't have dairy farms, soybean fields or acres of corn; the migrant workers were an important, if silent, part of our agricultural system.

"Each year in the spring, transient workers – or migrant, whichever you prefer – come in and plant trees for the forestry department or any company or agency that is willing to hire them."

"Plant trees, out here?" I waved my hand around at the heavily forested land all around us.

"Every year believe it or not. Remember that fires, storms and even planned cuts leave areas of no trees that need to be replaced. The workers make their way from down by the Texas or California borders and by spring, they arrive here. When they get to the Canadian border, they turn around and head south again, just following the crop harvest. Most don't speak English, although their crew leaders usually have passable language skills."

I suspect I shook my head or something, because Amos continued, "They're here for about a month and basically spend long hours planting trees. They're amazing to watch, if you get the chance. I've heard they can plant up to four thousand seedling trees a day, per man; or more, if they've had some experience."

"Alright, I believe you. I just never knew - how come I've never seen them around?"

"They don't socialize much, I guess. And they are further out than Elk Ridge is, so we don't really see much of them. Sounds like we might today however," As he finished speaking, he was waved over to the table where they were giving out assignments. I was called over shortly after he left and was given mine.

I wasn't surprised that they quietly asked me to use my cadaver dog to check out the ravine first. If nothing came of it, they'd send me to another location with a live-find dog.

"Do you have someone who can walk along with me as my backup? I can run my own GPS, but it is good to have someone handle the radio and just keep an eye on us for safety."

Glancing around, the deputy asked a group of fireman if any of them would like to go out with one of the dogs. I watched as they looked me over. I knew what they saw; a middle-aged woman with gray in her brown, curly hair, and not exactly in top physical shape. I saw the assessment, the wheels turn, and a decision made. This was the easier task than doing a line-search through the woods. I felt a bit sorry for the one who stepped forward to volunteer.

"I'm Joe, I'd be glad to walk with you," He grinned and with a side glance at the others, finished with, "What is it you need me to do?"

"I'm Rebekkah, and the dog we'll be working is K-9 Jael. She's a cadaver dog and they want us to go check the area around this ravine. Joe, we don't need to broadcast she's a cadaver dog as families don't need to think about that yet, alright?" As he nodded, I held out the topographical map I'd been given, pointing out the ravine. Watching the blind nod, I knew the young man had no idea what he was looking at. I did, and it wasn't going to be a walk in the park.

"Okay, all I need for you to do is three things. Handle the radio communications with base here. Watch for hazards that I might miss that could endanger the dog or us, and step in if need be. And finally, run interference if anyone not associated with the search approaches. Oh, four things. Stay close enough so I don't have to yell to be heard."

Gathering my gear, I unloaded Jael. Just the sight of the dog had Joe, my volunteer field support, taking a step back. Slipping on her royal blue search vest and hooking up her leash, I looked him over.

"Joe, do you have any water with you?" I couldn't tell for sure, as he was in full turn-out gear.

"No, I'll be fine, really."

I bit my tongue, debating with myself. I needed a person watching my back who wasn't suffering from dehydration, but I also didn't want to alienate him right off the bat. "Well, tell you what, can you carry some extra bottles of water for me and my dog? We'll be expending a lot of energy, and sweating off everything we drink. It will really help me out."

I watched as he stowed the extra water in his pockets, and we headed south. I was happy that my compass bearing matched not only my mental map, but also the physical map that I was carrying. In this area, with the amount of iron ore in the ground, one could never be completely sure the compass would be on.

Once in the woods, away from the other search teams and specifically the family, I gave Jael her working command, "Go get caddy." Releasing the leash, I watched as she shot out away from us, glad to be free and working.

"How long have you been a fireman, Joe?" I asked it conversationally, but I had a pretty good idea I knew the answer. Not long.

"About three months, but I've finished all the courses and I've been on a couple of calls already." The pride was there, and I didn't begrudge him that. It took a special breed of person to run into a burning building and battle a fire. I didn't think I could do it.

"So I'm guessing you like it then?" We were walking along a small man-made trail, but I knew shortly we'd be cutting into the woods to parallel the ravine. I wanted to make sure we didn't miss the woods by having tunnel-vision on the ravine.

"Yes, I wish I could do it full time for pay. I've applied to a few of the larger stations down in the metro, but nothing so far."

"Too bad, I hope you get in. We turn here."

It was only fifteen minutes later I realized Joe was struggling. Young and healthy as he was, he was constrained by the heavy turn-out gear. Thirty minutes later, I called Jael to a stop to give him time to catch up.

"Let's take a water break. We all do when we stop. Just a safety thing, just like at a fire, you don't realize how much you're sweating off until it's too late." I was happy to see him comply, and guzzle half a bottle from the ones I had given him.

Two hours later, we came out of our search area with nothing to show for it but bruises from the dense woods. Joe was clearly spent. Jael, on the other hand, was still running and working. I was feeling the effect of the impenetrable vegetation we had bucked through, but I was used to it. There had been no radio calls about anyone finding anything, so it was likely I'd have to go back out.

Joe, upon exiting the woods, paused. I seriously thought he was going to kneel and kiss the sweet easy trail we had come in on. He didn't, but I knew that it was in his thoughts.

"Thanks for coming out with me Joe, you did a nice job. Why don't you go over and check us back in. Let them know I'll be over to debrief after I put my dog up, and if they need me to go out with my live-find dog, I'll be ready in about fifteen to twenty minutes."

With a strange look I can only describe as a fish-eye, he walked to the table where they were coordinating the search. What Joe didn't know was that, while he was feeling the hike today, tomorrow he wouldn't. I, on the other hand, would feel every branch I hit, every rock I tripped over, every foot step I made. The difference between youth and age; they recuperate faster.

The debrief went quickly as there was little to report. I met up with Amos who had come back from a less than successful attempt to locate a trail. We restocked our water, checked our packs and chatted while we waited for our next assignment. His came first and it was closer to half hour later when I was finally called over to the table.

A section of woods, owned by a couple from the Twin Cities, needed to be checked. The owners came up only for about two weeks out of the year, and these were not their two weeks. A phone call had garnered permission to cross the property line, and it was my section to search.

Glancing around, I realized Joe had disappeared. Returning to the table, I asked if anyone else was available to go out with me. A man, clearly my age or older, stepped up and offered his services. The first thing I noticed was he was wearing a hydration pack. He was already a step ahead of Joe.

"I'm Rebekkah James, I'll be working K-9 Ari today. He's an older dog, so we'll play it by ear how much work I'll put him through today."

"Deputy Jesse Deschene. I heard you give the young fireman his directions, so I'll try to keep up, keep my eyes open, keep you and your dog safe, and I have water with me." The twinkle in his eyes made me think of Al, and I knew we'd get along.

"Sounds like we have to drive out to get to this area, do you know the roads? Can you drive us there? I'd rather leave my own rig here instead of alone on the side of the road with my other dog still in it."

It didn't appear to be a problem, except I didn't realize how small the back of a squad car is. I'm not that tall, but my knees were hitting the protective barricade between the front and back seat. My pack in my lap, my dog squashed in beside me, I wondered if I'd ever get out again.

I did get out, but with help. After stretching my back, I put Ari's blaze-orange vest on and gave his side a pat. Our mission was to cover about eighty acres of woods. I had chosen to do a grid search pattern simply because the woods here were expected to be thick and little wind was moving. In fact, in the woods, I felt no wind. A tight grid was the only reasonable choice at that point.

Air scent or area search dogs rely on the wind to bring the odor to them. If there isn't any, we have to cover more ground on our feet to make sure the dog's nose gets to as many places as possible.

I explained the strategy to Jesse along with the reasons. We would go on an east to west line; reaching the end, we'd turn, move north about one hundred fifty to two hundred feet and run another west to east line. We'd continue on that pattern unless conditions changed.

Jesse, looking at the map did some amazing math calculations and informed me that would put us in a position to walk some five or so miles. I only nodded, not really sure if he was right, but willing to give him the benefit of the doubt. Shrugging, he checked his hydration valve, resettled his pack and we were ready.

I called Ari over and sent him to work with a single sniff of the scent article and the word, "Find".

Ari immediately checked for a ground trail. None. With little wasted time, he started working into the woods we had parked next to. I set the grid line using my compass, but monitored it with both compass and my GPS tracking. With the

63

featureless terrain and lines of trees, the map wouldn't help me much yet.

Ari, not looking his age at all, worked out ahead, checking back with me only when he wanted some water. The three of us worked in companionable silence for nearly the first full leg of the grid. As we approached the natural boundary set as our end point, a small creek, I stopped, checked my bearings, the map, and the GPS before moving north to set up for our next west to east leg. Jesse, staying close, startled me when he actually spoke.

"Does your dog really know who he is looking for?" I glanced back at him and could see he was serious, not joking or challenging.

"He actually does. The scent article told him to match that odor with a person. He'll keep going until I ask him to stop."

It was quiet in the woods, even my dog making very little noise. Much of the snow had melted off, leaving only damp pine needles and dead leaves. Thankfully the area wasn't nearly as thick as the section Jael had earlier, so we covered ground fairly quickly. The only noise was when we periodically called out Don's name. When we did call, we'd stop and listen, hoping to hear a response.

Ari, used to his handler yelling out names as he worked, ignored us. He'd periodically disappear among the trees or behind brush or windfalls, and then suddenly the orange vest would pop out again.

As we reached the eastern boundary, which was the trail, I took a water break for both myself and my dog. I also took the time to slide my hands over Ari. Jesse, watching as he, too, took a water break, asked what I was doing.

"Checking for cuts, scrapes, burrs, or just anything that if left unattended could cause further injury or problems later. He's doing well however."

"If he did get hurt, what would you do?"

"See the small red bag attached to the outside of my pack? That is my first aid kit, for both him and me, or anyone with us. I'd take care of what needed immediate care, assess if he can continue to work, and either proceed or back out."

"How are you holding up yourself?" I arched my back, and then crouched down to stretch the muscles out again. I would likely have back spasms in a day or two.

"I'm doing better than I expected after seeing Joe come out of the woods earlier. Shall we go again?"

The silence seemed to envelope us as we went further into the woods, each leg carrying us deeper into wilderness and away from our vehicle and civilization. The trees changed from hardwoods to pines, and our breaks came a bit more often as we both were feeling the mileage. It was nearly two in the afternoon when I called a stop again, informing dog and field support I needed to eat something. Opening my pack, I dug out a small blue bag with a clear zip cover. Inside I carried power bars, crackers with peanut butter, and if my dog was lucky, jerky for him.

"Power bar or granola?"

"Are you sure? Do you have enough to share?" Jesse, I could see, was hungry too.

"Technically, they say you shouldn't share your pack with anyone, but I usually carry extra bars, and this way, you help me rotate my stock. It might be old, but should still give you energy."

We ate the bars, I gave Ari some of the beef jerky, and we checked our water supply. I carried not only the hydration pack, but also extra water bottles in the big pockets the BDU pants I was wearing. We were good for now.

As we checked our water, a vision of my mom went through my head. In the good old days, we used to call the bags of water we carried on our back, water bladders. My mom hated it when I would say things like, 'I need to fill my bladder,' or 'I need to clean out my bladder.' In her generation, people just didn't talk about things like that, even if it wasn't about my actual, well, bladder. She was infinitely happier when the vernacular changed to 'hydration pack'.

As we sat on the damp ground resting, I saw motion down the hill, across the small creek we had been using as our turn point. Then another movement brought me to my feet. They looked like small ants, scurrying over the land to our west. They weren't of course, they were people. Each carried a tool of some sort and canvas bags strapped over their shoulders.

Pulling out my small binoculars, I watched the tree planters. They moved easily, yet every few strides, they swung the tool they carried, slamming it into the ground and with a swift motion, bent over to push a small twig into the ground. A quick stomp and they moved on.

"They're using a hoedad – sort of like a flat spade set at a forty-five degree angle from the handle. It puts a perfect hole for planting the seedlings. I heard once that they can plant between four and six thousand trees a day that way. Makes my back ache thinking about it; of course, I think my back hurts anyway." Jesse drank some of his water and stood next to me, watching the planters work. It was truly amazing.

As we watched, Ari put up his head to see what we were watching. Brightness lit his eyes and his ears went as far forward as they could. People; there were people down there. The wind was wrong for him to smell them, but Ari was smart enough to realize any one of those men down there could be his subject. He just had to go down and sniff around.

Before I could stop him, he took off across the cold creek and with a happy bounce in his stride, headed for the planters. I was hot on his trail, realizing we really shouldn't eliminate the possibility they might have seen Don, or he might actually be with them.

Ari, his heart and drive making him forget his age, started fast, but as he crossed over the clear cut area where the men worked, he slowed down as he encountered what remained of the trees that had been there before.

Jesse and I caught up with him as he approached the first man and sniffed him. Undeterred when he realized it wasn't Don, he moved on. In the meantime, Jesse tried to explain to the first man what we were doing. It was a hopeless cause, he didn't understand us.

"Scuse me?" A man stepped up, shorter than I was, also carrying a hoedad and a bag as everyone else carried.

"You speak English?" Jesse asked. Upon his responsive nod, Jesse continued, "We are searching for a man who went missing. Have you seen anyone besides your workers?"

"No, no one but workers here – perro – the dog – he will not bite anyone?"

"No, he won't. He's looking for the missing man, he likes people." We all turned to watch Ari, still checking the workers. It was becoming more and more like seeing a dog version of "Are you my mommy?", only of course, Ari was asking "Are you my subject?"

Calling my dog, he returned to my side, and I could see discouragement on his face. All these men and not one was the one he wanted to find.

"It's okay boy. You're doing great." I gave his ear a rub and his side an encouraging pat.

Returning to our area and checking the map, we estimated we were nearly half done with the area. The dog was still doing well, even with the unplanned side excursion. I knew I was tiring, but still believed we could finish it. Jesse radioed in our position and PAR, or personal accountability report, to base, also including the information about the planters in case any other search teams were around that area.

We started again, heading east, back to the trail. Two more sweeps and all I could think was we were almost three quarters done. My legs and back were starting to give my age away.

It happened in a moment. I can't even say I heard it, but in that millisecond before it happened, I saw my dog react. And then the world changed.

One moment I was walking, the next, Jesse had thrown me to the ground, his body protectively covering mine.

I don't recall ever having that happen to me, and as I hit, a searing pain shot through me. I wasn't sure if I had broken my ribs or been shot. They say being shot feels something like getting kicked by a mule and I was sure that is what I felt, the kick of a mule.

68

The air was completely knocked out of my lungs, leaving nothing to talk with. Trying to drag in air was a big problem due to the combination of the man on my back and the pack that was already there when he landed on me. Not to mention that the pain in my mid-section was agony.

I'm not sure how, but I managed to pull in enough air to hoarsely whisper "get off of me." Jesse didn't move, so I determined I needed to move him. I arched my back, pushing up and hoping to dislodge him.

"Hold on, don't move" His voice was extremely calm, too calm actually, and yet under it, I could hear the steely order.

I had to move, or, more truly, he had to move. I was struggling to breathe. "Please. I landed on a rock." I drew in another ragged breathe in order to continue, "I can't breathe, please get off of me."

I once again arched up, this time actually causing Jesse to lift his head and then I heard it. A reminder of why I was laying there, on the ground, my face in the dirt. Someone had shot at us. Jesse had saved my life, and I nearly cost him his by moving.

It was clearly aimed at us as the bullet hit the tree over our heads, showering us with bark and needles.

"But my dog, where is my dog?" I couldn't see Ari and it was freaking me out. Had he shot him first? I didn't hear any whining, I didn't hear anything.

"He's over there, to our right. Whoever it is isn't shooting at him. Don't move Rebekkah!" Instead, I lifted my head again, causing Jesse to lift his.

That was a mistake as another shot ricocheted off our tree, slamming into another one nearby. Jesse, none too kindly, reminded me to be still.

"I'll try to move off. Don't move. I'm the one wearing the ballistic vest, not you." Slowly, carefully, and taking far too much time for my lungs, he inched his way off of me. The release was amazing as I could lift myself off the rock.

With more freedom, I lifted my head again, this time trying to see my dog. Yes, there he was – still working. I had initially wondered if Donald Wussow, fifty-eight, in good health, had gone round the bend mentally and was shooting at us. Watching my dog, I knew Don wasn't out there. It was someone else. In a moment I remembered what I saw just before the first bullet zinged at us. My dog had thrown up his head and stood frozen, staring to our left. He had smelled him, but didn't race toward him. He wasn't our subject. But why was he, or they or whoever they were, shooting at us?

I had never been shot at before; I never wanted to be again. It was frightening, it was… I wasn't even sure what word to use. Normal people didn't have this happen to them! As the thought struck me, I suddenly realized that any searcher out today could be at risk. Not just me, not just my dog, or Jesse here, but every member of my unit who had come. I was the president, the leader of the group. If anything happened to them, it would be on my head. Even the planters, wherever they were, could be in danger.

The next thought that came was who would take care of my mom if something happened to me. That thought alone kept me still, and doing the only thing I could do. I prayed.

"Dear God, we spoke earlier today, on the drive here. I asked for safety for our subject and the searchers. I hope I was sensible enough to include me in that request, but if I forgot, please include myself, my dog and Jesse over there. I think he saved my life. Please tap whoever is shooting at us on the shoulder and remind them of the seventh commandment – the one about 'thou shall not kill'. Thank you and Amen."

As I lay there, I heard Jesse on the radio, explaining our situation to base. I had the GPS with our coordinates, but I wasn't sure if I should move to give it to him.

"Jesse, I have our coordinates, do you want them?"

"I hit the emergency response button on my radio, does the same thing. I'm going to try and talk to this guy. He may not realize I'm Law Enforcement or that we're on a search."

Before he could say anything, we heard someone yelling. In Spanish, then a word or two in English filtered through.

"Señora con el perro – lady with dog – dónde estás?"

No gunshots ripped through the air, instead, tree planters came running through the woods. The crew leader was the one calling, and I watched, tears in my eyes, as my dog greeted the man with happy bounces.

"Here, we're here!" I called back. They had just saved our lives, I was sure. First Jesse, and now a group of men I couldn't even communicate with had risked their lives for me.

"Okay? Señora, okay?" The look of concern was clear on his face as he patted my dog.

"Si – yes, we're alright. How – did you hear the shots?"

It was confusing, but between Jesse's calm measured questions and the half English, half Spanish response, we understood that our new-found friend, Arturo, heard the shots from our direction. The first shot they ignored, but by the third, they were concerned for us.

"Arturo, did you see anyone as you came here?"

"Si; yes. See man with long," He spread his hands far apart, then put them up as if he was going to fire a rifle, "um, pistola, um, gun!"

Jesse nodded and with some arm pointing, determined a direction of travel while I stood back and let the rest of the tree planters meet my dog. I tried not to let on that I was shaking so badly the tree was the only thing that held me up.

"I need to radio this in. Not sure what we have, but it sounds almost like a pot farm or something. I'm going to ask our friend here if he could stay with us until the deputies show up, but the rest can go back to planting. Are you alright?"

"Yes, my stomach hurts like crazy from that stupid rock; had to be the size of Gibraltar. I'd like to thank Arturo – he saved our lives."

He was incredibly shy as I tried to explain my thanks. He patted Ari, and in his broken English, I understood he was worried about the beautiful dog; he didn't want such an animal hurt. With those simple words, he won my heart. I dug into my pack and found a business card for McCaffrey House and asked him if he and his crew could come for dinner on Friday. It seemed such a small way to say thank you, so I was pleased when he indicated they would try.

As we waited for the cavalry, in the form of other Law Enforcement officers, to show up, Jesse let me know our missing man had been found. Hypothermic, but alive, about half mile from the maples he tended so lovingly. I was glad of that.

An additional radio call let him know that they would want me to stay in case I had anything to add to what happened. Glancing down at my dog, visibly tired, I asked if there was any way to get my truck closer to me so I could put him up to rest.

"They say if you can walk back out to where we parked the squad your truck should be waiting. I have to stay here, Rebekkah. Are you alright to go on your own?"

I went, walking slowly and with a definite limp. My dog, at over ten years old which was comparable to over seventy in human years, made me look like I was over ninety.

As I arrived back where we had left the squad car, I found not just the squad and my own truck, but every emergency vehicle imaginable.

Marge wrapped her arms around me and while I love hugs, I yanked away. It hurt, and badly. Amos helped me take off my pack, while Al loaded Ari and fed and watered my dogs. Someone volunteered to drive for me to get something to eat in the nearby community.

It was then I realized they didn't know what happened, or really, they had heard about the shooting, but not that it was me. Explaining the situation, Amos flagged down a fireman with an ATV and asked him to drive me back out. They'd stay with my truck and dogs.

It ended up they didn't need my testimony anyway. I told them of Ari's initial alert reaction to someone over to our left, but beyond that, I had spent most of the time with my face in the dirt or looking for my dog. I had not seen anything or anyone. I felt rather stupid as I listened to Jesse explain where the shots had initially come from, what type of firearm he believed it to be, and then Arturo, through a translator, telling them what he saw.

Finally, around seven thirty, I was able to leave. An ATV took me once again out to my truck, where Amos and Marge waited. All I wanted at that point was a bathroom and a hot bath; in that order. It wasn't until Amos asked about food that I realized I wanted that as well.

Stripping down in the handicap stall of a local restaurant, I found a deep purple bruise. I'm sure it was the size of a volleyball and covered my entire stomach area. And it hurt. It hurt to stand, it hurt to sit, and it hurt to bend over especially. I only hoped it wouldn't hurt to lie down.

Over dinner, I learned that Don, our missing person, had been found by line searchers. It appeared he'd be alright, although no one seemed to know what happened, or why he had wandered.

When I arrived home late that night, I found a note from Gary stating that my mom was doing well, but he wanted me to get her in again. I was happy to see the note. It was real. What had happened out there in the woods today wasn't. It couldn't have been. Yet, I had the bruise to prove something had happened.

# *Chapter 6*

*For there is not a word in my tongue, but You know it.*

A s I settled back into my routine, that odd day seemed more and more as if it didn't happen. The only tangible part was I was still very sore. Gary had checked me out and I had no broken bones or damaged internal organs. I was just bruised. And it still hurt to sit and bend over.

It was when Megan left me a note saying she had a call, very broken English, asking if they could still come on Friday, that I remembered my invitation.

Calling back the number, I reached a hotel in a nearby community. Explaining why I was calling, they took a message to say yes, come at six for supper, and directions to our local church. I then called Pastor Dave who loved the idea and promptly contacted every family in the community to ask if they could help.

Two days later, E.R. SAR received a note from the county to thank us for our help. Although it seemed normal, yet somehow abnormal that it didn't mention that the president of E.R. SAR had been shot at and a material witness to a crime. Yet I knew it wouldn't. It just seemed odd.

Then another card arrived, and I smiled at the perky puppy on the cover of the card. Inside was a hand-written note.

> *"To one of the bravest women I've ever met. I hope (and pray) that you're doing alright. I wanted to tell you how impressed I was with your calm and your courage the other day. And to ask if I could take you to coffee or something to apologize for throwing you to the ground like I did. I've included my card with my email and number. I hope to hear from you soon!"*

Staring at the card, I felt another smile form. I could be wrong, but I think I was being asked out on a date; and by a very nice man.

"Rebekkah, you look like the cat that ate the cream. What was in that card?"

"An invitation to coffee, Connie. Say, where were you the other day? I had hoped you would come to Amy's big maple party."

"Well, I had a date of a different sort." And with a flirtatious grin, my friend left the room, letting the café doors swing closed behind her. She didn't want me to know, which of course made me want to know who she had a date with.

Going back to work, I found myself periodically checking on the card, wondering if it, like that odd day in the woods, was real. It was in staring at the card, I realized I actually should answer it.

Making a phone call scared me. It seemed so personal, so instead I decided to email.

*"Jesse..."*

I stalled out immediately. Did I address him by his first name, or as "Detective Deschene"? Officer Deschene? Sighing, I waited for inspiration. It came in the form of two little old ladies who told me to stop daydreaming.

"Martha, Margaret, can I ask you a question?" It was, of course, a silly thing to ask. Martha knew immediately something was up and positively glowed at the anticipation of giving someone else advice.

I explained as best as I could without giving a lot of details; and waited as the two women cogitated together. Finally,

76

Margaret said something quite simple, "How did he address you in his correspondence?"

He hadn't. And it was a perfect solution. I wouldn't address him either with any kind of name or title. Giving the ladies a hug and promising to be out of their way shortly, I typed once more.

> *"Thank you so much first, for saving my life, and then for the thoughtful card. I'm still feeling like it was a dream – or more like a nightmare – that didn't really happen. But then I met two very special people – you and Arturo. I thank you also for the invitation, but have maybe a better idea. Are you available Friday to join us at the Elk Ridge church for a big potluck we're throwing for the tree planters who risked their own lives for ours? I really hope you can come. It's at six p.m. If that doesn't work out for you, I'd love to take you up on the coffee invitation."*

I included my contact information and hit send, hoping it wasn't too forward. My mom would be very upset with me if I were too forward with a man, even at my age.

I was so deep in thought, that I was completely startled when Megan touched my shoulder.

"Rebekkah, can I talk to you?"

"Sure, here?" I glanced around the kitchen where The Sisters were bustling about, doing food prep for the evening meal. The butcher block table had become my impromptu desk because I could stand and work until sitting became easier.

"Can we go to the office or the library? I'd like to talk to you privately if I can?"

We chose the library, putting a "Do Not Disturb" sign on the door.

"Should I worry, Megan?"

"No, at least, I don't think so! No, I need to tell you something which is good news for me anyway. Rebekkah, I'm pregnant! We didn't expect it; we were told after my last I couldn't anymore. It just happened."

"And you're happy?" I could see she was. She was ecstatic. And her comment to Connie about staying away if she was ill suddenly made sense.

"I'm happy. A little nervous, as they are worried about complications, but I've got a great doctor. I'll be okay. Tommie is excited too, he loves kids. The reason I wanted to tell you is, well, at some point I won't be here, I'll need to take time off. Will that be okay with you?"

"You know it will be. You didn't need to ask, you're important to us here. Megan, you're part of the family!"

"I wasn't sure if you perhaps planned for Connie to take over for me. Lately, it seems when you're not here, she does. I didn't know what to do the day you left for your mom." She stopped as my eyebrow went up.

Legally, of course, Megan's job was secure when she took family leave time, but I knew this conversation wasn't about her rights. It was to confirm her place here, in the McCaffrey family.

"Megan, you are basically my second in command for the running of McCaffrey House. I'm sorry. I've been negligent in telling people that. Agnes didn't want to be responsible for it as you know, and you took to it like a duck to water. You've been an integral part of this team for quite some time now. It's time, I guess, to have an employee meeting."

The last thing I wanted, of course, was to have to tell Connie, my friend and mentor, to straighten up and fly right. Perhaps a meeting with everyone would be the best way. I posted a notice up to have everyone go to the library on Thursday at one p.m.

Prior to the meeting, I sent an email to my fellow owners and our advisory board. Well, all except Martha and Margaret, who I talked to privately over tea. They didn't have e-mail. It was during this meeting I learned that Martha was having some difficulties adapting to Connie's personal schedule.

"She tends to stay up or go out late, and then doesn't get up to help in the mornings. She also leaves such a mess. She cleans it up if I say something, but not before. To be honest, Rebekkah, I haven't really known how to tell you."

On Monday, everyone showed up except Connie. It dawned on me that we'd never officially made Connie an employee of The House. She just helped out. That, I saw, would need to change.

Going ahead, I explained to those present about the need for leadership, and responsibility to our fellow employees and our guests to support that leadership. With Megan's permission, I then let them know of a change soon to come.

"Megan is going to have a baby," I paused as all the women in the room oohed and aahed over her for a few moments before going on, "During the time she'll be on family medical leave, I'll resume the duties she's taken over for me. When she returns, she'll go back to her current position."

"Only if Connie isn't here," A quiet voice from the small group interrupted me.

I stopped, and while painful, I sat down with them to make it more personal before I spoke again.

79

"How many here have had a problem with Connie?"

It was silent, but then, Agnes spoke up, "I have. She seems to be a nice person for the most part, but periodically she'll, well, take over. Not to do the work itself, but to tell us how it should be done."

I watched as all the heads nodded. It was in my court now, and I hated the very thought of it. Friendship and loyalty were things I was raised to respect and cherish.

"I'll take care of it. Connie isn't officially an employee of McCaffrey House. She's never signed the agreements all of you signed. That was a mistake on my part. She hasn't been told the rules of the business. That's where I'll start. If she wants a job here, she'll need to adhere to the standards. I think it will all be fine."

After everyone left the library, I remained. I don't know why, but I was reminded of a SAR training many years ago. The first year I was in Search and Rescue actually. They put everyone in a circle facing each other under a magnificent night sky. The constellations were brilliant, the moon shining bright. We all had our compasses in our hands and were told to check for north and lock the position in our heads. Then we were told to close our eyes, and someone turned us around, rather like a pin the tail on the donkey game. When we were stopped, we were told to open our eyes and point to north.

Hands were pointing in a wide range of directions. Only a few were correct. Unbeknownst to the people in the circle, the trainers had put in ringers – people who quietly changed locations within the circle while the eyes were closed and people were being turned.

Many of the people, when they opened their eyes, looked for the person they were across from when they first located north. Only a very few rechecked their compass and pointed to the correct direction.

I felt like that for some reason. Not quite lost, but not understanding where north went. The familiar landmarks that pointed the way weren't there anymore.

The lesson that night under that beautiful starlit sky was, check your compass. Landmarks will change, things will move, we'll get disoriented. Rely on your compass. I laughed ruefully at myself as I had just had that reminder recently on our navigation training.

The reason I laughed was I realized I was still learning that lesson many years later. Only it wasn't about my navigational compass anymore. It was about my spiritual compass. My north shouldn't be based on people, places or things. They distract and confuse. It should be based on the only thing that is completely unchanging; God.

# Chapter 7

*You have beset me behind and before,*

*and laid Your hand on me.*

Friday dawned bright and clear, and showed signs of a true spring warm-up. My mom was up and ready to tackle her day as I got ready for work. She was making homemade pies for the big potluck tonight, which made my mouth water. My mom made the best pies, even better than Margaret did. Of course, I'd never tell Margaret or Martha, but it was true.

Arriving at McCaffrey, I learned that we had a plumbing problem that was being dealt with by Harold, our maintenance man, as well as the local plumber. One of the down-sides to running the Bed and Breakfast was the interesting things that people flushed down the system.

Checking on their progress, I could see I was just in the way and turned my attention to making sure the people who used that bathroom were aware of where the other facilities were. No one seemed incredibly put out, but it bothered me a great deal. Especially when the plumber tracked me down to inform me it wasn't what was flushed down, but what was coming back up. The septic line had frozen up.

"How can that happen? For heaven's sake, winter is almost over!" I was likely a touch crabby, which I knew I'd feel bad about later, but not at the moment.

"Actually, it appears the faucet in the tub was leaking. Leaking cold water into a line, it hits the cold pipe and slowly built up ice layer by layer. We can steam it and fix it, but the faucet will have to be replaced."

"Well, Bob, is it something you can take care of today? Please?"

Getting the details, as well as the estimated cost, I notified the other owners. Most of the everyday decisions for McCaffrey House were left in my hands, but a bill of this size, I wanted everyone aware of it.

That dealt with, I was about to start on my own office paperwork, when my cell phone went off.

"Elk Ridge Search and Rescue, how can we help you?" I was tapping my fingernails on the table top, feeling like everything was conspiring to keep me from my work. It wasn't, of course, but for some reason, I was feeling stressed.

"Rebekkah? This is Jesse, Jesse Deschene. Is that you?"

"Oh, yes, this is Rebekkah. Hello! Did you get my email?" I felt suddenly fluttery instead of stressed. It was in that moment I realized I had been upset because I hadn't heard back from my email to him. It had nothing to do with all the external influences.

"Yes, I did. I'm sorry I didn't answer right away, I wanted to make sure if I could come, and I can. In fact, Arturo contacted me to find out about directions, so they'll be following me. We'll see you tonight!"

As I hung up, I looked up to see Connie watching me. I saw that odd look once again, and decided it was as good a time as any to talk to her.

"Connie, do you have a few minutes? Can we go into the office for a moment?"

She nodded and followed me to the small alcove. Megan was out in the front room, so we had a little time to ourselves.

"Connie, I realized this week that we need to formalize your employment with McCaffrey House," I held up my hand as she started to jump in, "I know that you don't plan this to be a long-

84

term thing, but for our insurance and of course just keeping the state happy, we need to show you as an employee. Are you alright with that?"

"Well, this is sort of coming out of the blue. Is it because I'm staying with Martha? Have there been issues?" Connie did look puzzled, but also not very happy.

"Connie, the problem is actually the fact you're living in the apartment in exchange for helping out with McCaffrey, but we've never formalized it. To have you work here, we need to show you on the employment records so you're covered by insurance." I had always disliked insurance and dealing with it, but now it came in handy as a scapegoat.

Connie nodded, and I wondered what was going through her head. It felt as if a wall had gone up.

"Wow. I'm just wondering if there is something behind this, besides the business." When I didn't respond, simply because I had no idea what to say, she continued, "Are you jealous of the fact I'm dating Benjamin?"

Had she hit me, it would have been less surprising. I had no idea she was dating our sheriff, and if I had, I had no reason to be jealous of it.

"Connie, are you listening to what you just said? First, I have no idea who you are dating, nor do I really care. No, maybe that isn't true. I do care, because I care about you. That being said, Sheriff Rafael is a big boy who dates who he wants, and from what I understand, that covers a lot of territory, so I am concerned that you'll be hurt again." I paused, feeling unsure of how to proceed. All I had wanted was to formalize her employment, not get into a personal confrontation.

"Second, no, please let me finish," I said as she started to interrupt, "This has nothing to do with your personal life Connie. It has everything to do with the life of McCaffrey House. Right now, no one knows what your position is here. They aren't sure if you are employed or simply a friend of mine who gets to live here for free with no responsibilities. Can you understand the position that puts me in?"

Connie was silent, and I wondered if she was angry or thinking, or both. I waited; and waited, determined to make sure she'd speak first.

"So, what are my options?"

"You actually have options, but we just need to formalize what you decide you want to do. Do you want work for McCaffrey?"

Once again, I waited. I could see the answer, however. She didn't truly want to work for McCaffrey. She wanted to have the freedom that she finally had a taste of; maybe not forever, but for now.

"Connie, you are someone I care about, you know that. But I also hope you can understand what I'm dealing with. If you want to stay in the apartment, we have to have some sort of agreement. If you want to work for McCaffrey, you'll have specific scheduled hours and assignments. You will be expected to abide by the employee guidelines that everyone else does. If you don't want to do that, then we'd have to work out what the value is for staying in the apartment." I left the implication unsaid. Work and stay, or stay and pay.

"How much time do I have to make a decision, Rebekkah?" My heart quivered as I saw the discouragement and the frustration. I wish I could take back everything I had said. This woman had helped me so much in those first hard years of SAR, I felt almost like a traitor. On the other hand, I had to think about the business.

"I'd like to know by the end of next week. Connie, is it because it would require you to have a schedule that you wouldn't want to work here?"

"Honestly? I don't know why it scares me. To be tied down by a job? I don't know. Or what would that job be? If it is simply doing dishes and laundry, it would be very hard." She had a faraway look, and I suspect she was thinking, really thinking, about her future.

"Rebekkah, I know you can't let me live here for free. I know that there has to be some contractual agreement. It was one thing for a short time, but I need to find my own place, move on, or buckle down and work here to pay for my lodging. I know all that. I just need to think about it. Tell me, what would my job be?"

"Fair enough and I'm glad you're not still thinking it's about me being jealous. I think Benjamin is an extremely attractive man. Every woman, single or otherwise, in town does. He's a good friend; no, he is a great friend. But he's not a Christian, and I've known him long enough to know he likes his freedom. Go carefully Connie."

I pulled out a chart and passed it to her to look at. She studied it and then handed it back.

"Those are the jobs that have to get done every day. With our current staff, we get them done, but it's a daily challenge. The only team that doesn't need help, really, is The Sisters. They run a very tight ship and keep things going smoothly in the kitchen."

"That all being said, what I would propose to you, knowing your personality and the fact that you are really an artist at heart, is to work part time under Agnes, helping her do whatever needs to be done. And part time with Martha and Margaret in the kitchen, learning to cook."

Connie came up sputtering, and I put my hand on hers, before speaking again, "Sorry, that came out wrong. I know you are an excellent cook. What I'd like you to do is learn to cook as they do, for specific needs, larger meals, and how to manage the costs at the same time. Part of working with Agnes, by the way, would be to take over hostessing. She hates it, but has done an admirable job."

"Connie, here is the real rub. If you decide to take on a job here, you wouldn't be in charge. You'd be under Agnes, who is technically under Megan, who answers to me, and I answer to the rest of the owners. You'd also be required to abide by the company policies for employees." I pulled one of the packets out and handed it to her.

"I'll look it over, and think about it. I'll let you know before the end of next week. By the way, I think you're wrong about Benjamin. I think he'd settle down for the right woman."

I just smiled and nodded. Since I had known him, a number of women had tried just that. While he hadn't quite left a trail of broken hearts, he definitely left a trail of disillusioned women who thought they had what it took to tame him. I tried to stay out of that part of his life, so I had no idea if he took great pleasure in his triumphs or simply moved on without any real understanding that he had foiled many a marital-minded woman.

Returning to the kitchen, I realized the time had been flying by and I should have gone home to pick up my mom and her pies for the potluck. Checking out with Megan, I left in a hurry, only to run into the very person we had been discussing; literally.

I slammed into him and I was reminded that not only was our sheriff good looking, he probably worked out every day.

"I seem to always be in your way. Is everything alright? Your mom is okay?" The concern was genuine. He had always gotten on well with my mom, which never ceased to amaze me, considering his reputation.

"Yes, everything is fine; I just have to go get her for the potluck tonight. Pecan, pumpkin and apple pies are waiting at home. Are you coming tonight?" I knew he would, even if it was at the church. It was a free meal, and what bachelor didn't want to take advantage of that?

"Yes, I hear you have some new friends - which, by the way, you've never really talked about. I'm sure you likely can't say much, but I hear you held up under fire quite well." He grinned and dropped his arm across my shoulder, "I hear that you never even panicked. That's my girl," and with that, he walked away; likely to go meet up with his date for the night; who was likely my best friend Connie.

I arrived at the church almost two hours later with my mom and the pies intact. They nearly didn't survive as we had to fight off a dog that was sure she was going with us. It never ceased to amaze me how fast Jael could leap straight up.

Pastor Dave arrived to help my mom out as I pulled up, and took the pies to carry for her. I wasn't sure if it was my mom or the pies he was truly worried about.

"Rebekkah, glad you got here early. We're going to have a great turnout. This was such a great idea!" Jane, a friend from church, scooped me out of the parking lot and scurried me into the church, barely giving me time to take off my coat.

By the time our guests of honor had arrived, we were ready. I don't know if I did, but later I heard the rumor that I lit up like a Christmas tree when Detective Jesse Deschene walked in.

For me, it was the first time I had the opportunity to take a good look at him. My memory of that day was twinkling eyes and calm, cool, and in charge. I wasn't truly sure which attracted me more.

Jesse, dressed in Dockers and a polo shirt, wasn't anything extraordinary; he was average in many ways, except one. He had an amazing smile. It was exactly what I remembered from the day we were shot at. It's what I saw as soon as he walked in.

Arturo Vegas and his tree planting crew came in behind Jesse, and I saw again the shy man, shorter than I was, but cleaned up and looking much more like someone you'd meet on a street in town. His crew, too, had that same shy look and it finally dawned on me it was likely because they weren't able to communicate.

The issue was solved when three different folks from the church split forces and served as interpreters. I had no idea anyone there spoke Spanish. This far north, this close to the Canadian border, most people took French as a second language in school.

I took Arturo and Jesse around to introduce them, and felt a distinctly funny feeling as Benjamin was suddenly at my side. It was clear that he knew Jesse, and they had to have talked. How else would he know if I had panicked under fire or not? I personally thought I had panicked, nearly costing Jesse his life by fighting to get him to move as well as trying to see my dog.

The two men were soon in conversation, so I took Arturo to where his crew was in the food line. Potlucks at this church were always as if people pulled the stops out to make the best food they could. There were some very good cooks in the church, although I did tend to bypass the lutefisk. My own opinion was, if you had to soak the lye out of your food, you shouldn't eat it. Besides the fact, it was fish; or had been at some point.

"Arturo; thank you, and thank your crew again for doing all that you did. You didn't have to, but you risked your lives for us." I glanced over at Tim, who translated easily for me.

"We are glad to help." Arturo smiled that shy smile, and continued, "I have um, esposa, - wife! Si; wife, at home. I think, what she would say." I interpreted that to mean, what he did was because he knew his wife would have wanted him to help.

"Do you have children – oh – niños - Arturo?" I tried to pull from the recesses of my brain what little Spanish I remembered.

"Si; cuatro, four little niños!" He said it proudly, and I wondered about this man who spent so much time away from his family in order to earn a living.

I sat with Arturo and his crew, Tim and his wife joining us to help with the language barrier. Arturo, I learned had been raised in California, and started every year there, picking crops. As the harvests in each state finished, they traveled north.

"How do you know where you'll go next?" Tim, now clearly interested, asked. And with his interpreting, I, too, learned the answer.

"He says that they actually work for a labor company that contracts them out. They bid on projects for the workers, and then as the crops are finishing in one area, they notify the next agency or farm or whoever is hiring them, that the workers are on their way."

"I had no idea, did you?" I quietly asked Tim. He shook his head in the negative. The men who sat there were all younger men, in the twenties and thirties. "Do they do this every year, year after year?"

The answer was apparently not the same for all of them. Some returned with other crews, some didn't. Our conversation turned to their families, and Tim hardly got any food as he spent most of the time asking and answering questions. The men showed us pictures of their wives, sweethearts, their children, and one even showed me a photo of his dog at home. Their cellphones were their lifelines to heart and home.

Towards the end of the evening, Arturo touched my arm and explained they needed to leave, but wanted to ask me a question.

"Señora, the perro, your dog, give him pet from me. Very real – like king." Tim leaned over to explain 'real' meant regal.

"Yes, I will. Please take care of yourself. If you come back next year for planting, please, let me know." I handed him another card with my own contact information.

The planters said good night and as I watched them go, I wondered about a life I had no idea existed in Minnesota, and what it must be like.

"Rebekkah, I need to go as well. We hardly had a chance to talk, but I thought I'd let you know, we did get a lead on the guy who took the shots at us. A group of guys appeared to have a pot plantation growing back there, unbeknownst to the owners of course. We must have tripped an alarm or triggered a game camera or something that they were just waiting for us."

"Well, I have to say next time, I'll be far more careful when I go into the woods. I hope you catch them. Do you really think they were trying to kill us, or just scare us into leaving?"

"Frighten us. Whoever was pulling the trigger was a marksman. I checked the hits on the tree and they were consistent and close to each other," Jesse cleared his throat and then said, more quietly, "Are you still interested in going out for coffee or maybe a dinner sometime?"

"Sure, I'd like that. Just let me know when and where!"

"Have you known Benjamin long?"

"I guess ever since he came to Elk Ridge. Why?" Something in his manner made me start to wonder what Benjamin could have said about me.

"Well, he couldn't say enough about you. I rather got the impression he really likes you. To be honest, it appeared his date wasn't thrilled about it either. I don't want to, well, hunt on posted lands. Are you and he..." He let it trail off, so it took me a moment to realize what he was asking.

"Oh! No. Dating Benjamin? No, he's dating my friend Connie right now. We're very good friends, but no, not... no." I realized I was babbling. Take a breath, I thought to myself, then I finished with, "No, I'm not dating Benjamin, but we are good friends."

He nodded and with a final reminder he'd call me for that coffee, I watched him leave. A moment later, I watched as Connie and Benjamin left, her arm linked possessively through his.

"Rebekkah, why are you looking so, well, worried?" My mom nudged my arm, trying to get me to help carry the empty pie plates.  Apparently all of the leftovers had been packed up and sent along with the planters.  No leftover pie for an unorthodox breakfast.

"Worried?  I'm not worried; just tired.  How are you doing?  Your pies were amazing as usual."  We walked out to the truck in silence, and I wondered what look was on my face that she interpreted as worried.

# Chapter 8

*Such knowledge is too wonderful for me;*

A few days later, Connie signed the employee forms, agreeing to work part time with Agnes and part time with The Sisters. The early reports were that she was much easier to have around when everyone knew what the expectations were. And in reality, I could see that Connie herself seemed happier. Of course, part of that might have been because she did seem to have exclusive rights on our sheriff.

As I adjusted the schedules for Connie, I realized that for the first time since launching McCaffrey House, I had staff and time to take some time off for myself. A whole week of true vacation time, paid even.

Digging in my desk, I found a brochure for a workshop every cadaver dog handler dreams of; a trip with their dog to a body farm.

Every year I had printed out the notice, hoping to go, and not being able to go. Sometimes it was just the timing, as when I lost Gus-Gus, but most often, it was simply out of reach for my budget. I had made the decision, the promise to myself that this year, this year I would go.

I had been planning for this very trip ever since, telling no one about it for fear it wouldn't happen again. I had squirreled away every extra penny, knowing it wouldn't be cheap. It required not only the workshop costs, but a roundtrip of nearly three thousand miles, meals and of course the hotel while at the class. I had done it though. I had the money.

A few calls later, and I had Bev convinced to go with me, as well as Marge. It saved each of us money sharing expenses, but even with that, I knew that the trip would easily eat up the thousand dollars I had in savings.

There was one other worry; my truck. It had taken to needing repairs nearly every time it required an oil change. Had they been normal maintenance, I could have understood it. I put on thousands of miles on the truck, often in just a month or two.

These repairs, however, were odd things that were starting to cost me more a month than the actual truck payments. Could I trust this truck for a trip of that distance?

The answer was made for me. Three days before I had to pay for the class, my truck broke down, again. It took all my savings to get it running again. Now, I was faced with having to cancel my trip; another dream gone by the wayside. Angry and frustrated, I found myself in a familiar position; on my knees.

"Rebekkah, can you help me?" My mom blinked at me in an odd fashion as I pulled myself up off the floor. Kneeling was getting harder and harder with my bad knee.

"What do you need?" I followed her into the room we called our family room, where the television and our favorite chairs sat.

"Help me move my chair. I think my eyes are changing, I can't see the TV anymore." I had my misgivings as I pulled her chair two feet closer, but she was happy, so I let it go. It seemed far too close to me, but perhaps her eyes were bothering her.

Returning to my room, I looked at the numbers again. The money just wasn't there. The next day, as I went through my daily chores, the difficulty of the decision was weighing me down. I had to cancel, I didn't have a choice.

Driving home, I finally accepted that I couldn't go. I would notify Bev and Marge that my truck couldn't make it and I couldn't afford to go. It left me feeling very depressed and empty.

I handed mom our mail as I headed for the computer. Email would be easier than trying to explain on a phone call. I couldn't cry in an email.

"Rebekkah, I can't read this; what's this one for?" Mom handed me an envelope that I hadn't noticed when I sorted through the mail the first time. It was addressed to me, but the return address was missing. Ripping it open, I watched as a miracle fell out of the envelope. It was a check from a dear old friend, with a note saying she was thinking of me, and hoped the money would help with my search and rescue work. It was for exactly the amount I needed to register for the class. While it didn't cover the travel, it was enough to give me hope.

"Mom, it was for me. It's a check to help me to go on my trip." I registered the next day, paying for the class, and trusting God to come up with the rest.

Twenty-four hours later, I had a call from the college hosting the event. The scholarship I had requested earlier had been granted. As they noticed I had paid for the class, they would refund the money. Martha, standing near me as I took the call, grabbed my arm as I nearly dropped my phone.

The final blessing was still to come however. Adam called to let me know that he had heard about a vehicle that might fit my needs. It was newer, had fewer miles, but because of some hail damage the owner was willing to lower their price. My bank gave me the nod, and when we left for our trip, it was in a slightly used but incredibly dependable Suburban.

We packed it up with gear, crates and dogs and still had some room to spare. As Bev sat in the heated leather seat, she informed us that it was like riding an overstuffed couch down the interstate.

God wasn't through however. As we made our first stop for gas, I called home to let mom know how things were going. The first words out of her mouth were, "Did you make a deposit before you left?"

Apparently someone anonymously supplied the last of the funds with a deposit directly into our account. It arrived the day after we left. My needs were supplied in full measure, pressed down, and running over.

Driving across the country with good company and a vehicle that just ate up the miles was amazing. I hadn't been away from home for so long, it felt distinctly odd. But as my mom was doing well, Megan had McCaffrey running smoothly, I finally felt good about taking some time off.

The only sadness I felt was that I had left Ari at home with my mom. Jael was the future; Ari was moving slowly into retirement. Still, it hurt to watch his face as he knew he was being left. Besides that, however, I knew I was going to have a wonderful time.

It was when we stopped in Tennessee for lunch that I noticed it. Jael had a lump on her face, as if someone had stuffed a golf ball into her cheek. I gently touched it and she flinched away. It felt warm, and it had happened so quickly, we all agreed it must be a bug bite. A little Benadryl, she'd be fine soon.

She wasn't. By the time we reached the hotel that night, the swelling hadn't gone down, and if anything, it had gone up a bit. I carefully iced her cheek and gave her more medication.

The problem with antihistamines is they dry out a dog's nose, and the ability to smell is greatly affected. I had traveled nearly fifteen hundred miles to arrive with a dog on medication that could possibly prevent her from even training. Sometimes, I wondered what God was thinking.

As we met with the staff and learned our schedules for the next several days, I notified them of my dog's swollen face, and that she was on medication. Each sympathized and left it up to me if I wanted to work her. Between Bev, Marge, and me, we made the decision to go ahead. It was likely a once in a lifetime chance.

As I turned her loose for her first search scenario, I realized that, although I had told everyone around me, I had forgotten to tell Jael her nose wasn't supposed to be working. She sailed into a small barn and within a moment, she had given her trained final response, a perfect Egyptian cat-like sit. The instructor, watching her for a moment, finally said, "Well, I guess her nose still works! Reward and keep working."

By the end of the day, I carefully noted in our training logs that K-9 Jael had performed five blind finds, with a success rate of one hundred percent. And the golf ball in her cheek hadn't dissipated at all.

Sitting through the class room sessions, I still worried. A bug bite would have gone down by now. She didn't seem in any severe pain, she was still eating like a horse, but I did notice by the fifth problem, that she was having a harder time catching her tennis ball. So engrossed was I in my thoughts, I hate to admit, I missed part of the lecture on bone identification.

I figured it out when, over dinner, several of the students were talking about it. The people at the table came from across the United States; from New Jersey, Pennsylvania, Florida, Michigan and of course, the three of us from Minnesota.

"You three are from Minnesota, aren't you?" One of the handlers asked, and at our nod, continued, "Have you ever trained with the unit that does disaster work over in Wisconsin?"

"I didn't know there was a unit that did that over there. I wanted to train my first dog for it, but he wasn't cut out for it. My second dog, Gus, I had hopes for, but his legs were too short to navigate rubble. Jael, well, I think she could do it, but wasn't aware of a training area near us for it."

"I'm from Michigan, and I had heard there was a training facility in Wisconsin. I'll get the information to you if you want. It looks pretty neat, and the trainer either was or is a FEMA level handler."

"Thanks – I suspect several of our unit members would be interested in some of the training. We don't get too many disasters around us, but the training sure couldn't hurt!"

The idea was like a small bee in my bonnet, and I was happy the handler remembered to give me the information. Checking online, I realized it was only a few hours from the Elk Ridge area. She included the trainer's contact information as well and I made a mental note to contact them when we got home.

That night, the swelling on Jael's face went up. I gave her more Benadryl, more ice and prayed for the best. We would be doing more intense problems the next day, but still not actually entering the research part of the area where the bodies were.

As the day progressed, Jael continued to work problems well, but instead of ramping up as she had always done at workshops previously, she was slowing down a bit. Not noticeable to anyone but myself, by the end of the second day, I was worried. I thought

I could see her flews, the dog version of a lip, looking flaccid and floppy, but I wasn't really sure. Arriving at the hotel that night, I realized it was because the lip was now swollen too.

The last day, we were going to enter the research area, the moment we had all waited for. To see our dogs be able to work odor of a full body in decomposition. The thing that most of us forgot was that we would also be seeing the bodies ourselves.

Our instructors took us in first without our dogs, explaining that if both dog and handler were shocked or fearful or nervous upon entering, it did no one any good. This way, the handler could get over the shock factor first. It made sense, and I know for the first time since arriving, I questioned my own sanity for wanting to do this. Was I really as strange as people said I was, even jokingly?

Then I looked around at the other K-9 handlers there. They, too, were there to learn, to expose their dogs to something that wasn't readily available to K-9 handlers every day. They all seemed normal. The sad fact was - most K-9 teams only experienced the odor and sight of a full body on a real search.

This training gave us the opportunity to learn what our dog would do in a controlled training environment. If they would be nervous, fearful, or even destructive, now was the time to learn it, not on a real search.

"Remember folks, it isn't just the odor, which is powerful, but also the visual. Don't be surprised if your dogs don't do a trained response, or if they show aversion to the visual impact of a body. All we ask is, don't let your dogs urinate, defecate, taste or otherwise disturb the bodies."

There was a pause, and in careful tones, he continued, "The bodies in here were people who had lives, family; they experienced love, laughter, pain, sorrow and all the other things you've experienced. We treat them with respect, call them by their names, and want you to do the same."

It was a graphic moment for me, for everyone there. We had come with the thought of training our dogs on a body, and somewhere lost a small part of our humanity. It was a good reminder that each person we look for is just like those in the research facility. A reminder to use their name, not just the word subject or missing person; they are real and a beloved child of their Creator.

The gate was swung open, and I have to admit that my first impression was the odor of crayons that seemed to hang in the air. Then it was the person, Miss Mavis, who lay directly in front of us. Her soft tissue was long gone, but leathered skin still covered parts of her skeletal structure. Her smile was the smile of a skull, all teeth and looking real, yet not real.

Waiting patiently, the instructors simply let us absorb visually what would have horrified or fascinated many. I can only speak for myself, but I was humbled, and I'm not sure why. It was into the silence the instructor spoke.

"Most of the folks here are here because their families couldn't afford a funeral. They were paupers. But in coming here, they are providing us and you, an opportunity that they weren't able to do when they were alive. Please consider that when you bring your dogs in. Stay on the paths, although you can let your dogs approach each person. Keep them on leash however."

And then they began pointing out each deceased person in the research area, calling them by name, and explaining when they were brought in. Each was in a different level of decomposition;

each dressed as they had come, some still wearing watches and medical bracelets.

It felt peculiar, standing there, and yet I was glad the instructors had taken the time to do this. It was a good thing to remind us of who these people were in life, so we would continue to think of them as they were.

I went to get my dog, being second in the rotation. I felt, in fact I was sure, my dog could handle this new training. She had never seemed to be affected by what she saw. She didn't seem to think all that much after all. Ari, I knew, would have been saddened by the death around him. I was glad he wasn't there.

Entering the fenced area, I watched my dog shrink back, but not from what she saw. She was completely overwhelmed by what her nose was taking in all at once. The odor, which to me was sort of a waxy smell like bad crayons, was of course due to the adipocere.

Adipocere, the substance created by the breakdown of a body's fatty tissues, is literally waxy in texture. Also known as grave wax, it can both help and hinder death investigations. While it often preserves areas of the body, it can also mask how long a person has been dead.

In this case, it merely made the entire area smell like death. To my dog, however, it was just an overwhelming odor of what she was trained and rewarded to find. I let her acclimatize, as they had told us to do, by just standing and waiting for the dog to make the first move.

A moment later, Jael did. She, as I expected, didn't seem to have any concern over the appearance of the grinning skeletons, but instead started walking directly onto a pile of disarticulated bones, sniffing deeply.

The only thought that went through my head was "or otherwise disturb the bodies." I was about to give my leash a hard correction when I heard a whispered instruction behind me.

"Cue your indication," The instructor, reading my body language before I probably had a conscious thought, stopped a mistake on my part. A handler should never correct their dog when they are doing what we trained them to do. My dog was trained to find deceased and decomposing humans; that is what she was doing.

"Jael, SIT." I gave the cue and Jael whirled around and sat on the pile of bones, facing me. Taking out one of her toys that I could hold onto and hopefully not drop onto the ground which was saturated with the biohazard of decaying flesh, I let her take it for a moment before taking ahold of it. She promptly let go and we continued on. She bypassed a newer body to go to more bones, less decomposed than the first. Another reminder for me to cue, another "SIT" command and Jael promptly sat.

I felt confused. She obviously knew this was cadaver odor and she should sit, why wasn't she doing it on her own? The third body, this one less decomposed then the first two she had approached, and she finally, hesitantly, sat on her own.

The realization was finally dawning on me that my dog was smarter than I was, even if she didn't know it. She had entered an area where there were some thirteen bodies, both buried and above ground. She had never, in her life, been around such a strong stench. I was asking her to filter through it and find one body at a time. She was doing it in the best way possible for her. Starting with odor she was comfortable with; old and aged; and then moving slowly up to newer and stronger.

In my head I knew that each body would actually smell differently simply because the decomposition process was at a different stage. Here, I was seeing it in action, and yet I was still struggling to understand it myself. My dog, by starting with the bare bones was, on her own, building her inventory of odors.

I praised her and we continued down the next path which led us to yet another, even newer person. This time, the sit came more quickly. It was as if my dog suddenly was my dog again. And the light bulb went on. She had reached the odor threshold that I trained most often on. I felt chills as I realized what a breakthrough we just had. Or I had, as my dog didn't need a breakthrough.

With that fairly solid sit, we approached Miss Mavis, who was the least decomposed of all the people in the research area. I wondered how my dog would handle this body. Miss Mavis still looked human, and had to smell so much stronger than the bones Jael had been going to.

I didn't have long to find out as my dog walked right up to Miss Mavis and touched her smile with her nose. Without hesitation, my dog wheeled around and sat, her full tail plumed out over Miss Mavis's abdomen.

I praised my dog to the heavens, not caring that my entire dog now had to be decontaminated. Not just her feet as initially planned, but her whole undercarriage and tail. It was well worth it however as we left the research area.

We played with her tennis ball all the way back to the truck, and there, I carefully used a small metal pan to wash my dog off. The decontamination process was to eliminate the odor and any dirt still clinging to her. At the same time, I pulled off my own boots and put them in a plastic grocery bag. The last thing I wanted was boots that smelled of death resting on the clean carpet of my new-to-me truck.

Our training euphoria was short-lived as we headed home that afternoon. By the time we reached our stopping point in Lexington, Kentucky, halfway home, Jael's face was looking larger on one side, and she was increasingly whiny. By morning, my world fell out. My little German Shepherd's face was grossly distorted. She looked like the dog version of the Elephant Man, with half her face swollen and the other half still normal.

We were still six hundred miles, and still some twelve or more hours from home. While I called Dr. Mikkelson, Jael's veterinarian at home, both Bev and Marge began internet searches on their 'smart' phones to find a vet in the middle of nowhere.

When we pulled into the next small town and I entered the clinic, the right side of Jael's face was so swollen we could no longer see her eye. She looked like half a hippopotamus. Heat radiated from her, and I was panic-stricken.

The vet, looking at my dog, asked the obvious question, "How is she about having her mouth handled?" I looked at my dog, realizing that a dog in her situation could be reactive out of just plain fear.

"Normally she's fine, she's pretty gentle, but..." I let it trail off, not sure how to say 'be careful'. She just nodded and gave her vet technician a nod. My dog suddenly began to rise up from the floor where she had been standing on a scale. With a moment of panic, I thought for sure my dog would fly off the scale. Instead, she just leaned into me, and I knew she was more than ready for help.

With shots to stabilize her, antibiotics and more antihistamines, we were on the road again. My poor dog was miserable, and I was right there with her. To have such an amazing training adventure together end like this didn't seem quite fair.

Dr. Dan Mikkelson was waiting for us when we got home. Leaving Jael in his care, I was simply relieved she made it home. I unpacked the truck and played with Ari, who thankfully didn't ignore me in punishment for leaving him home. I needed to love up a furry friend.

It wasn't until I came in to take the call from the vet clinic that I realized mom had moved her chair again. It was now only about one to two feet away from our twenty-seven inch screen television. I took the call, staring the entire time at my mom in outright fascination as she leaned in to look at the television.

"Rebekkah? Jael had a puncture in her mouth, between her gum and cheek. It looks like something jammed up there, not sure but there was a bit of gummy substance I pulled out."

I thought back, and remembered a pig's ear she had been given. Crated next to Bev's dog, she had likely snatched it up and stabbed herself that first day on the way down. Typical Jael behavior to try and keep the goodie from the other dog.

"Does it look like a piece of rawhide or pigs ear?"

"Yes, that is what it made me think of, but I didn't think you fed them to your dogs. Anyway, she's ready to come home. You understand we had to drain the infection, so she has a tube stitched into her face. This means she has to wear an E-collar until the tube comes out."

What Dr. Mikkelson didn't tell me, likely because he couldn't possibly know, was that Jael wasn't one to be deterred by a cone. Her first encounter with a doorway was impressive. The cone hit the door flat. There stood my dog, pushing hard against the collar, trying to make the door open by sheer force of a plastic cone wrapped around her neck. She wouldn't listen as I tried to get her to back up so I could actually open the door, which swung

107

inwards. I finally wrapped my arm around her chest and pulled her back, freeing up the door to open.

More impressive was her first time out to go potty after she arrived home. Racing into the back yard, I watched as she put her head down to sniff. The collar, opaque white, went flat against the ground. There stood my dog, staring at the ground – or at least, I assumed she was staring at the ground as I couldn't actually see her head inside the cone. She didn't move, she just stood there, the white cone flush against the grass.

"Jael – lift your head, stupid," Up came her head, and off she ran. Only to stop and sniff again, and a moment later, there she was, stuck to the ground again. I wasn't sure if I should laugh, cry, or just be embarrassed by how dumb my dog was being.

"Jael, lift you head!" Up she came again, and off she ran. I wondered if this would be a daily thing or if she would eventually learn she had to lift her head in order to see where she was going.

Coming into the house was yet another learning experience. For me that is. Jael, used to just pushing her way past or through anything, wasn't expecting the collar on her head to catch on the door frame and stop her cold.

Undaunted, she pushed harder while I tried to tell her to back up. No, she had never had to back up before; she wasn't going to start now. Within seconds, I heard a creak, a snap, and she was through. And a piece of white opaque plastic spun into silence beside my feet.

All in all, Jael adapted to the cone much better than the rest of the household. She could catch her tennis ball in mid-air. She figured out how to use the cone to flip her toys so she could catch them again. Amazingly, she didn't seem to fight having it on.

The sight of her messed up face with the drain tube hanging out of it, however, was hard. Typical of any dog, she didn't know she looked funny. And unlike Ari, she didn't care if she did.

Ari, after accepting the fact his sister was wearing a new type of battering ram, simply tried to stay out of her way. And so did the rest of us. Still, I ended up with bruises and nicks on the backs of both legs from Jael charging up behind me, expecting to run past me and instead catching the edge of the cone on me instead.

Bedtime, however, was the worst for me. Jael, as if on purpose, had discovered that if she turned just right, the cone would make an awful thickety-thackety-thickety sound as it slid across the bed's frame. Rather like a child running a stick along a picket fence; over and over; every night, over and over.

Needless to say, we didn't get much sleep, Ari and I. Jael, on the other hand, always seemed bright and chipper in the morning. I came to understand the meaning behind "The Cone of Shame". The shame wasn't Jael's, it belonged to the rest of us.

I love my dogs, but by the end of her imprisonment in the cone, I was ready to rip it off myself and not care about the tube that hung out of her face. The cone was no longer simply opaque white; no, it now was edged and striped with silver duct tape to keep it together.

Interestingly, while I had the impression Jael hadn't cared, the day it came off, I found out she did. Jael, ever since she had started visiting Dr. Dan's office, would, instead of offering herself up to the exam table, hop into the chair next to it.

I know in her mind, she felt the chair was there for her specifically, and the table was obviously for someone else; like me. Each time, I'd have to lift her from the chair up to the table.

That day, as we came in, the cone banging and catching on everything Jael could find to hit with it, Jael didn't hesitate. As we entered the exam room, me ready to grab her off the chair, she instead threw her front paws on the table and I know if she could have spoken, she'd have demanded Dr. Dan to get that blinking thing off of her.

To date, that is the one and only time my dog offered herself onto the table. Ever after, she went back to hopping on the chair first.

# Chapter 9

*It is high, I cannot attain it.*

A few days later, I came home to find my mom had once again moved her chair. This time, it was pushed back about six feet from the television. I was also informed she had made an eye appointment. I wanted to make a smart comment about what took so long, but refrained.

As I made a note in my calendar of her appointment so we wouldn't forget, I wondered about a certain coffee date that hadn't happened yet. My mom had informed me upon my return from my trip that the call had come, but I wasn't there. I was at a training half the country away. The disappointing part was, now that I was back, there had been no follow up communication.

"Rebekkah, do you have a minute?"

Glancing up at Megan, I could see that pregnancy was definitely adding to her waistline. She was happy, but like my mom, tired more often than not.

"Sure; Megan. What's up?" I hoped it would be something routine, finished in a moment, because I had a number of items on my to-do list for the day.

"I hate to bother you, but my doctor and Tommie both have been pushing me to talk to you. I'm having some retention problems with this pregnancy. My doctor says I shouldn't work so many hours, or if I do, I need to take breaks, lie down, and put my feet up." The concern in her face was about her job, I knew. They relied on her income as well as Tommie's.

"Well, we have an apartment right in there with a very comfortable couch where you could lie down as you need to. If you prefer to start working part days, we could do that too. Your health is more important right now, Megan."

"Thank you, but I'd like to try to just lie down as I can, if you think Martha and Connie wouldn't mind. I don't want to intrude on their privacy."

Martha wasn't the one I was worried about; however, Connie proved very open to the idea. As the days flew by and Megan took more and more breaks into the apartment, I could see that my time was soon coming where I would be back full time at McCaffrey.

It was while I was waiting in the lobby of the eye doctor that the call I'd been hoping for came in. Jesse called back finally. We chatted for a few minutes before he finally asked if I would be willing to meet someplace for coffee. He knew of a little coffee shop midway between Elk, where I worked, and his own community of Deer Lake. With a fluttering in my stomach, I agreed to the time and place and hung up as my mom came out of the exam room to pick out new frames. I hardly paid attention as I was more concerned about what I should wear for my own appointment in two weeks.

A week later, mom and I we were back at the clinic. The glasses weren't correct, she still couldn't see. Little was I to know, we'd be back again in another week. No, I was too wrapped up in my upcoming date to be thinking about what my mom was going through.

Arriving at the small coffee shop, I was surprised how upscale it seemed. It was in a town no one would ever hear of unless they lived there, but their coffee shop was bustling. Jesse was waiting and this time I noticed he was in jeans and a long-sleeve t-shirt with his county's logo on it.

Ordering for us, he paid and took us to sit at a table outside to enjoy the sunshine and blue skies. I have to admit that I don't remember everything we talked about, but we talked for a couple of hours. It was during the talk; however, I started to realize the differences between us.

On the drive home, I had time to consider them, and objectively realize that, while I liked Jesse and he was a good man, he and I were far apart in many of the things that were important to me.

With that rather depressing thought, my cell phone went off.

"Elk Ridge Search and Rescue, how may we help you?"

"Hey Rebekkah, we have a search and we'll need whatever you can pull together. Not sure if we have a suicide or not, but there was a big family argument, the missing person left on a four-wheeler which has been located by the family, but he's not been located yet."

Benjamin's voice on the other end of the phone meant it was in our county, a local family. Taking the details, I started the calling tree for the unit. Who could come now, who could come later, and who wasn't available. After those calls were made, it was calls to other K-9 SAR units, slowly spreading the net out to get additional searchers and dogs to come help.

I had to go home first to get my dogs, check on my mom, and head out again. As I leaned into the family room, I saw that her chair was once again within a few feet of the television. It gave me a headache just thinking about it.

We were in July weather now, and so the first thing I checked was that I had plenty of bug spray and wipes with me. The dogs had a homemade concoction made of a bit of citronella oil, bath oil, and petroleum jelly that I could rub on their ears and down their backs to keep them safe from the biting bugs.

Additionally, I verified I had spare batteries for the portable fans I kept in the truck. The temperatures would be climbing well into the nineties, and with the humidity only ten points below that, it would be a horribly sweaty day. The last check was that I had plenty of bottled water with me.

All of which took only fifteen to twenty minutes. Climbing into the truck, I wrote down my mileage and put it into gear. Benjamin called me back as I pulled out of the driveway, dogs and gear loaded.

"Rebekkah; an update. Deputy Parks is on scene and as usual, there is a bit more to the story. The family argument happened last night. They got up this morning and he was gone, just left them a note. Not a pleasant note either. It sounds like a suicide. There is a firearm missing. Do you want to stand your unit down?"

It was a long-standing rule for almost all volunteer SAR units that if there was the possibility of being a potential target, we could decline the mission. Each person in the unit had to make the decision for their self.

"I'll make the calls. I'll still come, Benjamin; I have a hard time saying no to a family. However, will you have enough deputies to send out with us, just in case?"

"We'll figure it out. Tell your handlers no questions asked if they decide to stand down. And those that still come tell them no uniforms."

In the end, everyone from E.R. SAR agreed to respond. A few from units further away declined, and it truly was a no questions asked. It was a risk versus benefit consideration. What are you willing to risk in order to gain something? In this case, it would be risking our lives. And the only benefit would be to possibly save someone else's life.

Arriving on scene, I found out the first K-9 team had already deployed with a law enforcement officer walking with them. This wasn't the first time we had searched for a potential suicide-by-cop. It seemed strange to most of us, this idea that the person might not be able to pull the trigger on themselves, but are willing to shoot at a police officer in hopes they'll return fire and kill them.

Our goal was, if this was the scenario, that the handlers and their dogs remained safe. A well-armed officer would deploy with each team to defend them and also take that shot if required. The handlers, by not wearing anything remotely looking like a uniform, would look more like someone out walking their dog. Even the officer, while still wearing their badge, was not in full uniform. That would simply draw fire back toward the handler again.

Deputy Ron Parks walked up to me and even now, years later, I would always think of him as the deputy with the voice like the mice in the Cinderella movie; high, squeaky, and vaguely irritating. He couldn't help it of course, and he was a good man who did a good job. I studied him, noting the dark pants, the dark shirt with his black bullet resistant vest covering the county's logo on his left chest. In his hands was an automatic weapon, his badge at his waist.

"Ron, just so you know if it should come up, the red bag on the back of my pack is my first aid kit. If I get shot, that is the first aid kit, okay?" At his nod, I tapped his vest with my finger and continued, "If you get shot, just so you know, I'm running like a rabbit the other way. I'm not wearing one of those."

Ron smiled and nodded. While I had said it in a light-hearted voice, he knew I was somewhat serious. I don't know what I was thinking, placing myself into a situation that I had just experienced and hated a few months previously. And there were no tree planters out there to rescue us this time.

"Rebekkah, I've asked Amos to see if he can get a trail from the four-wheeler. Here is the map, let's get your handlers over here and talk strategy for the air scent dogs."

We leaned over the hood of a squad car, reviewing the many places the subject could have gone from that point last seen on the map.

"Benjamin, why did he leave the ATV?" Karen touched the sharpie-marked circle on the map.

"Fuel. Apparently it ran out, so he abandoned it."

"I'm wondering about this terrain feature here; is it really a drop off like it looks like?"

Benjamin waved a man over and introduced him as our subject's brother.

"Chad, they are wondering about this area. It appears to be a drop-off, is it?" The topographical maps rarely lie; the tight brown lines indicated a very steep incline. However, man often changed terrain features with the use of big equipment. It was best to ask.

"Yep, it drops down into that marsh there. Nasty place, I can't imagine he'd go there. If he went anywhere, it would be our hunting areas, like over here." He placed his hand on another area which looked far more level, far more accessible.

"Rebekkah, you've got the old dog; that looks like a good area for you to start. Karen, why don't you take Section B over

116

here," Benjamin, using the sharpie, was carefully diagraming search areas on the map. Hasty areas to check first; if nothing turned up, we'd be hitting the bigger areas harder later.

"When Chris gets here, let's put her in Section C1. I have a deputy for each of you, but I don't want anyone going out without an armed deputy. For now, please stay on trails if you can. If your dog alerts into the woods, call it in first. Our subject likes dogs, but we're not sure how he might feel about all of you."

"Will you be putting line searchers in?" Amos poked his head over my shoulder to ask. I actually didn't need to hear his voice to know he had come up, as Powder, for whatever reason, decided at that moment to bay. I glanced down because it never ceased to amaze me that when they bayed, they sucked in their massive lips, leaving a small opening for the sound to come out.

"Not yet. I need to know more before I put a bunch of people out there."

An hour later, I was in the woods with another Law Enforcement officer at my back. Ari was working well, but I could tell he was tired. It was getting harder for him to work these long searches. Two hours, and I knew it was time to pull him out. He was panting heavily and when I put my hand on his side, I could feel his heart rate was far too high and he felt warm.

The heat was getting to me as well, but I knew it was more than that for him. He wasn't a young dog anymore. In fact, I suddenly realized that he would be eleven years old in another month.

"Ron, I need to pull out. My dog is exhausted. I haven't seen anything in here from him, let's head back."

Arriving back at base, I felt guilty for not finishing our area. That meant another dog team would have to walk out and take over for us. I could work Jael, but everyone was still working under the assumption Derek was still alive and moving out there.

"Worn out?" Benjamin nodded at Ari, who was lying on his dog bed in the truck. I had a fan blowing toward him, but the air wasn't exactly cool, so I wasn't sure how much good it would do for him. It was hard to see him like this. His area search certification was expiring soon, and I knew at that moment, we wouldn't ever be able to complete another one hundred and sixty acre test again. Tears, unbidden, filled my eyes.

A strong arm wrapped around my shoulder and gave me a squeeze. Nothing was said, and I was very grateful for that. Taking a deep sniff, casually brushing away the tears, I smiled and gave Ari a good pat before shutting the door of the truck.

Benjamin, always able to lighten the mood, put his hands on the screens that were covering the windows of my truck. My mom had made them with magnets so they sealed out the bugs, but let air into the truck.

"I wonder what the county would think if we got your mom to make some of these for the squad cars..." I laughed; glad he got my mind working in a different direction.

"What can I do?" I glanced around, and could see that there wasn't much to do. All the K-9 teams that could go out had gone out. Unlike training, on a real search, the radio could get eerily quiet. People were focused on their job and not on checking in.

"I know you don't like to, but could you talk to the family about the dogs?"

Brushing hair that had come loose from my ponytail, I walked over with Benjamin to where the family waited.

"Everyone, this is Rebekkah James, she's with Elk Ridge Search and Rescue. While she likely can't say much about what is happening in the field right now, if you have any questions about the dogs, feel free to ask."

There was a moment of silence and I wondered if I'd get off that easy. This family was in crisis. I had seen the note their son, brother, boyfriend, and father had written. It was cruel, even hateful. But they loved him and wanted him to come home.

"Thank you, all of you, for coming. I just don't think Derek would hurt anyone, especially the dogs. But I understand why they are worried." It was the brother I had met earlier. Chad, yes the name was Chad. I just nodded, knowing there wasn't anything I could say in response.

"Do you have a dog here?" A woman, based on her age, I was guessing it was Derek's mother.

"Yes, I do. He's going to be eleven next month, which is very old for a German Shepherd. We just came out of the woods. This heat was getting pretty hard on him."

"Yes, I understand getting old. Did he find anything at all?"

With a glance toward Benjamin, who simply nodded, I answered as honestly as I could, "No, where we were at, we didn't. I can tell you everyone out there is working as hard as they can for you."

With a nod to the family, I walked back toward my truck. It was very hard not to get sucked into the emotional lives of the families. If we did, it could affect our decision making and give us tunnel vision. I had been on searches where that had happened, and it became a driving passion that burned out searchers and actually ruined one or two dogs who were asked over and over and over yet again to search the same areas and kept achieving the same results.

At the end of the day, nothing had been found. No clues, no signs. Arrangements were made to come back, as Benjamin was not putting anyone out in the dark to search. The family pressured him to continue into the night hours, and normally, the K-9 handlers would have agreed.

Typically, night searches were best for the dogs as air conditions generally were better. It was cooler and moister. This did not hold true, however, if someone might be out there willing to take a shot at whatever moved. Especially as most handlers put lights on their dogs in order to have better visibility on them. In this case, Law Enforcement made the right decision. Of course, that was just my opinion.

We never dreamed the search would go on not just for another day or two, but weeks. Everyone was getting tired, yet the acres just kept piling up, and no reactions from the dogs, no clues were discovered by line searchers, and discouragement was taking over.

I had made the decision that I wasn't going back. I had a life to live, a job to do, and my dogs were getting worn out. That search from years ago had taught me a good lesson. Still, when Benjamin called and asked me to come back yet again, I couldn't tell him no.

Arriving with only Jael in the truck, I was informed we had a major clue uncovered by one of the line searches earlier in the week. Chris pulled in just behind me. She and Onyx had certified for cadaver earlier in the year, and it was obvious Benjamin meant to keep this search small and quiet, although I could see there was a large group of fireman standing nearby.

"Here is the thing. Someone came forward and said they saw someone who looked like Derek walking out on that minimum maintenance road there. They didn't see where the person went from there, but on a line search earlier this week, they found Derek's wallet. There are three areas we want to check based on the location of the wallet. There is a creek that runs under the road, and further on, a large clearing with the best view in town. Finally, a wooded area over to the south that has some minor trails that run through it."

"Rebekkah, you have the water certified dog, I'd like you to check along the creek, and then move up to the wooded area. Chris, you take Onyx up to the clearing."

As he spoke, one of the firemen came up, and I realized it was the chief, Johnny.

"Sheriff, do you want us? Parks called us to come, but I don't want to mess up with the dogs if they're going out."

"It won't mess us up, Johnny. These dogs are cadaver dogs; they'll only be looking for the odor of someone who is deceased."

"Okay if I put them into that wooded area? Once you're done at the creek, you can work ahead or behind them."

I nodded, and a short time later, I was working Jael toward the creek. Firemen trooped by us as we reached the bridge, some hesitating, watching the dog work. I sent Jael to check along the sides of creek, and she ignored the firemen as I assumed she would.

I watched in fascination as my dog returned repeatedly to the bridge. Bridge was an exalted term for what was really a road placed over a large concrete culvert. Along the edge of the road as it crossed over, there was a spot to sit on the concrete overlooking the water, but no real bridge existed.

Still, Jael returned to the same spot, that place to sit, and sniffed it. She'd move away, down the embankment, and return again to that spot. Realizing she had something odd, I just marked it and headed her toward the wooded area.

As we rounded the corner of the road and got to the corner of the search area, the radio crackled to life. Derek had been found. The firemen, while performing their line search, had located him. He was deceased by a gunshot wound to the head.

Feeling incredibly depressed, I was about to stop my dog when I saw her alert, hard and strong. She would have had this one, if I hadn't told them to go ahead with the line search. I know it sounded very selfish, but I couldn't help it. Still, I had an opportunity here that I hoped we could take advantage of.

"Ron, ask if I can approach with my dog. She's scented him; I'd like her to finish this."

Ron glanced at my dog, straining at the end of the leash I had quickly put on her. Incredibly, he responded, "Chris and Onyx too?"

"Yes, if we can. If we aren't going to disturb the scene or anything, it would be good to get the dogs in there if we can."

Ron called Benjamin, and then nodded at me. I turned Jael loose and she soon was working the scent cone, ignoring the firemen who were now leaving the area, leaving only a small group to stand over the body until Law Enforcement could arrive.

Jael, reaching Derek's body, gently pawed at his side. There are moments in life when I wondered about my dog. Derek looked very intact, considering his mode of death and the timeframe. Jael, realizing her subject wasn't going to respond, came running to me and grabbed my right pocket before running back and sitting next to the body.

Incredibly, she had understood that Derek was, or had been, a person, not just cadaver odor, and had fallen back to her foundation training of a bringsel indication when finding a living person. Training we hadn't practiced in years.

Tossing her the ball away from Derek, I took her about twenty feet from the area to reward her. A short time later, Chris arrived and let Onyx work the scene. As I watched, I realized there was no way on God's green earth to ever explain this to anyone. The men there, the Law Enforcement officers and firemen, they understood. But the real world, the normal people, they wouldn't.

Onyx, working the odor so well, suddenly came to a complete stop. She had seen the body. Her entire body was

123

trembling, and it wasn't from excitement. I remember the instructors at the body farm describing this very reaction, and it was incredible to watch it happen before my eyes.

Chris, somewhat embarrassed and frustrated, squeaked out in her best dog reward voice, "Onyx – what do you have girl? Is that Mort?" Mort was Chris's command word to find the odor of cadaver. Onyx only cowered down at the words.

"Chris; quiet, low tones. She's petrified of the visual. Don't make it any more freaky for her. Stay calm and let her just work it, okay?"

Putting my dog in a stay, which wasn't hard as she was playing with her tennis ball, I walked closer to Derek's body. Amazingly, I hadn't detected the odor yet myself which I was glad of, and I was careful not to look too closely.

I crouched down and just went still. Onyx, used to me, slowly put one forepaw down, then another. Each step was done with dramatic quivering and maddeningly slowly. As she finally reached a point about a foot from us, she suddenly turned from looking at me and stretched out her muzzle to touch Derek's jean-covered leg. She then lay down, looking at Chris. Her final trained response was solid.

"Good dog Onyx; that was perfect." I kept my voice low and Chris, picking up on it, also praised her dog calmly. Onyx, receiving her reward of a flexible Frisbee, took it and moved away.

"Should I make her go back?" Chris was staring at her dog as if she had suddenly grown an extra head.

"I wouldn't. If she starts to approach on her own, calmly praise her, but don't force it. They told us at the school the visual can be way too much for a dog, I just never realized how much. And Onyx had no problems doing her mannequin sign-off."

"Well, maybe the odor was different, and let's face it, that visual over there is very different than a mannequin."

"Yes, it is." As we spoke, Onyx suddenly paused in playing with her Frisbee and turned back towards Derek. I watched as my own dog suddenly shot up and started toward us.

Turning, I realized, too late, that they were lifting the body to put in the body bag which arrived as we were talking. Chris was so correct; the visual was far different than a Rescusi-Annie that we used for training.

"Good dogs, yes, that's Mort, Caddy, yes, good dogs." We both praised our dogs for responding to the odor, and as the guys lowered the body, Ron motioned to Chris.

"See if she'll approach again before we zip it up. Don't mean to rush you, but I just heard the family is on their way. Benjamin tried to stop them, but they want to see their son where he was found. We can't do that to a family."

Chris, calling Onyx over, gave her the command to find Mort. Onyx, with only a little hesitation, went over, touched Derek, and lay down. She was past the visual fear, at least in this situation.

We had our dogs leashed and off to the side before the family arrived, Benjamin walking with them. Their son was already in the bag and in the rescue pod to bring him back. The only thing left to see was where the soil had been burned by the beginning of the decomposition process and the rifle. As the men moved out of the way, something about the scene didn't look right, but for the life of me, I couldn't connect what it was.

125

It didn't take long, but soon the family left in tears, following the pod being pulled away by an ATV. With permission from Benjamin, Chris and I put on decon equipment and began the macabre job of cleaning up what was left from a suicide.

We scraped the ground where the body had been, and it was then it hit me; what had looked wrong. The area should have been stained with the impact of a gunshot wound to the head. However, all that was going into our sealed bags was the dirt where the body had been. I made a mental note to ask Benjamin about it later.

"Sad ending, but at least it is an ending for them." Chris spoke softly, as if we were at a funeral. I guess, in a way, we were.

"Was this area searched at all earlier?" I couldn't remember it, but we had, at different times during the weeks of the search, covered a lot of area.

"I hate to say it, but yes, I believe we had dogs over here." I knew as soon as we got home, we'd both be checking our search reports and comparing it to the GPS coordinates of this spot. If we had dogs miss the subject, we needed to find out why.

We left the woods, our strange harvest of dirt tucked out of sight in our packs. The dirt would be rehomed in glass jars for training the cadaver dogs later. For now, however, our dogs were romping together down the trail, relaxing after a stressful search ending. As we approached the bridge, I told Chris about my experience there. With an odd look, she said Onyx had done the same thing.

"Mere speculation, but do you think Derek sat there for a while, trying to make a decision? Maybe there was too much odor left because of that? Or, and this sounds weird I know, but if he was angry, suicidal, depressed... could he have left a peculiar scent there the dogs picked up on?"

"This many weeks since he disappeared?"

Chris had a point. Odor doesn't hang around that long unless there was something there to keep refreshing it, such as an article of clothing, an item the subject wore, or a body. And we knew the body wasn't there.

Returning to our vehicles, we loaded the dogs and checked out on the roster sheet. Ron and Benjamin stood nearby chatting, so I walked over. I really wanted to know something, and hoped they'd tell me.

"Benjamin, did he die there?"

The change in expression was obvious, even on our sheriff who could keep a poker face better than anyone I knew.

"Confidentially? We don't believe so. The family doesn't know this yet, so please keep it quiet. Also, the item found by the searchers was his billfold, cleaned out except his license. They found it on the edge of the culvert over the creek. It was just sitting there, a couple of leaves had fallen over it, but someone saw it."

"Chris, come here a second," I waited until she had joined us, and, skipping the part about the death scene, asked Benjamin to tell her about the wallet.

"So our dogs were picking up on what? The odor from the billfold? Or the chemical changes from his depression and desire to kill himself?"

"I don't know, but it sure gives a person something to think about. Thanks Benjamin."

The coroner's report reflected what we all knew, that he died of a gunshot wound to the head. The only odd part was the post-mortem interval, or the time since death, revealed Derek hadn't died within days of having been reported missing. His body hadn't been out there for weeks. In fact, they believed he had been dead only about three days.

Additionally, while he appeared to be in decent physical shape at the time of death, it was further determined his system was full of alcohol and drugs. Benjamin quietly shared the part that wasn't being released. There was so much in his system, it was unclear how Derek could have possibly pulled the trigger. He would have been passed out cold.

Simply because of where he was discovered, our unit decided to hold another debrief to review our search reports and mapping as a unit. It was unsettling to discover that several dogs, including members of Elk Ridge Search and Rescue, performed sniffs in that area, however nothing was ever discovered. Our hope was that he had come in after the searchers had left.

What happened during the intervening weeks from the time he went missing to when he was found would remain a mystery to everyone involved with the search. The family, as much in the dark as everyone else, simply were left to mourn his death.

# Chapter 10
## Where shall I go from Your Spirit?

On my home front, I was starting to wonder if my mom was actually losing her mind. She was doing odd things, like putting things away in weird places. While I wanted to laugh about it, sometimes it just wasn't funny. After yet another visit to the eye doctor, I was really glad when he looked her in the eye and asked when she last had a physical.

My mom was from the generation that didn't go to the doctor unless you were bleeding or dying. So, while she had gone to the doctor, it wasn't for a physical. The optometrist, looking at her address, simply dialed a number and within a moment, had made an appointment for her with Dr. Sheffield.

"Mrs. James, I believe you might have a problem with diabetes. You need to get yourself checked over. That is the only reason I can come up with for your eyesight fluctuating so much in such a short period of time."

Just as she had with finding out she had high blood pressure, she began her research. I soon learned that not only would I have to give up salt in our foods, but sugars. Like a smoker who has quit smoking, my mom became a crusader for healthy living. And this was all before she even had met with a doctor.

It actually became quite irritating at times as I learned that so many of the things I enjoyed eating were bad for me. Like Margaret's caramel rolls. The cream and sugar I added liberally to my coffee each day. Even one of my favorite foods, Chicken Alfredo, was bad. I was starting to think eating itself was going to be banned.

I, of course, had to admit that yes, I was a little overweight based on my height. I could stand to lose a few pounds, but having it forced on me just didn't seem palatable.

Still, I went to mom's appointment and sat in the waiting room where, yes, they had magazines with decadent foods displayed on the cover, and articles that promised to help me take off an easy twenty pounds. I'm sure it wasn't by eating the foods they pictured.

I lost track of time as I waited, but when my mom came out, I could see something had made a big impact on her. Raising an eyebrow, I waited for her to tell me what happened.

"I have it. I have diabetes. First; high blood pressure, and now this. Rebekkah, I've been healthy my whole life. What is happening to me?" Putting my arm around her, I didn't say anything. Like Benjamin that day with me facing an aging dog, there wasn't much to say.

"I have to go on medication again. I don't want to, but apparently they can't believe I'm not in a coma. My A1C was at thirteen point eight. I have no idea what an A1C is, but apparently thirteen isn't even on the chart!" It was then the tears started. I helped her into the Suburban and simply sat while she cried. Had I tried to hug her, she would have pulled away.

It all came pouring out on the drive home. Her blood sugar, which should have been around one hundred, was well over five hundred. And the A1C, which reflected her sugars for the past several months, was, indeed, off the charts. She apparently should have been dead by now. Just like the blood pressure, where she should have had a stroke and died.

"Well, mom, at least you know that your body is pretty resilient. From what you're telling me, you should have died several times over now. I'm glad you're ok, mom, really. And the meds likely won't be too bad, right?"

"They said it would help my tiredness. They kept asking if I had sores on my feet. I guess diabetics get sores and then they don't heal. I don't; have sores on my feet, that is. I only know I feel tired and my eyesight was going crazy."

Shaking my head, I only hoped that my body could be as tough as hers as I aged. Then I glanced down at myself and realized that I needed to lose weight too, or I'd be following on the same path as my mother.

Arriving back at McCaffrey House, I had the shock of my life. Megan had gone into labor, at work, and had to be rushed by ambulance to the hospital. There were complications.

The struggle between wanting to rush over and be there for her, and my responsibilities at McCaffrey was difficult. My job won out as I discovered that several families were checking in and I needed to jump back into my role as full-time manager.

Smiling, I handled the sign-ins, handing out keys to rooms and putting credit card transactions through. Also, explaining the layout of the House, when meals were, and presenting the maps of the extensive trails through the woods around McCaffrey.

By the time I finished the third family, I was sure I'd have to unscrew my smile. The people were wonderful; I just wasn't used to the job anymore.

Entering the kitchen, I poured myself a cup of coffee from the ever present pot, and stopped myself just as I was reaching for the creamer in the fridge. No, I'd try to be good. No cream or sugar for a while, see what happened.

Connie came in just as I was just about to leave, and I was surprised to see that she looked terrific. Not just that she was dressed up, but I was sure she had lost some weight and the haggard look had left her face. She simply looked good. Could dating Benjamin really do that for a person?

"Hey, Rebekkah! I was just getting ready to go out. Don't worry, my shift is over. I'm going with Agnes to see how Megan is doing. Are you okay here?"

"Connie, you look great! I'm sorry if I haven't noticed, but with all the stuff going on lately; I was wondering if you've lost weight?"

"Yep, twenty pounds so far. I feel much better too. I guess having a steady job and a regular schedule helps. You look pretty nice too."

I knew it wasn't really true. I hadn't lost weight, I was still just me. But seeing Connie like this, I could understand why our sheriff was dating her.

"Please take this, I got it to give to Megan, but didn't think I'd need it yet. Glad I did though!" I handed Connie a small box and a card. I hoped she'd like it, it was a little keepsake box designed to put a child's first tooth, first haircut, first whatever in it; within reason of course.

Watching them leave, I turned my attention back to my job as one of our new guests came over to ask about shops in town. Showing him where we kept some of the brochures, we chatted about the area, the places to visit, the sights to see. I could smell Martha and Margaret's handiwork as they were getting supper ready and I wondered how often I could eat here instead of at home before my mom would catch on.

"Excuse me, Miss. We were wondering how to sign up for one of your excursions. Your brochure mentioned that we could get a mine tour?"

"Mr. Walker, yes, you can. The tours are every Tuesday and Thursday until the end of August." The Walkers were a middle-aged couple, she in a wheelchair with multiple sclerosis. At moments like this, I missed having my dogs at McCaffrey. They had the ability to open people up and make them comfortable. Even Jael, with her erratic and sometimes bull in a china shop like ways, made people laugh.

Something clicked in my brain as I stood there, and I wondered if Ari would be up to coming back to work with me. Maybe not on a daily basis, but at least part time, and then I could find ways to train periodically as well.

Helping serve up dinner, I watched as Jack came to pick up Margaret. They had a ritual now, this picking up your wife at work thing. He'd come in through the garage, wait by the office alcove, and when Margaret came out, he'd give her a hug and a resounding kiss. He didn't care who saw them. I wondered if Martha ever felt lonely, as I sometimes did, watching. Another reason to bring my dogs back to work with me; with them, I didn't usually feel lonely.

Shaking it off, I smiled and served and cleaned up, ending up in the kitchen with Martha to eat our own supper. Chicken fried steak with pepper gravy. It was incredible. Better than I remembered. Likely because cream gravy wasn't to be found at home anymore; I felt like I was cheating on a diet. Except, I wasn't on a diet, my mom was.

Still, I watched on the sidelines as my mom lost weight; and more weight. Her vitality came back, her energy and her memory. It was like having my old mom back. Well, a younger version of my mom back. It seemed strange how this small thing called blood sugar could cause so much havoc in a person's body.

The diet changes weren't over however, as my mom set herself a new goal, to get off of her diabetes medication completely. A new round of research and soon, I found myself sneaking off to eat banned foods. I had become a closet eater. It was rather frightening, actually, but I liked a sugar cookie once in a while. Or cream in my coffee. And even powdered cheese snacks. I'd stop at convenience stores on the way home from training just to get a junk-food fix.

Through it all, I managed a few good meals at McCaffrey, and spent lunches with the rest of the staff, looking at photos of Megan's baby girl, Charlene Rae. I had never been a baby person, but apparently my entire staff was. I loved and cared about Megan, but staring at endless pictures of her baby did very little for me. Now, if she had a new puppy; that would have been different.

My life, as odd as it had seemed lately, appeared to be settling back into normal again. I spent my days at McCaffrey House, falling into my old routine easily. The first day I brought my dogs back into McCaffrey, I knew I had made the right decision.

McCaffrey House had always advertised that there were 'resident dogs', and photos of my dogs had been up since we opened. It was good to have them back as Ari would quietly approach someone in their wheelchair and simply stand next to it, not demanding, but not declining a gentle pat.

Jael, as if knowing, moved slower around the people with disabilities. She modified her behavior and was quickly a favorite of the House. She would tote her tennis ball to someone and carefully put it in their lap, asking them to toss it for her.

One day I watched, amazed, as she gave Mrs. Walker her ball. Janet, unable to pick it up, let it roll off onto the floor. Jael picked it up and carefully put it back in her lap. I was about to step in and stop my dog from pestering her when Janet's husband said, "Janey dear, she wants you to toss the ball if you can."

Tears formed in my eyes as Jael, for the fourth time, patiently put the ball back on her lap. Janet, unable to use her hands, scooped the ball up with her arm and half tossed, half pushed it to my dog, who happily caught the ball in mid-air a foot away.

They continued their game of fetch for a few more minutes, and each time, Janet improved in picking up and throwing the ball. Steve, her husband, walked over to me and thanked me for having therapy dogs available. How could I have ever guessed my wild-child of a dog would be mistaken for a therapy dog?

The second benefit was that I could get some SAR training time in now that I brought the dogs to work. Training, which had begun to fall to the bottom of my priority list, was moved back up again. By bringing the dogs to work with me even two days a week, I could do some training with them and let them perform their own therapy with our guests. It was a win-win for all of us. I only wondered if I could keep it up after Megan returned.

I had been so busy at McCaffrey House that I'd come home from work exhausted. It was busier than I ever remembered being in the first years when I managed the House by myself and I'd be wishing I could simply go straight to bed, but I couldn't. And then to have my mom preaching about how changing my diet would help, didn't help.

Perhaps it was because I was seeing my dogs more often again that I saw the changes coming over Ariel. It seemed more than just feeling his age as never before. As with my mom, I wasn't sure if it was a passing thing or if it was something we'd have to manage from now on. All I knew was; he was tired far too much.

I was learning that I couldn't set up large problems or take long walks, as he would stop part way and simply stand, hoping I'd come back to him so we could go home together. My heart broke every time, and I'd turn around and we'd go home.

Meal times were becoming even harder as well. Already a picky eater, it only got worse about what he would eat. Then came the day, he simply refused to eat. Looking out at a dismally wet fall day, I finally gave up and left for work, telling mom to try again later. It was their day to stay home anyway.

What happened later wasn't what I expected. The phone call from home wasn't to tell me he finally ate, or that Jael had stolen all his food. It was to tell me, in a sobbing voice, that Ari had collapsed out in the yard, in a pouring icy rain, and my mom couldn't get him up.

Rushing home, I found she had gotten him into the house, I wasn't sure how, but as I entered, my beautiful regal German Shepherd couldn't even lift his head. My mom had called the clinic and Nan, Dr. Mikkelson's daughter and receptionist, told us he was out on a different emergency call. I had no options; I took him to the clinic I hadn't dealt with for some years.

Carrying Ari to the truck, his head flopping as if he were dead, I was crying. This isn't the way a noble dog should go.

We arrived at the clinic, and I was immediately reminded of at least one of the reasons I didn't like them. They wouldn't let me go into the examination room with my dog. I was stuck in the waiting room. I had spent more time in waiting rooms in the past year than any person should have to.

They didn't have any current magazines, and they didn't even have a television with a boring talk show. My mom patted my hand and tried to reassure me. It wasn't helping much.

It was nearly two hours later when they finally let me in to see my dog. He was hooked to an intravenous line; lactated Ringer's dripping into him. They had taken blood, it was obvious, and while my beloved Ari actually lifted his head, it was about all he could manage.

"We took X-rays, here, you can look. We were wondering about obstructions as you said he wasn't eating, but he's clean, his system is clean. He looks good for his age, even his joints, nice sharp lines. Blood tests aren't showing anything, however he was dehydrated."

I waited, wondering what, if anything, they had found that would fix him. Apparently, that was the extent of their two hours' work. Nodding, I went out and called Dr. Mikkelson's office on my cell phone.

"Nan? When is Doc going to be back? They've done a lot of tests, haven't come up with anything. Ari is at least a bit more alert. Not sure what to do..."

"I talked to him and he said if you can bring the files and test results down, he'll look at them as soon as he comes in. Can you do that?"

I agreed and returned to the clinic's counter. "Can I take him home?" The receptionist disappeared and returned with the doctor. She reminded me of the physician at the emergency room that mom always got stuck with. The difference was the vet had brown hair instead of blonde that splayed like a messy fountain off the top of her head.

"Are you sure you want to take him home? I mean, he can go, but it might be better to leave him overnight."

"No, it is better if I take him home with me. If he's going to die, I'd rather he die at home than in a strange place and alone." I know I sounded upset, but it just seemed stupid. I could just as easily put him on an I.V. at home as here.

Ari, once again being the tough guy, wanted to walk out of the clinic. I had to let him. I'd never known a dog with such dignity and awareness of appearances as he was.

I got the call a few hours later from Dr. Dan. He had reviewed Ari's files and the first words out his mouth were, "I think its pancreatitis."

"But the gal at the other clinic put in her notes she had eliminated that, didn't she?"

"Rebekkah, I know your dog. I really believe it is, and there is a blood test for that. Can you bring him in tomorrow morning?"

"Yes", but meanwhile wondering if he'd actually make it through the night. I slept next to him, my hand on his rib cage, feeling the slow rise and fall of his chest. I really expected it to stop, but by morning, surprisingly enough, he was still with us. Helping him into the truck once again, we went to Dr. Mikkelson's.

It was a quick test, and he was right. My dog had nearly died of pancreatitis. His recovery was long and protracted, and I finally made the decision I had not wanted to. I retired my first SAR dog. He had served his community long and well, giving over ten years of his life to search and rescue.

I didn't tell him, and with the permission of my unit, I continued to bring him to trainings, and worked with him at home. But no more, when the cell phone went off, would he be responding. It hurt, too. The tragic looks I'd get as I had to leave him home were enough to tear my heart out.

I knew what he was saying, we had always communicated well with each other. He wanted to know why I was taking the snit-faced little brat instead of him. There was no answer that I could give him to help him understand.

There were days when he was amazing, doing well, eating well. I'd wonder; could we, just one more time, take another certification test? And then a day later, he'd be moving slowly, staring at stairs as the hated enemy. It was definitely a roller coaster ride of emotions. The ultimate question was how much longer I'd have him with me. It was a question I didn't want to answer.

It didn't help that as I was coping with it, we suddenly had more searches than we knew how to handle. In fact, there were more searches than most of the units in the state could deal with. It was as if the world had gone missing.

First it was a woman who had disappeared under circumstances that were possibly criminal. Then a toddler walked away and couldn't be found. After that it was an elderly man out walking in the woods who never came home. And then, yet another young woman vanished. Our unit was stretched thin and when we called in other units for mutual aid, we learned they were going to call us to help with their searches.

At one point, we had seven searches on-going all over a three day period. As I took the call for the seventh search, I knew we had no one to send. Taking the information, I contacted a unit some eight hours away to find out if they could assist us.

Thankfully, their area was quiet, and I found myself coordinating a search I wasn't even going to.

As I hung up the phone, I looked up to find our sheriff standing beside me. He had gotten a cup of coffee and two cookies out of the kitchen. Placing a cookie on my desk, he bit into his and waited until I picked up the contraband and joined him.

"How's it going? I hear you guys are very, very busy right now."

"McCaffrey or E.R. SAR? Both; actually. Both are busy, which is good for McCaffrey, but I hate saying no to a search."

"How is the old man?" Out of nowhere, another cookie appeared on my desk.

"You know, some detectives use money for bribes, or reduced sentences. It is pretty sad that all you need is anything with real sugar in it to get me to answer questions. And even sadder that you know it," I picked up the second cookie with little argument from my conscience before I continued, "And the old man is doing okay. Not great, but okay. This retirement thing is way too hard."

"I'm sorry Rebekkah. He's the best dog I know, really. I stopped by to see how you are holding up. Find out how things are going with Detective Deschene. Still going out with him?"

"You didn't bring enough cookies to get that answered. No comment is the proper answer. And yes, Ari is the best dog I've ever owned and known myself." I tried to say it lighthearted, but I knew the pain still came through.

He put a strong hand on my shoulder and gave it a gentle squeeze. Turning, he threw a parting shot at me that destroyed all the good will he had built up, "Well, I don't think he's a good fit for you anyway; Deschene, not the dog."

Watching him leave, I wanted to throw something at him. I didn't know if he knew or not, but after our single coffee date, Jesse hadn't called back. While I had made the decision we weren't compatible, by his not calling me back, I felt as if I was the one that didn't measured up. That instead of my making the choice to no longer date him, he had chosen not to date me first. It was rather twisted, but it made sense to me; and it hurt.

Looking down at the cookie crumbs, I wondered if that was the problem. I could never alter my plain looks, but I could lose some weight. Everyone around me appeared to be losing weight. Me, I just stayed the same. Maybe it was time to at least try.

# Chapter 11
## *Or where shall I flee from Your presence?*

Thanksgiving arrived, and we still had no snow on the ground. The lakes were still open, and the temperatures were well above normal. Wondering if that boded an easy winter or a hard one, I also noted that Megan would be back to work in a few weeks. While I was glad Megan was coming back, I also realized how much I missed talking to our guests, helping them with questions, even dealing with the issues. I actually missed my job, and had to admit a feeling of regret that I'd be soon giving it up again.

It was really brought home when Megan stopped in to show off Charlene. The place came to a stop as all the staff came over to see the cute baby. Connie, Agnes, Margaret, they all went gaga over the baby. Even my dogs wanted to meet the new arrival. Ari gently sniffed her over, pronounced her a member of the family with a gentle lick on the cheek and moved away.

Jael, meeting her very first infant, sniffed a tiny sock, and made her way up the baby's leg, taking extra care to sniff the diaper, then out to each tiny clenched first. She ended with a little 'whiffing' sound by Charlene's cheek, and the baby actually laughed. Jael, tail wagging, licked her cheek and then sat down next to the baby carrier, as if she had staked her claim.

Somehow, it felt like even my dogs were traitors by being so enthralled with Megan's new arrival. I wish I could drum up that kind of excitement, but for some reason, it just wasn't in me.

As if on cue, Benjamin arrived. I suppose the fact he was dating Connie accounted for his unexpected visits, but this time, he tapped my shoulder and nodded towards the kitchen.

"Not a baby fan, there, Rebekkah?"

"It's that obvious? Even my dogs apparently love babies. I guess God just didn't feel the need to put that gene into my DNA." Ari had joined us, more because he liked Benjamin. In fact, I sometimes wondered if he didn't like Benjamin more than he liked me.

"Megan appears to be ready to come back to work. She was asking about reservations, how things were going, and if certain people had come back as planned." I poured us coffee as I talked. Benjamin liked his black, and I, determined to be good, did likewise.

"You miss doing this, don't you." It wasn't a question, it was a statement, and I nodded. He gave me a gentle tap on my shoulder, "I've noticed that you've just blossomed since coming back and doing this job. You love interacting with people out there. And you're so good at it. You may not have a mommy gene, but you do have one for service. The world needs more of them."

"So, what did you come by for, if not to see Connie?"

"Just an update for you; we've got some leads on the Derek Nieland case, and I wanted to give you a heads-up. We may need your cadaver dogs to help locate the crime scene."

"Chris and me; both?"

"If you think she's up for it, sure. Nothing yet, but I'm working with some DEA officers who had some information," he paused, and then, leaning down slightly so he could look me straight in the eyes, he finished with, "Don't get too down about things. I know how easy it is to do, but it is that much harder to climb out of the pit."

I had hoped I was able to hide my feelings, but with that parting comment, I realized I wasn't doing as well as I'd hoped.

144

He was right, however, I knew I had to get myself off the 'poor me' trolley. The one thing that always managed to make me feel better was training the dogs. I called the unit, hoping to find someone who wanted to train. Just the thought of it recharged my batteries.

When most of the unit declined, it didn't help my depressed mood. As if sensing it through the phone line, Marge volunteered to meet me on Saturday morning and set up some cadaver problems at McCaffrey House.

We had not had a decent training in almost two months. There had been so many real searches we had responded to, it wasn't hard to understand why people wanted a weekend off from SAR. The end of the searches had finally come, and everyone from across the state were burned out. Yet, without training, we don't maintain a good state of readiness.

That was my reasoning, but I knew in my heart, I just needed to get out and train. My heart, mind and body needed a good airing that only being outside in the woods with my dogs brought.

I know my mom would have raised an eyebrow and suggested that perhaps I should have the same feeling about going to church, and while it was true, in reality I felt closer to God in the woods than in a building.

Driving down to McCaffrey on Saturday morning, I was happy. Ari, knowing what was coming, was happy as well. He had lost so much weight during his illness, but I put great faith in his ability to recuperate. He was eating normally again, although he still struggled with unstable motion and his hips were still very gaunt. His muscle tone had dropped to almost nothing, and I didn't know if he'd get it back. All we could do was try however.

Turning him loose, his nose went into immediate action. There was nothing wrong with his sniffer, thankfully. He moved out, and it was easy to see he was as excited as I was to be training again. He located the first source which Marge had tucked into a low-hanging branch. Sending him on his way for a second source, he immediately headed for the water's edge. With typical care, he began picking along the slippery rocks and suddenly, he went down.

One moment he was stepping across the wet rocks, the next he was tangled in them, his back legs twisted under him. He didn't make a sound, but instead struggled to get up on his own. Running over, I carefully pulled him up, not sure if he was injured or not.

Ari didn't care, he pulled away from my protective arms and minutes later, he located the source. Marge had dropped a cricket cage with bones into the water along the shoreline. In order to retrieve it, she tied it off to a dead branch just under the water.

I praised my dog, and watched as he swaggered back to my vehicle. He jumped into the truck on his own, something he hadn't done for a while, his adrenaline and pride still flowing strong. While the fall looked bad, I didn't worry too much as he didn't seem to be hurting.

Jael ran a different set of problems that Marge set up in the garage, and I was glad to see that she worked it easily, even the source hidden high up in the rafters. Loading the dogs, I thanked Marge and offered to bring her to the kitchen and see what we could find to go with a cup of coffee.

As we sat in the kitchen chatting, my cell phone rang. I thought I would have had some premonition, but I didn't. There wasn't any warning.

146

"Rebekkah, this is Grace Pearson, Tommie's mom, Megan's mother in law. We're at the hospital; there was an accident. Tommie and Megan…" the voice broke off into sobs, and soon a male voice, calmer, but still broken, took over the call.

"This is George Pearson, Tommie's my son. There was an accident; Charlene was with us, but…oh dear God, they are all gone. All gone…"

The world stopped revolving, I was sure. Megan? Dead? I had spent the last year worrying my elderly mom was going to die. Megan was half my age. She couldn't be dead. How could this be?

"I'm so sorry; I'm so sorry. What can I do? Is there anything I can do?" Marge, on high alert, put her hand on my arm, a question mark in her eyes.

"I don't know yet. We didn't know who to call I guess, but we found your card in Megan's purse."

"The children, too?" The words were hard to force out. I remember questioning how anyone could be so wrapped up in children, and yet, their loss had left me speechless. Megan had pictures of Jessie and Micah on the desk and talked of them with the glow of a proud parent.

I knew that Jessie was, gosh, around thirteen now, and played basketball. Micah was fourteen and a bookworm. To think of them as dead just didn't seem possible. I just couldn't think of them that way. Mr. Pearson's voice pulled me back.

"Yes, I'm sorry, I can't… they were killed instantly is what the state patrol officer said; A truck, broadside. They were taking a trip with the kids before Megan went back to work. Oh, dear God, why?"

There was a long pause, and I simply didn't know what to do. I was still stunned. I couldn't believe what I was hearing. On top of the shock, I had an overwhelming sense of guilt. When Megan had visited the last time with Charlene, all I could think about was how much I had enjoyed doing her job, and wished I could continue. There was no way to unthink that thought.

Seeing Marge still staring at me with wide eyes, I pulled a note pad over and wrote down what Tommie's parents were telling me. The last thing I wrote was, 'it isn't fair'.

"Mr. Pearson? Can I help? Can we take care of Charlene for you while you deal with this?" The words were out before I thought about it. I didn't like children, not really. What was I doing, offering to take not just a child, but an infant?

"Megan's parents, they died before she married Tommie. She doesn't have anyone. We don't have anyone else. I don't know who to ask, but it would be a God-send if you could you take her for a few days. Are you sure?"

"Of course, Mr. Pearson; Megan was like family to us here, and we will be there for her family. Where is Charlene now?"

By the time I had hung up, I realized I needed help. I had no idea how to take care of an infant, and yet, I knew that the Pearson's needed help. It was a moment of inspiration or stupidity, but I grabbed the phone and dialed Adam and Amy's home number.

"Amy, I need some help. This is really difficult, but, wow, this is even harder to say. Megan and Tommie and their children were killed this morning in an accident. No, I'm not kidding. Charlene was staying with Tommie's parents. It was a family trip to spend some fun time before Megan came back to work," I realized I was crying, and with Amy, I was honest, "I know it isn't my fault, but wow, that makes me feel guilty."

Amy made soothing noises, and waited for me to continue, "Amy, they need a place for Charlene to stay for a few days while they cope with this. They are in a horrible place right now, dealing with four deaths, four funerals, and apparently there isn't any other family around. I told them we'd take care of her for them. I can't, you know that. I'm not a mommy in any way, shape or form. Please, would you take Charlene for a few days?"

There was silence on the end of the phone. I knew it; it was a stupid idea. Amy wanted a child of her own to raise and love forever, not just one for a few days. I felt even worse about the situation, and wondered where to go to next.

"Rebekkah, I need to ask Adam, but my answer would be yes. If I can be of service, yes; oh, that poor family."

I met George and Grace at Megan's home. I had never been there before and the house, though small, was clearly cared for inside and out. Tommie had worked nights for a machine shop, and along with Megan's additional income, they had made a comfortable home for their growing family.

Grace, eyes shiny with tears, welcomed me into the house. It physically hurt to see the family photos on the walls, the children's toys, even a hamper of half-folded clean clothes. It was obviously a home people expected to come back to and live their lives; people who would never return.

George was sitting on the couch, holding little Charlene, giving her a bottle. I had forgotten how small she really was. It still felt unreal, dealing with the loss of entire family.

"I've packed her things up, not really knowing what you'll need or how much you'll need. She's been amazing, hardly ever

149

cries." Grace smiled down at her granddaughter, and it was heart-wrenching to watch.

"Grace, I want you to know that, well, how truly sorry we are, all of us here. Anything we can do to help, we'll try to be there." While I spoke, I realized I had opened up Grace's floodgates. A moment later, she was sitting next to George, sobbing.

Quietly, I took little Charlene from George and he enveloped his wife in his arms. I walked over to a window overlooking the front lawn and only saw more of the life left unlived. A basketball hoop with a ball lying nearby, obviously Jessie's. A swing set, outgrown by the older boys, would have been ready for the baby growing up.

When Grace's crying stilled, I returned to sit on an old wooden rocker. Charlene had been quiet, and I wondered if she had fallen asleep. She wasn't. She looked up at me with curiosity, if such a thing existed in a baby that young.

"George and Grace, I don't want to mislead you. While I'm picking Charlene up, a dear friend and her husband are actually going to take care of her for you, as long as you need them to. Amy and Adam Drahota have lived here much longer than I have, and Amy is a stay-at-home wife, so she'll be there to take care of Charlene, which I can't. Is that alright with you?"

George looked up from staring at his wife's hands, which were held in his. He, too, had been crying.

"Do they love children?"

"Yes. Amy is unable to have children, but they do love them. They are good people." Charlene was blowing bubbles, and I couldn't help but smile at her.

"She's very good, rarely cries," Grace reached over and touched Charlene's soft cheek, before continuing, "I am struggling, because I want to keep her with us, but we just can't right now. It's just too much."

I understood. I couldn't imagine suddenly having an infant in my arms. As it was, I needed to care for her for one night, as the Drahota's had an appointment with Amy's oncologist and wouldn't be home until late that night.

George helped put the car seat into my truck. I had already cleared Ari's space in order to put the back seats up in order to accommodate it. Strapping her in, I took their written instructions and all of little Charlene's things home with me.

That night as I rocked her to sleep I found myself singing the only lullaby I knew. I thought I was singing softly until my mom peeked in.

"Rebekkah, why are you singing Christmas songs?" It was likely an obvious question to anyone listening to me.

"Only one, Mom; it's all I could think of; don't give me hard time. She seems to enjoy it."

"Away in the Manger; I guess it is sort of a lullaby. Well, I'm going to bed. And Rebekkah, I hope you know I'm proud of you."

It felt odd, sitting there with a baby in my arms. It isn't how I'd ever consider spending an evening home. I carefully put her in the portable crib and, with Jael and Ari standing on either side of me, we simply watched her sleep. I just couldn't get past the reason she was there, however. And the loss she had suffered without any awareness of it.

The whole community was broken by what had happened. The funerals, held in our little church, were incredibly sad. A pall hung over the entire service, a feeling of anguished disbelief.

As we sat in the pew, I watched Amy and Adam come in, carrying little Charlene. The day I had brought her to them, Amy had shown instantly she would have made a wonderful mother.

Wrapping the baby into her arms, she sang a true lullaby, one that wasn't in the Christmas section of the church hymnal. Adam, leaning over her shoulder, only whispered, "She's beautiful, Rebekkah. Gosh, she looks like Megan."

I thought about Megan, and the first time I met her. She had been so shy, so unsure. I remembered watching her slowly blossom into a very competent assistant manager, and, as Adam had said, a beautiful woman.

Now, Adam and Amy had to turn Charlene back over to her grandparents. They met the Pearson's at the entry, carefully handing her to them. Amy, tears flowing, touched the baby's cheek and whispered to Mrs. Pearson.

Adam led Amy to our pew and helped her sit down. Her eyes turned toward where the Pearson's sat across the aisle from us, a look of naked longing in her eyes. I took Amy's hand in mine; hoping to distract her. It was shaking.

"Are you okay, Amy? I'm sorry; I shouldn't have asked you to do that. It was too much to ask."

"No, I'm glad you did. I want to be of service when God needs me to. I don't get to do it very often, so thank you." She squeezed my hand and I don't know if I could have made it through the funeral if it hadn't been for her kind words.

As we went into the church's basement for refreshments, I felt a hand touch my arm. Benjamin was standing behind me with Connie standing close by.

"I hear what you did for the Pearson's. That was really nice that you would think of that."

I kept hearing it through-out the day and all it did was made me feel worse. I wondered more often than not if what I did made things harder for Amy, or if I really helped the Pearson's. In the long run, I wasn't sure. They still had an infant to take care of, a couple in their early seventies.

McCaffrey House had changed somehow with the death of Megan. Our guests weren't aware of what happened, but the feeling of loss permeated everyone. The hardest hit, however, was Agnes. She had taught Megan in high school, and then she had tutored her over lunchtime and any spare time they had while working together here. Megan had become like the daughter she never had.

Knowing all that, I offered Agnes some time off, but she declined it, and I knew she'd just be home alone. Here, she had family and things to do. It was in losing Megan we all realized how much of a family we had become.

Connie, perhaps because she hadn't been as close to Megan, was able to think ahead of the rest of us and came up with an idea. When she approached me with it, I knew it was what we needed to do. First, however, I had to run it past Bill Carlton.

Bill had been my lawyer since I came to Elk Ridge. At one point, we had actually dated, which didn't work out. It seemed to be a common ailment for me. But the good thing was, we remained friends and he remained my lawyer. I didn't need his help nearly as often as when McCaffrey House first started, but thankfully a retainer fee kept him available.

Explaining the idea to him, he concurred it would be a very good idea, and agreed to handle it pro-bono if we decided to proceed. With his nod, I called a meeting of the staff and the owners, and let Connie take the floor.

"I know only a few of you well, and I really didn't know Megan that long, but it seems that everyone here has become family. As a family, we want to take care of our own, right? I was thinking that perhaps we could start a scholarship fund for little Charlene. I understand the Pearson's aren't that well off, and they don't have much for family, well, except us."

It was a simple plan, to start up a fund for Charlene, to help with some early expenses, but the goal was to help with her college expenses down the road. Everyone in the room was nodding in agreement. It was the perfect way to care for Megan's daughter for the long-term now that her parents weren't there to do it for her.

"Didn't Tommie or Megan have any insurance?" Margaret's husband Jack, also one of the owners of McCaffrey, raised his hand.

"They did, however after paying their debts and the funeral expenses, there wasn't much left." Adam, also an owner, spoke up. "The house had a mortgage and will be sold; that's what I understand. They may make a little on that, but not much."

"As an owner, I'd like to make a motion we go ahead with this fund and accept Bill Carlton's offer to manage it for us." Martha spoke firmly; it was the voice she used when she expected perfect obedience from someone.

"I'll second it," Margaret, used to obeying her sister, responded.

"We have a motion and a second; are there any questions or discussion?" Gary Sheffield, as one of the House's Advisory Board, had attended and agreed to run the meeting.

There were questions on how it should be handled; who should have signatory rights to the fund once it was set up; and how it should be managed. In reality, even with the discussion, everyone there was in agreement. Connie's idea was easily passed and before the end of the day, there was already nearly one thousand dollars ready to deposit.

Bill accepted the envelope with the first donations, the bulk of which came from Jack and Margaret. Glancing over at me, he asked if Margaret still made the best coffee and caramel rolls in the state.

Going into the kitchen, I poured him a cup of coffee as I remembered he liked it and put some rolls from breakfast in the warming oven.

"You look great Rebekkah. You've lost weight since I saw you, what, nearly two years ago?"

"I have lost weight, but it was really only about a year and a half ago. Mom got diabetes, you know, and well, our diets have changed dramatically." I was glad someone had noticed. I had lost nearly ten pounds since making the decision I needed to do something.

"You look well too. How are you doing? Ever get that little white dog you talked about?"

He laughed and shook his head in the negative, "No, no dog. The office is doing really well; I've taken on two paralegals to

155

help me keep up. I'm also dating someone now. She's a nice woman, loves to entertain and fits the world I live in," He paused as I pulled the rolls out of the oven and put them on plates for us. Grabbing the butter dish, two forks and two knives, I sat back down.

"How about you, Rebekkah? Besides losing weight and looking amazing? Are you dating anyone?" He watched as I carefully separated the roll out and stuffed butter down between the layers. "How did you lose the weight again?"

"By not eating rolls every day," I answered with a smile.

"Seriously, how are you doing?" He repeated the question, and I had to think about it. In that eighteen or so months since I had last seen him, so much had happened in my life. And yet, nothing had truly changed.

"I'm doing well. I had a date," At Bill's raised eyebrows, I laughed again. How to explain that statement? "I had a date with a man who saved my life on a search. I think we both mutually reached the conclusion we weren't, well, compatible. I met some amazing guys that plant trees every spring. I learned to make maple syrup finally, and I had to retire Ari."

"Oh, Bekkah, I'm sorry. He's your favorite, I know. Mine too, although I'm not much of a dog person – as you know."

As we talked, the door swung open and I was surprised to see Benjamin lean in.

"I'm sorry, didn't realize you were, well, anyway, I'm here to pick up Connie. She said she'd likely be in the kitchen, but maybe I'm early."

"Hello Benjamin! I came up for the meeting they had about Connie's idea." Bill stood and offered his hand. The handshake complete, Bill pointed at the two extra rolls still on the plate, "Hungry? I'll never eat them."

It didn't take a second for the offer to be accepted, and soon the two men were chatting with each other. I found myself laughing for the first time since I had the call from the Pearson's that awful Saturday morning.

It just seemed overwhelmingly funny. It felt like, at least over the past year, every time I was talking to a man, Benjamin would suddenly appear. If I had more courage, I might have asked if he was stalking me, but I knew he'd have an amazingly quick response that would leave me speechless. It was best to remain silent.

I refilled coffee cups and cleaned up the empty plates, and still they gabbed on. Whoever said women were the worst talkers hadn't been around men long enough.

Connie entered as I was washing off the plates, and I could see she was ready for her date. She had lost more weight, and her clothes were new and stylish. I was, of course, wearing jeans and a T-shirt. I'd never measure up to her sparkling personality and looks, no matter how much I tried.

"Benjamin, I see your date is here, so I should let you go. In fact, I need to get on the road for the same reason. Opera tonight and we can't be late!"

"You're taking Rebekkah to the opera?" Benjamin glanced at me, and I knew what he saw. A woman in jeans and a T-shirt and definitely not dressed for the opera.

"Oh. No. Sorry. Rebekkah and I are still good friends, but, well, different paths, different lives. I'm dating a gal I met online actually. Turns out, it can actually work." With another handshake and a few hugs, they were all gone, leaving me leaning against the kitchen counter with a wet dishrag still in my hand.

When Bill and I had ended our relationship, I had thought I was alright with being single. I had accepted it. What was wrong with me now?

Going home that night, I went into my home where I was met by an aging mother, an aging dog, and a dog that couldn't relax.

Oh, and a green leafy salad for supper.

# Chapter 12

*If I ascend up into heaven, You are there;*

It was at training the following week that I saw it. Ari was walking gingerly, as if his back leg hurt him. On the drive home, I heard him licking and licking himself. Unloading him, I saw immediately he had been licking his pelvic area. The fur was sopping wet from it.

Checking him over, I couldn't find a hot spot or anything that would account for him to be licking like that. I woke up during the night to hear him licking himself again. And again the following morning, which prompted me to find the dreaded bottle of lavender oil.

While many people like the smell of lavender; I hate it. My mom despises it. It isn't a welcome odor in our home. However, years ago someone had informed me that it worked wonders when a dog gets a hotspot. Not only does it have healing properties, it also keeps most dogs for licking the area, allowing it to heal.

Ari wasn't happy when I used a Q-tip to swab some oil on the fur of his hip. But it worked until I got home, when he started again. It became a nightly ritual, one I hated because my sinuses would immediately clog from the smell.

Finally, in desperation, I called Dr. Mikkelson. He was starting to get used to my calls, and my nervous worries about my aging dog. In this case, I could easily see Ari licking himself into an open sore which would never heal.

Much to my dog's distress, he took X-rays of Ari's hips and discovered the problem. His back and pelvis were no longer lined up.

"Rebekkah, do you believe in chiropractors?" My vet was looking at the X-rays as he spoke, but I knew he wanted an answer without the pressure of his looking at me.

"Yes, although I rarely go because I can't afford it, why?"

"Not for you, for Ari," I could almost hear him rolling his eyes. I ignored the sarcasm. When I didn't respond, he continued, "I'd like Ari to see an animal chiropractor. Are you willing to give it a try? This looks like it happened weeks ago, so it would take several visits."

I suddenly saw, in my mind's eye, Ari falling in the wet rocks into that cold lake. A few weeks later the lake was frozen finally. Christmas was just around the corner, and yet another thing was going wrong with my dog. I should have noticed him walking funny, and perhaps I did, but just thought it was still his instability. How wrong we can be.

"Are there any around here?" I was surprised when he nodded.

"Actually, Nan's husband just finished the training. If you're willing, you can bring Ari here. He just needs a signed referral from me, agreeing to the procedure, as well as from you. Since the laws changed in 2008, it is a pretty regulated form of treatment in our state."

Two days later, I met with Paul. Ari, after so many bad things happening to him in vet clinics, was trembling as we went back in. Dr. Dan had set aside a small room for us with soft cushion pads on the floor.

"Just let him off leash and let him sniff around and relax." Paul sat on a cube thing and watched my dog. Ari didn't cooperate; he just stood there waiting for whatever horror was going to come next.

160

"Okay, well, I'd like to see him walk. I saw his X-rays so I know what they say. I'd like to see what he says." I took Ari a walk down the hall and then back to the room.

"I see he does have some back end issues, what I'll do now is see what we can do to help him with some of that. Can you kneel down in front of him and just hold his head steady."

I did as instructed, which I know my dog appreciated. I felt his body tense as Paul placed his hands on Ari's hips, then the sound of licking as Ari tried to calm himself. A moment later, I felt my dog flinch and then suddenly relax.

Looking between his ears, I asked, "What just happened?"

"I adjusted his pelvis. It was really out; poor dog must have been in some pain." From that point on, Ari remained in a stage of tenseness to suddenly relaxing. It felt odd through my hands as he pressed his head into my chest and I held him gently around the neck.

It was over before we knew it. Ari, for the first time in weeks, or even longer, suddenly shook himself from head to tail tip.

"Yep, I'm guessing he hadn't done that for a while, not in the condition he was in. He should feel really tired and thirsty today, that's okay. Can you bring him back in, next week, same time?"

Nodding, I wasn't sure what to say. My old dog had limped his way in and was walking out. I had known that chiropractors can help, but that much?

"My father-in-law once told me you have to explain to Law Enforcement officers that what the dogs do isn't black magic. It is channeling the ability that the dog already has. That is what I do. It isn't black magic; I just remind the body where the parts are really supposed to be, and help them go back to where they belong. From there, the body does the healing."

I understood, but even if I hadn't, just watching my dog would have convinced me it was worth the visit.

Returning home, I found my mom in the midst of baking Christmas cookies. Not just any cookies, but my Grandma James' honey anise cut out cookies. A pan of the golden brown goodness sat waiting for the boiled icing she was just finishing up.

"Grandma's Cookies? Real cookies, with icing and colored sugar and everything?" Growing up the daughter of a military man, we moved every few years. We lived in many places across our great nation, but only two things made Christmas, Christmas. My mom's homemade manger scene and when the box arrived from Grandma James.

No matter where we were stationed, the box would come with honey anise cookies, lightly frosted and sprinkled with colored sugar. There was also a five pound box of pecan halves for my dad's favorite holiday treat, pecan pie; but it was the cookies we kids looked forward to.

When Grandma's health was failing, I sat down with her and carefully copied her recipe. My Grandpa had been a baker, and so the recipe was in weights instead of dry measure as they made such large batches. I remember it took us three full Christmas's after Grandma died to get the measurements correct. Who would have guessed it was so hard to convert ounces of dark brown sugar into standard cup measure?

The smell in the kitchen was Christmas for me. For some, Christmas is the smell of a pine tree, or turkey. For me, it will always be the smell and taste of the cookies.

Sitting down at the table, we decorated them, laughing and enjoying the time together. Diets forgotten, we ate the misshapen cookies without worrying about the calories. It was a wonderful time and I wondered if my mom planned it, just to get my mind off what had happened.

She couldn't entirely, but she knew that. The Pearson's, amazed at the outpouring of our community to Charlene's fund, had wept openly when asked to join Bill at the local bank to formalize the documents. We couldn't help but wonder if Christmas, for the Pearson's, would always be a reminder of what they had lost instead of the greatest gift ever given to mankind.

A few days later, as I pulled into the tree-lined drive to McCaffrey House, it was as if the House itself had decided it was time to put her mourning clothes away. The trees were lit with tiny white lights, looking almost like stardust on the needles, and then there was McCaffrey itself, lit in old-fashioned Christmas light glory.

I knew it was thanks to Harold and his intrepid staff of local high schoolers, but the transformation was actually magical. My spirit, so long in sorrow, was feeling the restorative powers of the season. The day with mom over trays of cookies had started the process, and here, looking at the beauty of lights, I felt my spirit lift and soar again.

Entering the main part of the House, I smelled it before I saw it. Harold had brought in the tree; I knew it. It stood tall and grand near the main fireplace, and I was excited to see that someone had remembered our Christmas tradition here at McCaffrey.

Beside each breakfast plate was one of our ornaments. As the guests came in, they could hang their ornament on the tree, wherever they wanted to. Our only request was that the lower boughs were left for those in wheelchairs. It was something we had done since we opened, having our guests help decorate the tree. Megan had ensured the tradition had continued over the last two years as I wasn't there on Saturdays as much anymore.

Going into the kitchen, I knew immediately who it was who had remembered. It was Agnes; and I knew it was to honor Megan when she carefully handed me a small box.

Opening it, I started to cry. Inside was a tiny ornament that looked like the cover of a "Pat the Bunny" book, with the words, "Baby's First Christmas". On the back was written, 'Charlene Rae Pearson".

"Agnes, I think you should put this one up." I handed it back and we all went back in to join the families staying with us as they put up their ornaments.

A couple I had checked in a few days before were making the decision on where to put their ornaments; one was a small husky puppy that brought back memories of the family who had given it to us. Eric and Jane, who had enjoyed a dog sled ride while visiting. Their marriage was on the rocks when they arrived, but each year, they had come back. I wondered suddenly if they were on our reservation list.

Megan's ornament was placed in a prominent place where it would be noticed and commented on. Not many trees in a place like this would have a baby's first Christmas ornament.

I returned to my desk to sort through the mail and uncovered a small envelope that was addressed to 'Lady with dog' in care of McCaffrey House. Intrigued, I carefully opened it, noting the stamp was from California.

Inside, a fuzzy sheep with a wreath around its neck stared out at me from the card. Inside, was written "Fleece Navidad", and a carefully hand-written note.

> *"We are wishing you a Merry Christmas, or how we say 'Feliz Navidad'. We are making our way north, following the crops, and hope to be in Minnesota by late April this year. I hope to see you and your dog (perro) when we arrive! My daughter Maria writes this for me, and she also wishes you a Merry Christmas."*

The card was signed with an assortment of names, but front and center was Arturo Vegas. Someone even drew a little stick figure of a dog. I couldn't help but laugh. It was a wonderful card, and I knew I had to answer it, even though it was clear Arturo was already on his migrant path back to us.

Finding the box of leftover Christmas cards we sent out every year to people who had stayed with us at McCaffrey House, I wrote a note in return, hoping the family would pass the message to Arturo. I also tucked in a collector card with a photo of K-9 Ariel, along with his information on the back. We had them made up on a donation a few years ago, and I only had a few left. This seemed like the perfect time to give one away.

"Rebekkah, do you know the church's schedule for Christmas services this year?" Agnes leaned in, and I came to earth with a jolt. For some reason, I had expected to look up and see Megan. She was the one who handled all that before.

"Yes, here it is; Pastor Dave emailed it to me; just a second," I pushed papers around and realized I needed to organize the office again. I had left things as Megan had done them, but it wasn't my system. Much as it felt strange, I needed to put it back to how I had it laid out some years ago.

"Here you go. Can you post this for me?" Pushing aside another paper, I uncovered another schedule, this time for the community of Elk Ridge. "Oh, post this one as well. They overlap, but that's okay."

I spent the rest of the day reorganizing the files. Megan's system was perfectly fine, but it was her system and when I needed to find a file for the church, I expected to find it in the file marked, "Community Church", not "Pastor Dave".

I was just finishing the last file when my cell phone rang. It had been quiet lately, but this close to Christmas, a search seemed odd even for Minnesota.

"Elk Ridge Search and Rescue, how can we help?" I slid the file into place and leaned back into the chair, hearing Benjamin's voice in my ear.

"Rebekkah, remember our conversation a few weeks ago? I'm wondering if you and Chris are available to do a sniff with the dogs this afternoon? We'd be on a time crunch."

"Something you don't want to talk about on the phone or can you go into more details?"

"I need the dogs to execute a search warrant to determine if there was a crime scene.  Are you okay with that?"

Crime scenes, by their very nature, place the handler in potential danger.  If they locate something, there is the possibility the person who committed the crime will come after you.  It also placed us at higher risk of being called into court.  I'm not sure which scenario frightened me more.

I had once taken a seminar where the Master Trainer sat me down in front of all the other handlers and started asking questions, just as they did in court.  Within five minutes, I was flushed, embarrassed and unable to figure out where I went wrong.

It had started with a simple question; what was my dog's final trained response?

"He sits at source."  I had been confident, sure of myself.  I wasn't one to say too much, as some did.

"Is that all he does?  Just sit?"  The trainer leaned in, cocked his head, and waited.

Feeling a little pressure to respond into the waiting silence, I made my first mistake, "If I can't see the source, I ask him to touch it with his muzzle."

"Okay, so your dog sits and does a touch as well?  Anything else that you can't recall?"

"No, he does a sit at source."  I tried to retract, which only brought the trainer to his full height.

"So, does he or doesn't he touch?" At which point, he suddenly broke off and, turning to the class who sat watching me squirm, said, "See how easy it is to make a small mistake and suddenly you sound like you don't know what you're doing?"

To say testifying in court wasn't something anyone wanted to do was an understatement. Just as the trainer had said, dog handlers had been torn apart by lawyers by asking them simple questions.

"I'll ask Chris, but I'll go. It's in regard to the Derek Nieland search, correct?" I interpreted the silence to mean it was and didn't ask again.

Within two hours we arrived at what appeared to be a ramshackle hunting cabin with a few outbuildings in worse shape, if that was possible. Even though it was just off a main road, it gave me the heebie-jeebies just to get out of my truck. I had the uneasy feeling we were being watched.

Benjamin met us at the vehicles, along with two Drug Enforcement Agents. In a low voice, he informed us we had only three hours to run both dogs across the property to the back of the cabin; that the warrant only covered the 'open areas' and we were not to cross over the curtilage. If the dogs showed a desire to cross it, we were to restrain them.

After explaining all of that, our final instruction was that any final trained response given by the dog would be recorded, but beyond that, we couldn't touch anything.

"Rebekkah, you likely know this, but for the benefit of Chris, Minnesota courts use four things to determine the extent of curtilage. I'll try to keep it simple, but they include the proximity of the area claimed to be curtilage for the home. If the area is included in an enclosure surrounding the home, what the area is used for, and of course what steps the resident has taken to protect the area from observation by the passerby."

Chris looked stumped at the long explanation. Seeing her confusion, one of the DEA agents simplified as best he could, "search the open areas, don't go near buildings, and don't pass the fencing over there." He pointed at a dilapidated barb wire fence that ran along behind the cabin.

With that instruction, we were ready. One of the agents walked with me, the other with Chris. We split the area, with Chris doing the west side and Jael and I doing the east. As I turned my dog loose onto a small trail that led behind the house and on the far side of a rickety fence, she worked quickly and we were soon on the far side of the area, which opened onto a small road.

Letting my dog range out, I heard a vehicle pull in behind us. It slowed as it came up beside us, and we both turned to see who was coming up. It was an older gentleman and he intended to stop and ask questions.

"Excuse me, what is going on here?"

"Good afternoon sir. Is this your driveway?" The agent responded easily, and I was happy to let him handle it.

"Yeah, my driveway; is everything alright?" I realized that neither one of us was clearly identified as being part of a law enforcement search. I had chosen not to identify myself or my unit out of concern if a bad guy was watching they might take retribution out on the unit. For the first time, I looked the agent over and realized that while he likely had a badge, it was under the coat.

"Well, I can't say much, but we are trying to help a family get some closure on the loss of their son." I could see he was about to reveal his badge when the old-timer jumped in.

"Oh, that is too sad. I think I should warn you that the land you're on belongs to some strange folks over there. I think they're drug dealers, to be honest. There are always strange vehicles over there, all the time. I just drove by and sure enough, a bunch more cars are over there. You take care, there, eh?"

"Yes, thank you, we will." I glanced over at the agent as the vehicle pulled away. He was laughing, and it took me a moment to realize why.

"Those are our cars he's talking about, aren't they? Two unmarked squads and our two trucks?"

"Yes, apparently we're the bad guys today. But he's right; this is known to be a drug house and the people who own it are, well, not nice. I was about to tell him who I was with and show him the badge, but oh well. He'll have a story to tell I guess."

As we approached the end of our search area, my dog's head shot up. I waited a moment, wondering if she had scented Chris and Onyx or something else. Then I saw her breathing change, and I knew. She had the odor of human remains.

"My dog has had a change of behavior. It appears she wants to go back toward the cabin, which I know we can't approach. What would you like me to do?"

"Let her go as far as we can, I'll tell you when to stop her. Can you stop her?" I nodded and he nodded back in agreement.

Jael, her head shifting with the changing odors reaching her nose, turned at a sudden wind shift. Once again I waited, wondering if the change in wind direction had lost the odor to her, or if she could still catch and follow it.

It took a moment, but she swung back into the wind, her head held high. Wherever the odor was coming from, it was from a distance, not close by.

We only could go another four or five hundred feet, when I was told to stop my dog.

"Jael – stop! Here, girl!" It was easy to see my dog wasn't happy, but she responded. I marked the GPS for where we stopped my dog and made a note what direction she was going and which way the wind was blowing at the time.

Returning to our vehicles, I swapped search areas with Chris, as well as agents. We told each other nothing about what we experienced in our area, with the minor exception that our vehicles had been mistaken for druggies by a neighbor. Benjamin radioed a squad to go talk to the neighbor, just in case he might have heard or seen anything.

Forty-five minutes later, we came out of the second area with no reactions from my dog, and with only about fifteen minutes left on the search warrant. We were soaked from tromping through snow and swamp land.

Benjamin stopped by my truck as I loaded Jael, taking a minute to offer her a treat out of a container I kept by her crate. It never ceased to amaze me that she never barked at him.

"We'll go back to the office and debrief there. Bring your GPS and computer, alright?" With a final rub of Jael's fur, he walked away to give the same talk to Chris as she came back in.

During the debriefing, we discovered that Onyx and Jael had both reacted in the same area. Our waypoints marked on our GPS units were nearly identical. The odd part was that Onyx had a different wind direction than Jael did, but both dogs were heading for the same place. With a ruler and pencil on a paper map, we were able to extend their trajectory. The pencil line went straight through one of the outbuildings we weren't allowed to access.

"How strongly do you feel about what your dogs did?" One of the agents, the one that walked with me first, asked.

Chris glanced at me. I just nodded for her to go first. She pointed at the map and began explaining how Onyx had reacted upon leaving the road at the back of the property. It was like listening to my own trip on the first section.

"I'd have to say, everything Chris just said was duplicated for my dog. The strength of her response was a level three on a scale of one to four; four being an actual find."

Even as I spoke, I wondered what had pulled the dogs in so strongly. Speculation isn't usually a wise thing to do, but as humans, we want to solve the mystery, to figure out the answers. Speculation is one way we do it.

There wasn't enough information for me to truly have any idea what might have happened. The odor might not be related to Derek at all. It might be someone else entirely. Or it might be an old cemetery further along. I did trust the dogs enough that I believed they were in odor of human remains. We just didn't know whose remains.

Benjamin, as he escorted us out of the Law Enforcement center, reminded us not to say anything, and thanked us for the work. Chris nodded and in a flurry of falling snow, dashed out to her truck. Thinking how glad I was that the snow had waited until we were done searching, I paused at the door. Benjamin caught my arm, and I nearly jumped a foot.

"Oh, sorry; I just wanted to talk to you if you have a minute?"

"Sure, what's up?" We stepped back into the foyer of the building, and watched the snow falling. I could sense that there was something on his mind, and knew it wasn't related to the search. If it was, we'd have gone back inside instead of standing on the other side of the locked interior doors. Whatever it was, he wanted it to remain between us.

"I don't know if you've talked to Connie, but, well, we're not really dating anymore. I wanted you to know so there wasn't any...," He paused, and I simply waited. I had no idea what he was worried about or why he felt he needed to tell me this.

"I guess I was worried you'd be upset. It really isn't anything to do with Connie or me, we just aren't right for each other. I'm not ready to commit to a relationship."

We continued to stand shoulder to shoulder, watching the snow. I wasn't sure how to answer him. I knew Connie's desire was to lock him into a long-term relationship, as he had guessed. I also know I had warned her it likely wouldn't happen.

"Benjamin, not sure why you wanted to tell me that, as I don't keep up with Connie's personal life really. I have to admit, I'm not surprised," Feeling him glance at me, I shrugged. "I don't keep up with your personal life either, but I do know a little about your track record."

"Do you? Well, one thing I've always appreciated about you is that you don't make it your business to know mine. Unlike every other woman in town," He tapped me lightly in the bicep. I suspected he was serious, although he said it in a joking tone.

"Benjamin, you know that it's because you give them fodder for the gossip mill. I often wonder if you do it just to keep everyone guessing. I've never heard anyone complain about being jilted, so however you manage it, you at least end it gently."

"Usually they end it you know. They realize, finally, that I'm serious when I tell them I don't want to move in with them, or have them move in with me, or that marriage isn't in my plans right now. I believe in marriage, but only when it is the right people, you know?"

"Yes, in that I agree with you. Rather a lonely time to break up with someone, right before Christmas."

"At this point, my life is in some upheaval anyway. It's for the best right now. Well, if I don't see you sooner, I'll see you at the Christmas Eve service." With another light slap on my arm, he went back into the secured area of the building, leaving me wondering what I was supposed to make of that conversation. And if Connie would be broken hearted or spitting mad.

# Chapter 13

*If I make my bed in the place of the dead,*

*Behold, You are there.*

The answer was, she apparently didn't care. There was no change in her at all, so I was forced to assume, as Benjamin had said, she had dumped him. I was worried about her and did want the best. I just wasn't sure Benjamin was it.

For some reason, I was glad though. Her dating him had made things seem awkward between us. I wasn't ever sure why, but it did. With the holidays upon us we were busier than ever, and we needed to work in harmony.

Our reservations dictated whether we stayed open or closed over Christmas, and this year, we were staying open. We had a full house, which was wonderful.

Deep into handling reservations, working with our guests, and making sure the pantry and the wood pile stayed stocked, I wasn't expecting the phone call.

"McCaffrey House, how can we help you?" I answered the phone in the kitchen as I raced from helping Agnes clear the buffet table.

"May I speak with Rebekkah James, please?" Worry set in instantly. It sounded formal, lawyer-like. In the millisecond before I responded, I went through my head all the bills and any complaints for McCaffrey. Nothing came to my mind.

"This is she, how can I help you?"

"My name is Leonard Vanderhaagen. I'm calling from Schilling, Vanderhaagen, and Milner."

"How can I help you Mr. Vanderhaagen?" I truly believed lawyers thought every word out three times before saying them. All except Bill; I'd never noticed him doing it.

"Yes, well, I am calling on behalf of George and Grace Pearson. I understand that you helped them take care of their infant granddaughter after the death of their son and his family?"

"Yes, that is true. May I ask what this is about?"

"I'm sorry to have to make this call, but George had a stroke two days ago. A debilitating stroke, which, it appears, will leave him in the permanent custodial care of his wife, Grace. To that end, they are no longer in a position to care for little Charlene."

It was the first glimmer of humanity I had heard, when he said 'little' Charlene. As the words filtered through, it suddenly hit me. Grace had lost first her son, daughter-in-law and two grandsons. Now, she was losing her husband and her only remaining grandchild. What was God's plan in this? It made no sense to me.

"I have no idea what to say. Megan, their daughter-in-law, worked here at McCaffrey. I'm so sorry for them. What is she going to do?"

"She asked me to contact you and find out if the couple that took care of Charlene would be willing to do so again. The problem is, she is under a great deal of stress right now, and couldn't find their name or contact information. We are hoping you would be able to help. Ms. James, I tell all of this to you with the permission and blessing of Mrs. Pearson, but it is still confidential at this time."

I gave him Adam and Amy's information, wondering if I was doing yet another thing that would hurt them. Was this God's plan for Amy? I had no idea; I only prayed I hadn't opened Pandora's Box on the Drahota's.

Hanging up the phone, I could not tell anyone anything, not even Agnes. Confidentiality is a sacred trust, one I couldn't break, much as I wanted to. It was a lesson learned from SAR as well as working here at McCaffrey. Instead, I called Pastor Dave and asked him to put a family, no names given, who needed prayer on his prayer chain.

"Rebekkah, no problem, I'll do that. Got a question for you. Do you think your mom could play piano for the Christmas services? Phyllis and her husband received two airline tickets to go visit their kids in Florida over the holidays. It was totally unexpected; leaves us in a bit of a lurch."

"Call her and ask. She's feeling so much better; she might like to help out." There was a pause, and once again, I had the sense that a man wanted to share a confidence with me.

"Dave, is there something else?" I could hear something like an "ahum" on the other end, so I simply waited. Familiar turf, as I had recently waited for Benjamin to do the same thing.

"I wanted to let you know, but maybe she already has," I had inspiration finally. Connie, it had to be he was dating Connie again.

"Are you dating Connie?" I decided not to wait him out this time.

"Yes, how did you know? Oh, she told you?" I had no idea how to answer him. She hadn't told me, she had just walked away from the confirmed bachelor who had given me the opposite speech.

Part of me wanted to ask him if he was insane, part of me hoped she was serious and returning to Dave because she realized dashing and daring aren't exactly marital material, whereas quiet and unassuming are.

"No, she didn't tell me, but I heard from another source she was no longer dating Benjamin." Did I hear a hint of something unpleasant in my voice? I hoped not. I wasn't sure what to make of Connie anymore.

"I know, I know. I hear you, I really do. But I like Connie. She has an amazing ability to refresh a room when she walks in, just by smiling and saying hello. I'm not saying it's serious or anything. I think she just needed time to find her way."

I hung up with Dave wondering why some people got so many chances and some didn't. Love, I once heard somewhere, is all about timing. My timing obviously still wasn't on target.

Or maybe it was; the time just hadn't arrived yet. With that comforting thought, I went back to wondering how things were going to pan out for Adam and Amy. Now they were a couple who must have had terrific timing, as they clearly loved each other, which had gotten them through some pretty bad times.

I received the news first, rather like telling the stork who delivered the baby. Amy called to give me the details that Grace Pearson had asked if they would be willing to take temporary custody of baby Charlene. The belief was that someday, if her circumstances changed, she'd be able to take on raising her granddaughter. I didn't ask how they made such arrangements, but apparently it was all legal.

That Sunday, they walked in with Charlene in Amy's arms. The glow of motherhood filled her being while Adam stood to the side, clearly an inch taller in pride as a new daddy. Amy's prayers had been answered in someone else's tragedy, but everyone there knew Charlene would be raised in love and care, and would know who her family was.

As I went up the aisle to sit in the pew behind the piano where my mom was playing the prelude, I had to do a double take. Someone else new was in the congregation this morning.

Benjamin Rafael was sitting a few rows up, and beside him was a young woman. Her long black hair was tied up with white ribbon, her face devoid of makeup. And in that simplicity was one of the most beautiful women I'd ever seen. She was also a good twenty years younger than our sheriff, but as I walked past, I saw him place his hand on hers.

Fighting the strange feeling inside, I wondered where he had found the newest love of his life. She was a complete stranger to me, but more astounding was the fact that they were sitting in church. He never came to church. Well, except if there was a free meal that didn't involve a sermon.

During the Christmas hymns and a warm flowing sermon on what Mary, the mother of Jesus must have experienced, I tried to stay focused. I loved Christmas; it was an amazing time of the year when people actually tried to strive for peace and to take care of their fellow humans. It was hard, as the human in me wanted to know who that lovely young creature was with Benjamin, and where on earth he had found her.

I didn't have much of a chance to find out. Most of the congregation was clumped around Adam and Amy, and I was sort of sucked into the crowd.

Turning to leave, I bumped into them. Her eyes were remarkable, and I wondered if she had some Asian in her background. "I'm so sorry! My name is Rebekkah James." I held out my hand, which was taken for a handshake.  I had expected her grip to be soft, but it was as firm as a man's.

"Priscilla Davis."  Even her voice was delicate and pretty, like her name and face.

"Welcome to our church, Priscilla.  Are you staying in the area?"  I glanced at Benjamin and had the feeling he wasn't sure when or where to jump in.

"I'm staying with Benjamin Rafael through the holidays.  It was very nice to meet you."  And they were gone.  I wondered about her statement of staying with him, when he had so clearly said weeks before that he had no intentions of moving in with anyone or having them move in with him.  It all seemed odd, and it was clear he had no intentions of clearing it up, either.

Talking to Amy after the strange exchange, we made sure that we would sit together at the women's Christmas Tea at the church.  It was being held two days before Christmas Eve, and it was always a fun day for everyone.  Glancing at the closed doors where Benjamin had left, Amy asked if it would be alright if she invited his new girlfriend, if she was going to be still in the area.

I agreed, feeling the weird knot in the pit of my stomach.  It was the right thing to do, to help her to feel welcome, but without knowing anything about it, it was strange as well.  I wasn't sure how I felt when Amy called me with the news that while Adam stayed with Charlene, she'd pick up Priscilla for the Tea.

I missed the Tea, the first time since coming to Elk Ridge.  My cell phone went off during the night, and, along with other members of Elk Ridge SAR, we were on the road for a search across the border, in our neighboring state of Wisconsin.

Driving through falling snow, I prayed for our missing person, as well as the family and all the responders going to help.

With the cold temperatures, unless our missing man was dressed for it, it was unlikely he'd make it through the night.

I understood from the initial call that the search had been on-going for most of the day, but because Christmas was only a few days away, many of their SAR members were out of town, or unable to leave family gatherings for the search, or had to head home because of family coming in. They had been spread thin, and were now requesting mutual aid. I had my dog with me, but knew their initial sorties were using live-find dogs.

E.R.SAR arrived on scene together as we had caravanned the whole way. We checked in and I found myself assigned as a field support to a handler I hadn't met before.

Being a field support, or tech, behind a new handler is sometimes a difficult job. Most handlers are used to working with someone from their own unit. They have protocols and expectations that we may not. I remembered a search where the handler got very frustrated with me for being too close to them. Whereas, I preferred my techs to stay closer; it bothered me when they hung way back. There was only one way to handle it; ask questions.

"Rebekkah James from Elk Ridge. Can I ask a few quick questions before we start?" At the nod, I continued, "How close do you want me to stay?"

"Talking distance, and my name is Quint, don't ask, my parents pinned it on me." I laughed, and told him I wouldn't ask that question then.

"What coordinate system and datum are they using for this search?" This was a critical question, because if I used the wrong system, any waypoints I entered on my GPS could show up in an abstract area on the incident command's main mapping.

"Do you actually understand all that? I still don't after years of doing this. I can tell you that we are on UTM UPS WGS 84. Don't ask me what it means, I'm just happy I can change my GPS and it just happens."

While I didn't pretend to completely understand it myself, I did have a grasp of the concepts. The global positioning system communicated with satellites which made them able to tell us where we are on the earth at any given time. The key is that here on terrestrial earth we need to use the same systems; or basically, the same map.

I turned on my GPS and keyed the menu to the systems settings. First, I had to check which Coordinate systems I had on my GPS. I knew what I normally had, but periodically we had trainings where we were asked to reset them, just to make sure we could.

The choice used when I first started in SAR was always the long-standing latitude and longitude, or Lat/Lon. As its name implied, it marked the earth in horizontal and vertical grid lines. The lines were then assigned datum points so you knew where in the Lat/Lon system you were standing. It had worked for many years quite well.

Then UTM, or Universal Transverse Mercator, came along. UTM peeled the earth like an orange and flattened the earth out, using zones instead of lines. I knew in Minnesota, where I lived, we were in zone fifteen. Crossing the border into Wisconsin, I was still in fifteen, but any further east, and I'd go into zone sixteen.

All very confusing, but what people learned quickly was that UTM has shorter coordinates, and therefore was easier to remember for most people. I set my GPS for UTM UPS. I couldn't remember as I stood there what the UPS stood for, but I knew it had nothing to do with shipping parcels, only to how it made up for the large grid-gaps by the North and South Poles. Or I believed that's what it did.

Next, I had to set my datum. Quint stood next to me, getting his gear ready as I pushed buttons on the GPS. Leaning over, he asked, quite randomly, "What does WGS 84 mean, anyway?"

I thought back to all the navigation and orienteering classes I had taken over the years. I knew that, once you set your coordinate system, you had to tell the GPS where the coordinate starts, or were to lay the data on the grid. It is all fine and dandy to say "draw lines on the earth", but unless you know where the numbering of those lines starts, anywhere is home. It would be sort of like saying to someone "Go three miles west and then two miles north," but not telling them where to start their journey from.

"Seriously? Do you think I remember this stuff?" I laughed, but I knew it would be clicking in the back of my head until it came to me. I hated that feeling of knowing you know the answer, but unable to come up with it.

"All I know is the WGS 84 was set in 1984. NAD 27 was done in the 1927 and can be tens of meters off of the WGS 84 datum sets. I think it is because in 1984, they had advanced means of measuring the earth. Or the earth is slowly changing, like for the magnetic declination."

"What do you use up by you?" I was glad he skipped over the magnetic declination. We had very little here, so it wasn't something I kept current on.

We had started our search, with Quint's Golden Retriever ranging out of sight ahead of us. I radioed in the start and our initial position before answering.

"We use USNG, or United States National Grid. It is really easy in comparison as you don't have to remember quite so many numbers when relaying the coordinates. They're starting to put USNG markers onto trails so if people are lost, they can actually tell rescuers where they are."

We chatted as we went along, working through falling snow and the darkness. Periodically, Quint would check a small hand-held GPS he was carrying, and I finally asked what it was for, as it didn't appear he was checking our location.

"I have a collar on my dog, it sends periodic updates to the receiver here and I can track where he's at. He ranges out pretty far, and this way I can see if he stops or if he's moving. You can actually see a scent cone develop if he's in odor."

He handed me the small orange unit and I could see on the small colored map a movement that represented his dog. It was amazing, and I knew I wanted the technology as well. Too many times we wonder what has happened to our dog, if they've gotten injured, sidetracked, or, our greatest fear, caught in a conibear trap or snare.

"How much did that run you?" I was sure I didn't want to know, but had to ask.

"We got a grant, but they run around $600.00 each."

I nearly choked. The hand-held I carried with me was only a couple of hundred. That seemed way out of our league.

"He's coming back at a run, not sure why, I didn't see anything that would indicate a find."

We knew in a moment. Scout had been hit by a porcupine. In December, it seemed unheard of. Quills were all over his face, in his mouth and he was in a world of hurt.

"Oh my gosh. There are too many for me to deal with out here in the dark. We need to get him back in. Can you radio ahead for them to get a vet for us?"

Back at base, Quint left with his dog, and I reported back in as an available resource if they needed one. As I stood there, I saw a mapping chart and my memory's filing cabinet finally found the right rolodex card. WGS meant World Geodetic System, and I had no idea why I even knew that. What I did know was that even knowing what all the acronyms were went nowhere if you didn't understand how the coordinate systems and datum types worked. I did agree with Quint however. I liked the fact I could set it up on GPS and not have to completely understand it for it to work.

I was soon assigned to another handler, and we went out to finish the area that Quint and Scout hadn't gotten through. His GPS had told them exactly where Scout was hit by the porcupine, assuming it was still there, which was nice.

The new handler was quiet and reserved. We didn't speak much, but I could see she was an old pro. She knew her dog, she knew her job. She didn't have a fancy collar on her dog; in fact, she didn't even have a light or any type of search vest on him.

They worked as a team and it was a pleasure to watch. I recognized now that Ari was retired, I'd be out here as a field support more often now, at least on live-find searches. It was good for me, of course, as I was always learning from other handlers, but it was also very hard. For the first time, I realized that in retiring my first SAR dog, an era had ended for me.

Hours later, we came back in only because we were told to. I think Patty would have kept going if they would have let her. Base, however, wanted to make sure everyone was getting rest. I

185

was rather glad, as I had a dog still sitting in my truck, and very few people could actually take her out to go potty.

Jael was more than ready for a potty break, and was simply happy to get out of the truck and stretch. Daylight was dawning, and so far, no one had found anything. No tracks in the snow, no clues, no alerts from the dogs. The firemen were doing line searches through areas already searched by dogs, and the mounted posse was running trails on their ATV's.

Grabbing some coffee, one of the volunteers suggested I try the energy circles they had at the other table. I hadn't heard of them before and headed over to the table. Donuts; they were offering donuts. Energy circles sounded far healthier, and I was going to be sure to tell my mom they served them for breakfast as I grabbed one.

Patty came up quietly and asked if my dog was okay. I nodded, as my mouth was full of donut. She just smiled, and then asked if I'd ever considered training her for disaster work.

"People have been asking me that a lot lately. Why do you ask?"

"I saw her and she looks a perfect size for it, small, light, agile. I help train a class not far from here if you're interested. It isn't like the FEMA with all concrete blocks. We try to train for what we'd deploy to around here, which is more like tornadoes ripping through a community."

"Yes, I'd like that. Someone had given me information on a class, but the email address I was given, no one ever answered it, so I sort of gave up."

It was only a short time later that we deployed again, with me as Patty's support once again. This time, we were out until nearly eleven in the morning before returning to base, as our area was completed. Taking my dog out once again, I realized sitting in the truck for over twelve hours was making her a bit stir crazy. I either had to work her, or find a field to let her run for a few minutes.

Patty showed me a nearby area where other handlers were letting their dogs stretch, and I let Jael run for a few minutes, playing fetch and just getting to move. We stood watching my dog as she chased down another ball.

"Definitely bring her to that training; although, does she like to tug?" At my negative headshake, she just said, "Train her to."

I left the search two days later. I had slept two nights in the basement of a local community center with a few other dog handlers and their dogs, eating energy circles for breakfast, cold burgers for lunch and carefully trying not to spend too much on dinner.

Jael had finally gotten a chance to work, but in reality, it was obvious they were simply throwing resources at the area. I learned two other dog teams had already been in the area before me.

While understandable, it is frustrating to the resources when that happens as they realize they have become a warm body to put anywhere. By not utilizing the resources appropriately, it wore them out and rarely advanced the search. At that point, the search was managing Incident Command, versus IC managing the search.

Still, everyone was giving it their all to help find the missing man. In this case, it was an elderly gentleman who had walked away from the family home and just hadn't come back. My problem was, I had a business that was busy, a mom who didn't have a ride anywhere when I was gone, and a dog that was getting tired of living in the truck. Amos left the day before as duty called him home; Karen and Chief a few hours later as she had family coming in. I always hated leaving a search unfinished, but it happened more often than not, and I just couldn't stay any longer.

I drove home with the contact information for the disaster training class, and I couldn't wait to learn more about it. I was glad Patty had explained it wasn't FEMA level, as I had printed out their K-9 requirements on a whim, and it ended up taking a third of a ream of paper. It was good there were people who trained to that; I just didn't believe it was my calling in SAR.

Arriving home, tired, filthy and in desperate need of a shower, I saw presents under our tree. It was then it hit me. I had left for the search three days before Christmas. It was Christmas Eve, and my plans for my mom's Christmas present were gone with the search. The order I had placed had been backordered, and I was supposed to have gone to the store yesterday to pick it up as there wasn't time to ship it.

I wasn't even sure they'd be open anymore today, or in the two hours it would take me to get there. Honesty, they say, is always the best policy. I told my mom what happened, and promised to get her present the day after. I could see I had disappointed her, but wasn't sure what else to do to make it up.

She had a way; she wanted to go to the Christmas Eve service, which started in just two hours. That, too, I had forgotten about, just wanting to take a shower and go to bed.

Instead, I cleaned up faster than I ever have in my life, and was ready to go with time to spare. Carrying boxes of Grandma James' Christmas Cookies for the social hour afterwards, we headed out.

Entering the church, it was no surprise to see it full to overflowing. Elk Ridge had two churches, a Catholic Church and our little Community church. But only one building. On Christmas Eve, they shared the service, and every year I was amazed at how well they managed it.

Running the cookies downstairs, I helped get things ready there before heading back upstairs. Seeing Amy and Adam, I remembered the Christmas Tea that I had missed as well, and wondered how it went.

Before the question came out, I realized that they had a guest with them. Grace Pearson, Charlene's grandmother had come to spend Christmas with them. The baby was doing well, that I knew, I wondered how Grace and George were doing.

Introductions were made a second time, with no time left for chatting. They went into the sanctuary, and I was about to join them when I saw Priscilla and Benjamin come in. Her looks still were a surprise.

"Rebekkah! Glad you made it back in time for the service. You remember Priscilla." I nodded and smiled. I didn't know why, but I felt like a country mouse next to her.

"I'm glad you're still here, did you enjoy the Tea on Saturday? OH – the music is starting, we'd better go in."

After the service was over, a service that I yawned through and nearly went to sleep during, I apparently fell asleep in the corner of the reception hall downstairs. Thankfully no one said anything, and when I woke up, it was all over. Nearly everyone was gone, leaving just the ladies cleaning up. It was with some trepidation I asked my mom quietly if I had been snoring, with a twinkle in her eye, she said, "like a buzz-saw."

I wasn't sure I believed she was teasing, but one of the other ladies explained I slept very quietly and everyone had known I had just returned from nearly three days of searching and understood.

That somehow made it worse, that part about 'everyone had known' meant that everyone knew I was sleeping in the corner. Shaking my head, I wondered if I'd stay awake to drive home, but somehow we made it safely. It wasn't until I was getting undressed that I found the note someone left in my pocket.

> *"Stopped to see how you doing, glad to see you could relax so well. I really have a hard time doing that, falling asleep in a room full of people. Must be a gift - Merry Christmas!!"*

It was unsigned, but I knew who put it there, it had to be Benjamin. No one else would have done it.

# Chapter 14

*If I take the wings of the morning,*
                    *And dwell in the uttermost part of the sea;*

With Christmas over, and the New Year beginning, I decided to try and train Jael to tug, as the woman at that search suggested. Teaching her to grab a bringsel so many years ago was hard enough. She only liked certain textures in her mouth; mainly the fabric on tennis balls. Other things she wouldn't even touch.

Figuring the bringsel training was a place to start, and knowing she was at least grabbing a fleece tug toy, I decided it would work to begin with anyway.

It was fairly simple to remind her to first touch, then mouth at the tug. I simply held it, and as soon as she touched it, I clicked and gave her a treat. Then I ignored a simple touch and waited for her to mouth it. Click and treat for a reward as quickly as I could.

It was the next step I knew would be difficult. She had never shown any inclination to tug. She'd play fetch all day, but the moment we tried to pull back, she'd let go, anticipating another throw.

It took nearly two weeks, but I finally had Jael consistently grabbing the tug toy. The next step was to encourage her to hold onto it. I struggled to think of a way to reward, or click, for her to tug if she never tugged. I needed a first step to reward.

It came unexpectedly, she mouthed and actually bit down, but as soon as I started to add tugging, she let go. Except her tooth caught in the tug, and she pulled trying to free herself. I had no idea if it was good or bad to reward something that startled her, but I did.

Jael released and stared at me, then at the tug. I could see her hamster wheel turning in her head, and prayed hard for a breakthrough.

Although it didn't really happen, she finally learned to grab and eventually hold; but tugging was not happening in her book. Contacting the trainer, Patty, about it, I asked the simple question, "Why is a tug so important?"

The answer was easy. On a disaster area, you don't want to use a food reward because there might be food everywhere. You don't want a fetch reward, as it is too dangerous for the dog to run around on a disaster pile chasing a flying object. Plus, you want interaction with the subject who is hiding under the pile. Tugging was something that was a fairly stable way to reward.

Frustrated, I went back to the drawing board. How do you get a dog to pull, and pull hard, as a reward when they don't like to tug? I tried every toy she ever played with, touched or even considered hers. Nothing worked.

As winter was flying by, I struggled with the problem. My dog would not tug. I could reward by simply giving her a tennis ball and she was ecstatic. I finally gave up, and went with the plan to hand her a tennis ball on the pile, whatever the pile was. Which got me to thinking again; shouldn't I be training on something? What should I use for the pile? I sent off the email.

The answer was emailed back. Start with a few pallets and get her comfortable walking on them. Then stack them up and get her on them again. Add other things with odd texture, like woven wire fencing, or flexible and unstable.

So we trained. I found some old pallets and Jael, who was agile and confident on so many things, didn't want to get on the pallets. No reward could convince her to traverse those things.

Every time she stepped onto a pallet, her feet slid through. Even I was getting concerned she was going to injure herself. But we tried every day until she was at least walking across them. Even if it was slow, she was trying.

The rest of the challenges seemed easy in comparison to the tugging and the pallets. Jael didn't fuss about odd footing, jumping onto a hanging board that floated around in air at the nearby playground. I even took her up and down the slide with me.

As the day drew close for the disaster training, our whole unit was working on different aspects of the training. Obedience was critical, and while we worked on it anyway, this was different. It required faster responses, longer stays, and yet completely controlled.

Jael, Onyx and Chief all were ready, we hoped, to not make complete fools of their handlers. We were sharing a hotel room and caravanning to the training. As we arrived, and started to unload, Karen glanced over at me and said, without any warning, "I never heard; how is your bark command coming along?"

I froze. Bark command? I hadn't trained a bark command. Was that in the list of things to work on? I realized, as Chris nodded, that I had missed it. I had been so wrapped up in getting my dog to cross pallets and tug on a stupid toy she still wouldn't tug with, I had missed the bark command.

It didn't take long to find out the bark was a critical puzzle piece, and one that Jael wasn't going to grasp quickly. We had spent most of her life teaching her not to bark at people. Now we were going to ask her to bark at someone. Life was going to be very confusing for a while.

The first day, we watched as dogs, highly trained and skilled, were run through their paces so we could see how it was done, and why certain things are critical to their function; such as the tug. I shrugged that one off, as I knew it wouldn't happen for me.

Then, it was trying our own dogs out on simple agility. I was happy to see the unit dogs had no problems with the odd, mismatched wood and angles that made up the agility. The tall ladder I wasn't expecting, and realized we would have homework when we got home.

After the agility, came the directional boxes. We all started small, with one box, or table. Jael quickly mastered the 'hup' command and learned to turn and sit to face me. Then, as they got that, we added a second table. Hop on; hop off; hop onto the next one; all under direction of the handler and not on their own.

"Broad motions guys; when you point to the next box and tell your dog 'over', use broad sweeping motions so there is no question in your dog's mind where they need to go next!"

It felt stupid, swinging my arms like that, but I quickly saw how fast my dog responded. She was doing well, and we actually moved to sending her back to a table behind. I knew at home we'd set up a full baseball-shaped diamond course for us all to train on.

That night, we all expected the dogs to sleep soundly. After all, we were exhausted. That wasn't the case. They apparently were over-stimulated, and spent several hours chasing each other around the room, barking and whining, and demanding to go outside at differing intervals.

"Tomorrow night, we walk them after class. They need time to wind down I guess." Karen said after returning from yet another unfruitful visit to the great out of doors.

194

"Good plan. I'm too tired to do that tonight however. Can we give them something to make them sleep?"

"Such as?"

"Warm milk works for babies…" Chris offered this up from where her head was buried in her pillow.

"Yep, that will give them the runs, good plan Chris!"

"Well, at least they'll actually do something outside then!" She had a point. All of the dogs had been going outside with nothing to show for it. The visits were getting old.

One minute, it was a mad house, and then, silence. And then the most blessed sound in the world to any K-9 handler. The big heaving sighs right before the dog goes truly to sleep. It is a marvelous sound. I tried it myself; it actually is a good feeling right before you go to sleep.

I, on the other hand, didn't go to sleep, even after the big dog crash. My knee, stressed by standing for so long and the long drive, was in dire pain. No matter what I did, the pain didn't want to stop, and instead traveled up my leg into my lower back. I didn't want to move for fear of disturbing the sleeping dogs, but I finally went into the bathroom and took a hot shower in the small stall designed for the purpose.

About four in the morning, I finally went to sleep, only to be awakened at five as normal by my own dog; the life of a K-9 handler. I dragged myself out of bed, fed my dog, took her for a quick potty break and tried to return to bed, only to hear Chief waking up Karen, and then Onyx at Chris.

It was no use; we all got up and took the dogs for a long warm-up walk. To warm up the human muscles, not the dogs. They didn't appear to need it.

After a hearty breakfast at a little tiny café, we drove back to the training area. Today, we would get to see the disaster pile and work on it with our dogs. Between us, we only had one helmet, but we all had our own leather gloves. We were ready.

We were to be somewhat disappointed. The one thing we hadn't done yet, and needed to do, was work on a bark box. I'm sure at least three of us in the group had a blank look on our faces. I didn't remember the "bark" part at all, let alone a box for it.

There it was - the bark box. It was a wooden box big enough for a person to sit inside with a door that slid up on pulleys when pulled by someone standing nearby. The box had a small hole cut into the door, and it was explained that the person in the box would tease our dog until they barked, then the door slid open, and they got their reward.

Imagine their surprise when, along with a variety of tug toys, they were handed a tennis ball to give to the hider in the box. I tried not to look intimidated that I didn't have a dog that would tug. I tried to explain she'd do headstands for that ball, but they still looked skeptical. Especially when I added I didn't have a trained bark.

Dog after dog ahead of mine raced up to the box, and most, after trying to dig their way in and failing, finally resorted to barking. One or two already knew the game and barked crazily at the box until it opened and they were rewarded by tugging with the man inside. It all looked so easy. Even Chief and Onyx stormed up and gave barks after only a small encouragement.

I got Jael out of her crate, where, by the way, she had been barking at every single person who walked by, and took her to the bark box. I held her tight and told her "watch it – watch it" as the man in the box waved her barely visible ball at her. She wiggled, she squirmed and at the right moment, they lowered the door and I released my dog.

First, they told us to shut up and let the hider do all the work; then they reminded us to shut up and let the hider do all the work. I think they told us at least three or four times.

What does Rebekkah do? She talks to her dog, begging for her to give a bark. Yes, that was me, drawing my dog off the box and the hider who was there to do all the work.

"We have duct tape in the garage if that would work better for you," one of the trainers called out. I shut up. They had me gather my dog back up and start the process over again.

Jael, in beautiful fashion raced straight for the box, and like all the other dogs, tried to figure out how to gain access. Failing that, she turned toward me. I opened my mouth and felt a slap across the back of my head. I shut my mouth.

The hider, doing their job, called Jael's name and stuck the ball out just under the door so she could see it. She went racing back, but no sound emanated from my dog. The same dog who had been barking like a maniac in my truck was now mute.

The trainer took over the position in the box, hoping it was a matter of timing. Nothing; Jael simply wouldn't bark. We were just about to give up when she whined. Everyone there began praising her, but she only wanted her tennis ball.

"It's a start. Reward any sound, she'll figure it out." I only hoped they were right. The other beginner dogs all figured it quickly. My dog was a backward student if there ever was one.

That afternoon, we finally got to go down to the pile. I'm not sure about the others, but all the confidence I had when I drove down evaporated at the sight of it.

While they had been pounding Foundation Skills into our heads, we finally understood why. Typical of many human beings, we wanted to nod and say yes, but let's get to the fun part of the disaster pile. The trainers, however, knew better. They knew this was the place where all that other boring training paid off.

There wasn't any way a person could prepare for what we saw. It was if a small trailer house, or possibly two, had been torn apart by a tornado in the woods. It varied in height, but the biggest thing I noticed was how unstable it looked. Yet, in a minute, they ran a trained dog over it, and three observers climbed up to watch. It had to be stable.

Our newbie dogs were started on the small pile on the end, learning to sniff for a person in the pile who would reward them. The baby pile really wasn't much but some pallets, broken cinder blocks and a few odds and ends of furniture, but it looked scary to the dogs. They approached and questioned their handler's mental state for asking this of them.

I brought Jael out and hoped for the best. Giving her the find command, I slipped her collar off and sent her to check the baby pile. I was so proud of my dog as she circled it, sniffing intently. As she reached the board under which her subject was hiding, she paused. She carefully navigated along the edge of a board, but refused to attempt the pallet that would bring her straight to the subject. Feeling frustrated, I explained to the trainer about her problems with pallets.

They just shook their head and said she'd better get used to it if I wanted her to do disaster work. Not for the first time that weekend, I questioned why I was there. It didn't appear my dog had any aptitude. Onyx and Chief were both all over the pile without batting an eye.

That night, I told Karen and Chris my concerns. Chris simply shook her head and told me one of the trainers told her that my dog was doing well, she just needed some work.

As Jael did her final pile drill before we left, a trainer from out of state asked me to stop her. Going up to her, she held up my dog's petite little foot.

"No wonder your dog is nervous of pallets. She's got the smallest and smoothest paws I've ever seen on a Shepherd. She'd never be able to spread them to span the distance between slats like the Retrievers, and she just slides on the wood. Still, that is just a training and practice thing. Get a lot of pallets and hide her toy in them so she has to cross them often, every day. She'll figure out how to place her feet."

We went home the next day, three days of disaster training over with. It was the trainer from out of state who talked to me before we left, explaining that I had a terrific little dog who had the skills, I just needed to add the confidence on the pallets. It was likely that comment was the only reason I decided to keep trying.

The bark came along slowly, but it came. Once she found it, however, she used it for everything, which drove my mom nuts. Training a quiet command wasn't nearly so successful.

The pallets, on the other hand, were less quick to happen, but she worked hard at it. As she gained confidence scrambling over them, I hoped to pass that test by July.

It was during her disaster training when I realized that I'd gotten the email that our tree planters would be back in town by the first week of May. I had been so wrapped up in working on my dog, that I had lost track of the time.

Calling Dave, I asked if he thought we could do another potluck for whatever team came up. I explained it might be a totally different group, but I knew Arturo was still a crew leader because the family had been emailing me with updates on his progress. I had been having a good time communicating with them.

The potluck was planned, and I had the information to Arturo's family to pass along just in time.

The crews arrived the first week in May, as planned. I was able to meet up with Arturo and brought him a goodie basket of treats to share with his crew, along with the invitation to another potluck at the church that Friday night.

It turned out to be another great event for the community, and Pastor Dave pointed out to the men that if they were Catholic, Father Michaels was always available if they ever wanted or needed him. I sat with Arturo and we talked of his family. It was hard to believe it was just a year ago he had saved my life. He asked about my dog, my beloved perro. I told him he had retired, and was getting very old, but doing well. I asked if sometime I could come watch them work, and if I could bring my dogs as well.

The evening ended too soon, but the men had to go to work in the morning, and we parted on good terms, with an invitation for me to visit sometime that week.

Saturday dawned bright and spring, while still shrugging off the remnants of winter, was beginning to bud and blossom. I was in good humor when I arrived at McCaffrey House, waving at Harold as I drove in. He was busy pulling burlap off bushes and I knew he'd be busy outside all day today.

Entering the office, I checked for any messages first before heading for the kitchen to help there. Martha and Connie were busy working, but Margaret wasn't to be seen.

"She's sick, got the flu or something. She sounded horrible on the phone. Connie and I have it taken care of, but if you can do a couple of things, it would help." Martha, queen of the kitchen, threw orders out.

Within minutes, I was helping stir, whip and fold things I wasn't even sure what they were. As we worked, Connie leaned near me and asked if we could talk sometime today. Nodding, I wondered if it would be a conversation I should worry about.

Breakfast over, Agnes and Bella tackled the rooms while Connie and I cleared up the buffet breakfast and sent the dishes through the washer. As we worked, I asked if this was a good time to talk, not being completely sure if she wanted privacy or not.

Connie paused and looked out the French doors to the view of the lake below, still not completely clear of ice. Finally, she nodded.

"Rebekkah, Dave let me know he told you that we're dating again; sort of, anyway. I guess I just wanted someone to talk to, I don't have a lot of friends here, I don't always feel as if I fit in."

"I'm sorry, Connie, I know I'm always busy, which doesn't help, either." We continued to work as we talked.

"I'm not even sure where to begin. Maybe when I first got here? I wasn't in a good place. I had started to hate myself and that was bleeding over to other areas of my life and the people I thought I cared about." She disappeared into the walk-in refrigerator with the butter and cream. I waited for her to return and continue.

"I found myself avoiding Dave. He was too good for me, too decent. So I, well, I guess I rebelled. I wanted to show him how bad I really was."

I glanced around and seeing that we had actually cleared in record time, filled two cups of coffee and sat down in the kitchen. I had no idea if I wanted to hear the rest of it, but it appeared Connie needed to tell me.

"Not much worked, to be honest. I couldn't carry it through. Even with you, I tried to show you it was a mistake to take me in. Instead, you just, well, I couldn't handle all the kindness. I had gotten so used to people using me I didn't know how to deal with people like you and Dave."

She got up and refilled our cups, holding up the sugar for me. I shook my head no, and she returned to the little table.

"You look really good Rebekkah, no, I mean that. You've lost weight, haven't you?"

I laughed; I couldn't help it. I had lost nearly twenty pounds, and she was the first to notice or at least say anything. "Yes, I have. You were my inspiration, you know."

"I shouldn't have been. I was losing weight because I wasn't eating right, and when it started, I just kept it up because I was getting compliments. I've lost too much, I'm almost gaunt. Benjamin told me I looked hard, which was sort of a shock."

"Benjamin isn't always the most tactful person in the world."

"No, but he's been honest with me. You were right, of course. He is a great guy, I love being around him, but he has no intentions of settling down. I had hoped to hurt you by dating him. I know you're good friends, even if you do argue." I started to interrupt her, to explain we were friends, but not in an intimate way.

"I know, you've never dated him, likely never would. But I wasn't sure how to hurt you. I'd see him talk to you like, like deep friends. With me, it was all surface. Then, it seems like whatever you do, people praise you for. What you did for baby Charlene!"

"Connie, your idea for Charlene was amazing, it was all your idea."

"I did it to make what you did seem small in comparison. What I forgot was, what you did came from the heart, without thought for yourself. What I did was so people would say how Connie was so wonderful."

"No, Connie, really, I'm not that great, I've made some huge mistakes. In fact, I think we've had this conversation before. You've made your mistakes in life, so have I, they are just different ones."

"Rebekkah, through the past year, I came to realize I'll never measure up to you; Ever." Tears ran down her cheeks, and in consequence, I started to cry.

"Connie, can I tell you my side now? I've watched you over the past year. Dave said it best. He said you have the ability to refresh a room just by walking in and saying hello. I don't. I walk in, people don't even notice me. Do you remember that Emergency Medical Services conference we went to years ago? We sat at that table with the people from Moorhead for several hours. Then the one gal went and got everyone something to drink, remember? What happened? As she handed them out, she got to me, looked at me as she had no idea who I was or how I got there; she hadn't brought anything for me. Yet, I'd been there the entire time. I'm a wall flower, which is alright most of the time."

I paused, dried my eyes and sniffed before continuing, "When you came, and lost the weight, you looked terrific, like a model. Then you started dating Benjamin and having a real life, and I thought to myself, that I'd never measure up to you."

We looked at each other across the table, Connie with her sparkling personality that no one ever forgot, and the quiet country mouse, which was me. We were as opposite as people could be, but still best of friends.

"Okay, so our commitment to each other is, we will no longer use each other as our yardstick." Connie smiled as she said it.

"Agreed; I like that plan." We hugged and sat back down to finish our coffee. "Connie, I still plan to lose some weight, but it won't be about you anymore. I just feel better with the extra weight off."

She nodded and we sat in companionable silence for a few minutes, before Connie asked what she had wanted to ask all along, "What do you really think about my dating Dave. Do you think I can ever clean up my act in order to deserve him?"

"As you know, I'm likely the last person to ask about love and life and marriage. The Bible says "while we were yet sinners, Christ died for us." He didn't wait for us to deserve him. I'm not sure about marriage, if it is the same, but for me, the questions I'd ask are – is the man I love committed to God, do I love him no matter what, and does he like my dogs."

"I think I love him, but I've not made too many great decisions based on what I thought love was."

I had no advice really, so didn't offer any beyond what I had said. I cared about both Dave and Connie. Were they a good fit? I wasn't sure. Dave was calm, steady, strong, and focused. Connie, well she was spontaneous, loving, emotional, and needed someone with strength, good strength. I only hoped if they did move forward, both were ready for the other.

I wasn't surprised when the rumor mill went into high gear that Connie was now dating Pastor Dave. There were different camps of thought, all of which filtered back to me through Agnes and Bella, who each were in a different camp themselves.

One group felt Pastor Dave should have a higher standard for the woman he would date. Some years ago, everyone had hoped it would be me, but after one date, we both realized it wouldn't work. I wondered now if there were different factions on our dating as well.

The others felt that Connie should be given a chance at redemption. I liked that camp, as it wasn't about measuring up, but in mercy. Agnes was part of the redemption group, simply because she had seen the changes in Connie since she had arrived in Elk Ridge. Bella, for some reason, chose to ignore them.

# Chapter 15

### *Even there shall Your hand lead me;*

My day to visit the planters was fast approaching, and I made arrangements to switch days at McCaffrey so I could go. I was looking forward to it, and was surprised to get a call from Al, asking if he could come with me. He was off duty, and just wanted a day out.

We met at a junction near where the planter's base camp was, and Al hopped in with me. He had explained during the phone call that he had never seen them work, and was glad for an opportunity.

It wasn't far, and we arrived while they were preparing to go out. Even with our introduction at the potluck supper, the workers had returned to being shy and reserved, Arturo included.

Seeing a Forestry worker nearby, I checked in with him first, explaining the relationship we had with Arturo from the previous year. I wasn't sure if Dennis, as he introduced himself, was there to supervise, or if the planters were on their own, but I thought it best to talk to him anyway.

Arturo's reserve dropped as I unloaded the dogs to greet the workers, some who stopped to pet them, some who clearly weren't sure of the dog's intentions. Arturo crouched down and whispered "Real, perro," as he stroked Ari's fur. My dog, I'm sure, remembered the man who loved him up so gently. He pushed his head into Arturo's chest and just absorbed the attention.

With the greeting made, I loaded the dogs back up, and the planters headed out. Al, in the meantime, was gleaning all he could from Dennis.

"What are they planting today?" Al was looking over the seedlings still at the base area.

"White Spruce today. That is our main planting as they are pretty hardy and don't require much follow-up once they are in the ground."

"Don't the deer or moose eat them? I planted some young sticks like this a year ago and the doggone moose cleaned me out."

"Then you didn't plant White Spruce; moose really don't eat them. Now, we will mix in some other species they do like, such as White Pine, Red Pine, and Oak, depending on our objective for the site."

"I don't have a clue what they were to be honest. My wife picked them up and told me to plant them. I'll have to try Spruce next time."

"Dennis, are there reasons for planting different types of trees? I mean, besides marauding moose?" I was curious myself, now.

"We consider what the forest needs are; for instance, we do need to get some hardwoods, like oak, in there. They require cages or bud caps to protect them from those marauding moose as you called them, or the destructive deer," I had to laugh at his addition to my picturesque phrasing.

"We have to consider what we plant and how it will mature out. We actually do plantings for specific purposes; such as moose project sites where we'll use a variety of species."

"I always thought that the trees were planted in tidy rows and all of the same type. Live and learn."

"Well, in the past, the plantations, or where we plant the trees, were a single species in tidy rows. Although that still does happen, more and more we are planting a mix of trees, which, while not in straight rows, will still be in some semblance of order," He paused and pointed out a stand of forest to our south, "In the real world, trees don't grow in straight lines, and there are usually a mix of trees, from deciduous to evergreens."

"How many trees will these guys plant to the acre?" Al was watching the planters as we talked, and I knew he was thinking what I was thinking. Back-breaking work; and one wondered how much they were paid for it.

"Again, depends on our project goals, but in here, we'll be aiming for about six to eight hundred per acre. For wildlife projects, like the moose, we are closer to around four hundred and fifty."

"How do they do that all day long? That is insane!" Al, as if having sympathy pains, had arched his back to stretch the muscles.

"No clue to be honest. I have a great deal of respect for these guys. Their work ethic is amazing. Four of us foresters planted a section last year, and between all of us, we planted almost seven hundred and fifty trees in a day. Those guys out there, they'll plant an average of four thousand in the same amount of time. That is per person, not for the entire crew of, I think there are about twenty out there today."

We all stood and marveled at the efficiency of the workers. To be honest, I was feeling a tad guilty as I had never liked to sit by, or even stand by, and let others do all the work. They simply took a few strides, put that hoedad thing into the ground, bent over to shove a twig in, stomped, and moved on.

209

To think about bending over four thousand times in a single day was incredible. And swinging the tool into the earth for each tree; I couldn't imagine how rock-hard the muscles of the men out there had to be; or how fast their bodies had to be aging.

"Why can't they use one of those mechanized planters Dennis?"

"Take a walk over there. You'd never get the equipment in, period. This is the most economical and surest way to get the job done. We have about one thousand acres to get planted in this project."

Al looked stupefied for a moment, and I wondered why until he spoke again, "My math is rusty, but that is, from what you just said, around eight hundred thousand trees to be planted?"

I felt stupefied myself. Where on earth do they get that many trees to begin with? And how much did it cost? Of course, it was a U.S. Forestry planting, so whatever it cost, it was our tax dollars at work. At least I liked the result of this expenditure.

"Yeah, that would be about right. But we have twenty workers out there who plant about four thousand a day. Average it out, it will only take them about two weeks to get this project planted, and then move on to the next one."

"Where do you get that many trees?" I was still stuck on the sheer number of twigs that had to be brought in for this project. I watched as he glanced at his watch, and realized we had taken up far more of his time than I had realized. "Do you need to go? We just came out to see Arturo and see how they plant; we don't need to be bothering you with all these boring questions."

"Heck no, not boring at all. Most people don't care how all this happens, and to be honest, I find it as fascinating as you do."

210

"Well, in that case, where do you get eight hundred thousand trees?"

"We order our trees in the fall from nurseries, and they pull them while still frozen and dormant. We then store them in a cooler, although some places use a huge culvert buried in the ground to use for tree storage as well. We rely on the migrant workers to do the planting. You have to understand, we're sort of their last port of call before they head back south. Because of that, they are often here later than ideal planting time."

"You can't request them to come earlier?" It was a good question, one I hadn't thought about.

"Not really. We work through a planting company who actually arranges for the workers. We submit a contract laying out what we need done, and they submit bids back to us about mid-winter. The company then set up jobs for the workers so they work as steadily as possible until they get here. So if harvests are late, or there are bumper crops or weather delays picking, they arrive here later than we'd like. The problem with that is the trees may actually start to send out new shoots before they're put into the ground, and that isn't the best."

As we had stood there, I noticed, likely because of how my brain works, that the planters had started out in nice, even rows, but as time had gone on, they appeared to be everywhere, the rows lost. Dennis must have anticipated my next question, because he spoke before I had a chance to ask it, "We have standards in our contracts on how far apart the trees need to be planted. For instance, our contract has this section to be planted six by eight feet apart. We will do plot checks all over this site before they finish up and move on."

He pointed out to the workers, and continued, "I'm serious when I say those seedlings are so tiny, it is hard for me to pick them out. I do the plot check and then call your friend Arturo over, thinking there aren't enough trees in an area, and he'll just start pointing out every single one I missed. They do this so often, they know what to look for. He's a good man, Arturo."

We watched for a while longer, and when they were almost like ants, I saw one turn toward us and wave. We waved back, and thanking Dennis, we headed out.

"That was the most amazing couple of hours I've ever spent in the woods."

I nodded in agreement; although I had spent far more amazing hours in the woods, I understood exactly what he meant.

"Rebekkah, can I ask you a personal question?" I'm sure I blinked a few times, wondering how personal a question Al could possibly ask me.

"I guess you can ask, but depending on how personal, whether I'll answer it or not."

"Okay, here goes. Not even sure how to ask, or why I want to ask you this, but, do you know anything about the young thing Benjamin has been escorting around town?"

It was an interesting question to preface with saying it was going to be personal. Benjamin's new girlfriend wasn't exactly on my list of personal concerns.

"Other than her name is Priscilla Davis and she's hands down one of the most beautiful women I've ever seen live and in person?"

"Yeah, besides that," Al shook his head at me, likely wondering if I was hiding something.

212

"No, that's all I know about her. I haven't seen her since Christmas, is he still dating her?" Why was I even asking the question?

"Apparently one of the guys was down at the state capital for a hearing and was rather shocked to see our intrepid sheriff, dressed to the nines, escorting her into the Guthrie."

"Wow, I'm not sure what astonishes me more, him dressed to the nines or going to the Guthrie. What was playing?"

"Does it really matter?" I guess it didn't, but they had a diverse listing of things to go to, so while I had a hard time envisioning Benjamin at a Shakespearean play, perhaps a blues concert he might go to.

"Alright; no I don't suppose it does matter, but it's his life, Al, not ours. She seemed like a lovely young woman, why are you worried?"

"I don't know, except she shows up, no one knows her, he doesn't say much about her, but apparently she has some meaning in his life. I've never known him to take anyone else to the city for a night on the town."

"By the way, why would you think this fell under personal for me? Just curious."

"Because you're friends. He seems to talk to you more than anyone else." Al had me there. I had no idea who he talked to or about what. He did periodically stop in to talk, but it was usually in conjunction with picking up Connie, or at least until they stopped dating. I hadn't really seen much of him since.

"Well, I'm sorry, I didn't mean to go off like that, but I like Benjamin. He's a good guy, if a bit unorthodox in his lifestyle.

I've never known anyone who could date so many different women and remain single."

I let that one go; I was tired of being tangled up in everyone's lives. I needed to focus on my own.

# *Chapter 16*

### *And Your right hand shall hold me.*

My own life, if one called it that, seemed to settle once again into boringness. I had to recertify Jael for her land and water cadaver, but beyond that, it didn't seem like the search season was ever going to happen. Usually by May we had at least one or two searches. We even talked about it at training one week, forgetting the old adage about speaking too soon.

The call came a week later, from our own Sheriff. Once again, they wanted the cadaver dogs. And once again, it was for the Derek Nieland search. And once again, we had a limited timeframe to get it done.

Chris and I arrived at the Law Enforcement center of the next county over, along with our dogs and two field support in the form of Al and Marge. Benjamin met us in the parking lot and filled us in as we walked to the meeting room for the briefing.

"The place we searched last time is still of prime interest, however, we still don't have access to it. We have no probable cause for a search warrant of the home and curtilage. And, as you know, cadaver dogs only provide reasonable suspicion, not probably cause."

It never ceased to surprise me that drug dogs could provide PC, or probable cause which allowed for that precious piece of paper called a search warrant. All other odor detection dogs only provided reasonable suspicion, which needed corroborative evidence to move to probable cause, and therefore a search warrant.

"So, how did you get the search warrant last time?" I wasn't sure he'd be able to tell me, given the nature of the case, and he didn't. He just shook his head. There was evidence or testimony he wasn't willing to share.

"We are hoping to eliminate a different area today, an area owned by folks who have given us permission to do the sniff with the dogs."

Following him into the briefing, I noticed the two DEA agents were back, along with officers from the local county.

"Thanks for coming back today, we have a new area we'd like your dogs to do a sniff on, just across the road from the property we were at last time. The funny thing is, by crossing that particular road, we also cross county lines which is why we are here today."

The details were given out, and as I looked at the mapping, I realized it was strategic. The land was due west of the property, and the wind today was blowing from the east to the west. They wanted to confirm what the dogs had done, but hopefully also to do some triangulation. Was the odor from last time from the suspected property, or from someplace further west?

It wasn't a huge area, so we parked down the road from it on a small forest access and walked in. Chris went first, followed by both DEA agents and a county officer assigned to us. Benjamin sat on the bumper of my truck with me as we waited.

"How are things going lately? Seems like I haven't talked to you since Christmas."

"You never answered my note; thought maybe you were ignoring me." I laughed, remembering the note.

"It was unsigned. It could have been anyone, but you're right, I knew it was you. It didn't seem to require a response. Please forgive me. And no, it isn't a gift."

He paused, and then he too laughed, remembering his reference to sleeping in a crowd.

"I have never done that before. Too many control issues, I suspect."

"Yep, I can see that about you. To answer your question, things are okay. It seems like things are a little crazy, had some things thrown at me lately that I'm still working through, but I'll be okay. And you? Besides all the weight you've lost?"

"Thank you for noticing, you are now the second person who has said something. I was starting to wonder if we'd have any searches this year. Not that I'm complaining, but it has been a slow start. McCaffrey more than makes up for it, however, as we've been busy. I suspect I'll have to consider hiring someone, maybe part-time to start with." I picked a dandelion that was growing by the truck and twirled as I spoke.

"Glad to hear you're busy. Rebekkah, do you think I'm gullible?"

The question startled me, to say the least. It is the last word, or at least one of the last words I would ever have used to describe Benjamin.

"As in, easily taken in? No, I wouldn't. Unless you wanted to be," I sent the dandelion flying, wondering where this was leading to, wasn't sure I wanted to know.

"Why would anyone want to be taken in? That doesn't make any sense."

"Okay, think about how many people are, taken in, that is; people one would never think would be. Usually it is out of loneliness or needing love, I think. An older person has a wayward grandchild show up on their doorstep, say all the right things. The lonely grandparent says to themselves, "He's changed, he really does want to spend time with me," but somewhere, deep inside, they know it isn't true. But they go along with it because they're lonely, or in need of love and attention; and the next thing you know, they're bilked of their life savings."

There was silence, except for the chirp of birds and some crickets. His silence was almost scary. There we sat, side by side, and I wondered what was going through his head. Had he, actually, been imposed upon by someone like that? I finally looked at him, but he was saved from responding as I could see Chris and her entourage returning.

Nothing was said except to be aware of a barb wire fence buried in tall grasses. One of the DEA agents pointed to his pants, which revealed a triangular tear.

Pulling my dog out, I worked her from north to south and back again, so the wind was blowing across our search area, and not directly into her nose. Within minutes, I saw the change in her behavior.

Jael had been consistent when in odor of human remains. Her motion slowed, her head became almost snake-like as she searched for just the right place to put her nose to capture the most odor. Her breathing deepened, and her tail began a slow swishing. But the most noticeable change was her focus. She became so intent, the rest of the world just went away. Like a bloodhound on a hot trail, she'd have walked off the face of a cliff if I didn't watch for her own safety.

In this case, it was a busy road. As her behaviors hardened and became stronger, I saw her head suddenly bolt up, take a huge deep inhalation, and like a spring, shot off toward the highway.

"STOP!!" Using every ounce of lung power I'd ever had, I screamed it at my dog. For a moment, I didn't think she was going to stop, but she did, just on the edge of the shoulder, with traffic flying by at sixty miles an hour. She was heading straight for the property we couldn't access.

"Good dog – HERE, NOW!" Frustration was evident on my dog's face, with her ears and head constantly turning back toward where the odor was coming from.

"Guys, does the curtilage include the shoulder or the ditch of the highway?"

One of them smiled and said simply, "No, it doesn't." With that, we waited for a break in the cars, and darted across the road. I kept my dog on her long line and let her work the shoulder and down into the ditch. She lunged against the long line, trying hard to race up the embankment to the property line, which was marked by that same tumbledown fence.

Realizing I wasn't letting her cross over it, she finally whirled around and sat, staring me down. My dog had located odor; I wasn't letting her at source; she had earned her tennis ball.

"Good dog, I believe you. Come on over here," I tossed her ball to her and we playfully ran north, away from the cabin and whatever those disreputable outbuildings held. To be honest, I was sickened by the thought of what could be over there.

I played catch all the way back to the vehicles, where Chris just nodded in the direction of the cabin. I nodded back. Both dogs were, once again, consistent.

"We'd like to get some lunch ordered in and go over all this with you, is that alright?"

We sat down to a delivered, hand-tossed pizza from a local place that I made a mental to go back to. It was good pizza. Benjamin, sitting across from me, watched as I put away two hefty slices, and I knew he, like Bill watching me eat a caramel roll, wondered how I lost the weight. Salads and exercise was the answer.

"Here is where we stand. Both dogs have had reactions in the exact same areas, weeks apart. At this time we only have reasonable suspicion and aren't in a position to obtain a search warrant for the property. We had our GIS department make a map while we were eating, showing the sniff from before and today, overlaid with the winds. You'll find this interesting, I think."

We all leaned over the map, a very fancy and impressive map that any good Geographic Information Systems could put out, if a person had access to one all the time. Most counties did now, of course, but back in the day, if we were lucky, we would get a photocopy of a street map that sort of included areas we were searching.

They had put Onyx in yellow and Jael in red, the wind lines in green. They had continued the course of the dogs had they not been called off.

The lines to indicate where the dogs would have ended up had they continued all intersected at a very specific location. A small shed on the north side of the cabin's driveway, and set back into the woods.

"What do you do now?"

"We start trying to find someone willing to talk. All we need is one, and then we'll have our basis for probable cause. The

220

question I have for both of you is, if we call, can you come at a moment's notice?"

Chris, who had a family and part-time job, still nodded. Once a person becomes involved in these cases, it was hard to give them up. You wanted to help solve them if you can.

"I'm usually available, but I would request if you have any inkling you'll be going in for a search warrant, you get us online before you go in. I'd rather we either be there or at least on the road there and be told to stand down, then called after you get it and find we're unable to go for whatever reason. It could mess up your case badly."

"Good point, I'll make a note about that. I don't have much of anything else right now, but thanks for coming out again. By the way, that was an amazing stop on your dog."

"Not really, she should have stopped a lot faster than she did, but when they get into odor like that, they are like heat-seeking missiles and hard to stop."

We left by the same door, and as I drove away, I suddenly remember the unfinished conversation with Benjamin and wondered what that was all about. Perhaps the young woman Al was so worried about? I might never find out, but it was intriguing; nearly as fascinating as a search for a crime scene.

# Chapter 17

*If I say, surely the darkness shall cover me;*

Returning to McCaffrey, I caught up the paperwork, the mail, the bills and started tackling the inventory when Agnes peeked in at me.

"Are you very busy?" I glanced down at the desk, and realized I had accomplished quite a bit already.

"What do you need? Me to come there, or you in here?"

"You to come here; we have a guest who wants to see the owner. While I know the The Sisters are owners as well, it just made more sense to have you come out."

I nodded, and wondered what could be wrong this time. Generally they only wanted to talk to the manager or owner if something was wrong. As I walked out of the office, Jael and Ari got up and followed me out. I slowed slightly so Ari could catch up, and noticed he looked confused for a moment. I only hoped it was my imagination.

Entering the main part of the House, I was happy to see it wasn't a complaint, but a friend; Eric Rosten, although I didn't see his wife, Jane.

"Mr. Rosten, how are you doing? Where is your lovely wife?" I reached down for a hug, and soon my dogs were being given ear rubs and loving attention.

"She's out parking the van, she'll be in soon. I'm sorry we didn't make it for Christmas or dog sledding this year, but we decided we wanted to do a canoe trip again. You still offer them, right?"

I nodded and had a fun time getting them checked in while Agnes went out to help Jane bring in their luggage for the week. Just as he turned to go, he asked about Megan, as he was so used to working with her.

Telling him about Megan was hard, but I was glad to report that Charlene was doing well, and that Adam and Amy made sure they took her to see her grandparents at least twice a month.

"Is there some sort of fund for her? I had thought I saw something at the gas station in town when we stopped to fill up."

Opening the drawer, I took out a small card that we had made up to give to people who asked about it. It explained the situation of Megan's daughter, and offered a way for people to help.

Since the accident, I knew that the account had accumulated nearly ten thousand dollars. Adam had shared with me they didn't plan to use any of it if they could avoid it, so it would be there for her college fund.

I greeted Jane with another hug and helped Agnes with the luggage to their room. Chocolates were on the pillows, quote card on the dresser, all was ready.

As I returned to my office, I saw Ari standing so still, and then, as fast as it happened, it was gone. He had a strange motion of his head, almost as if he had fallen asleep on his feet, but woke up just as quickly.

Shaking it off, I went back to work. Still, I couldn't help but glance over to where he lay on his big orthopedic bed I had bought for him. Jael was on a similar one nearby, purchased only because she kept stealing his.

That night, after running Jael through some basic search problems, I sat down to take an evening off and just watch old movies. Sitting in my recliner, Ari's head in my lap, I felt it. His body quivered, as if he was getting minute electrical shocks that I couldn't feel. As soon as I looked down, it was over.

It had started with those slight tremors; as fast as they happened, they were gone. Not knowing what they were, I contacted Dr. Mikkelson, who had me bring Ari in. His chiropractic visits had been going well, and we were only coming in once a month now for his adjustments. It had helped him tremendously, but the reality was, Ari was going on twelve and had lived a hard physical life. How much more time we'd have, I didn't know.

Finding nothing specific wrong, he had me start a small log of when they happened, what we were doing when they happened, and if Ari was in any discomfort or seemed to notice them, or have adverse reactions afterwards.

The log, which started with only a few entries in the first few weeks, began to fill up quickly. We called them his 'episodes' as I had no idea what else to call them. They came when he was standing for any length of time, and while at first, I didn't think Ari was aware of them, I began to notice that when they were going to happen, he would come to me or my mom if I wasn't home.

As we coped with this new and unexpected part of an aging dog, we knew that we were getting off fairly easy for the time being. Some owners dealt with far worse concerns. So far, even during his absence seizures, Ari kept his dignity. Even when the episode was a bit worse than normal and he'd nearly fall down, he came out with his head held high.

In addition, his chiropractic visits seemed to actually help the seizures for a short time. And Ari loved to go visit the vet clinic now, as most of the time it was to see Paul and have his relaxing adjustments and small massages. Life wasn't so scary there anymore. Watching them together, I was sometimes jealous as Ari, after getting things gently eased back into place, would visibly relax. One could almost hear him sigh with relief.

He spent more time sleeping on his big bed at McCaffrey than with the guests, but that was okay. I could see he was getting more concerned about being bumped or grabbed. Jael picked up the slack and seemed to enjoy visiting.

When we could, she and I were working hard on prepping for her disaster certification, as well as her cadaver recertification which was due in September.

Her directional box signals were coming along well, and we finally had a bark when she found her person. The agility I wasn't worried about as she now clambered up ladders and across high dog walks and turned around on small boards, all under command, and so far, under control. They had told us if a dog goes to fast, it was a sign of nerves and many evaluators wouldn't pass them, so we worked hard on "slow – slow" commands.

The pallets were finally conquered, although I knew she'd never dash over them like the dogs with the big webbed feet did. But she'd give it her all.

The day arrived, and I headed for Wisconsin, dog loaded in my truck and ready to go. Hard as it was, I left Ari to home, knowing that two days of traveling would be simply too hard on him.

An hour from home, the search call came. A possible suicide off a bridge, could we come immediately? I called Chris and a K-9 handler from another unit. Chris, much as she wanted to, couldn't, and the other handler was at a seminar in Texas. Feeling just a touch frustrated, I called Patty to let her know what was happening. She said if I could still make it for tomorrow, they'd keep my slot open for the test.

Turning east instead of south, I headed for the Kawishiwi Bridge instead. I arrived and was directed to another location, downriver of the main bridge. Arriving there, I was re-routed to yet another area, where I met a young patrolman who had to radio for information.

Waiting, not quite patiently, I wondered how long it would take me from when I left here to get back to the testing area; three, no, closer to four hours. It was now five in the afternoon, we'd arrive at nine or after, plenty of time to get a good night's rest.

Twenty minutes later, the patrolman came back to my vehicle and redirected me back to the main bridge, there had been some confusion, but someone there would help me.

My patience had long run thin by the time I finally made my way back to the bridge, where I was asked to wait, as they were still checking on details.

It was another good forty-five minutes later when they asked me to bring my dog down to the water's edge and see if my dog could pick up anything. Seeing the enormous expanse between the sides, I explained I'd likely need to work both sides, which they agreed to.

Unloading my dog, I strapped on her PFD as well as my own. Hooking a long line to her, we went down toward the water, which was higher than I expected. Over the next few hours, we checked first one side, then the other, with no results.

As daylight was waning, I explained I didn't want to work my dog under the conditions after dark. As I relayed this to them,

227

I heard a radio crackle to life, standing everyone down. Glancing around, I was told to just pack up and head out.

"Who do I send my report to?" A quick mini-conference and I was given the name of an investigator, and further pushing, an email address. It was too late to drive four hours to a hotel near where they were testing, so I asked about hotels in the area. Thankfully one of the deputies on scene was able to provide a location to one nearby.

It would mean a very early start in the morning, but at least we'd get a good night's sleep as originally planned. Arriving at the hotel, I saw the sign "No Vacancies" was lit up. Going inside, it was confirmed, and they knew of no other hotels, motels, inns or anything in the area that wasn't booked for a fishing tournament the next day.

Pulling myself together, I just started driving, hoping to find something along the way. About midnight, I finally found a campground and pulled in, paid five dollars for a single night, and slept in my truck.

Getting up the next morning wasn't easy. I was battered and bruised from brush cutting to search along the river, cramped and cold from sleeping in my truck. The only upside was my dog was rearing to go.

I found a small bathroom, but no shower. I had done my normal tick check of dog and myself before I fell asleep, but sleeping with a dog that could hide ticks in the oddest places meant I was still felt creepy-crawly in the morning.

I hit the road at six and arrived in time to take a test I suddenly didn't feel prepared for, and was too tired to care about. Likely this was a good thing as, for the first time in my life, I wasn't stressed about taking a test.

With Jael in an unusually perfect heel, we performed our Fundamental Skills Assessment. First, we tackled the agility course. Jael, as if she had been prepped ahead of time, stayed at my side as we approached the first obstacle. I knew the goal was to complete all of the obstacles and that I was never to be ahead of the dog, not even my hand to give direction; and it was all to be off-leash and controlled. Unlike competitive agility, if the dog raced through an obstacle, we would have to do it again. Agility for disaster means going slowly and safely over rubble that may not hold the dog. Slow meant life.

Cuing my dog to proceed, we crossed over a chain link fence section raised above the ground. Jael crossed properly, she didn't try to jump or step off until I gave her the off command.

Then came the unstable surface; in this case, it was a wobbly flexible board resting on a frame. Again, Jael crossed it without incident. As we approached the ladder, my first twinge of concern hit me. Jael liked to race up the ladder. Cuing the climb, I waited at the base as she started up, with me muttering "slow, Jael, slow," as she climbed. And she did. Perhaps it was the strange ladder, but the test continued as she had to walk down the high twelve inch board that was some ten feet long, and part way along, I had to stop her, and turn her.

She stopped and sat, waiting. Cuing the start again, I immediately ordered her to turn. She did. As if feeling the relief, however, she trotted at a higher rate of speed than was truly acceptable down the off-ramp.

From that point, she aced the agility, completing the teeter-totter and finishing by going through the tunnel with a turn and a covered end.

With one part of the testing done, I let her relax and play a moment before turning our attention to the directional boxes, or really tables about two feet tall, set up in the shape of a baseball diamond. Starting at home plate, I had to send my dog to either first or third plate, depending on the course assigned to me. From there, they went to pitchers, back to second, return to pitchers. The final legs of this test were to return to the starting box and finally to home. In this way, they knew the dog would go at an angle, right, left back, and forward under command.

Jael started well, reached pitchers on target, but as she jumped on it, it tipped, sending her and it flying. One of the evaluators dashed in and reset it while I sent Jael back to first base.

Resending her to pitchers, the table flipped again. I could see my dog, making a decision; Part of the test required the dog to land on the table, turn, and face the handler to await their next instruction. They had to wait for a minimum of five seconds, so I always counted seven, to be sure.

Jael sat next to the upturned table. Glancing at the evaluators, I asked what they wanted to do. We had five minutes to do the test, I wasn't sure if this counted against us or not.

The evaluator went in again and set it upright, then called to me to simply cue the hup onto the table. She left the field as I gave the command. Jael, my darling dog, simply glanced at the table, looked back at me and remained seated.

"Jael, HUP," I called again. I wasn't even sure what to do; the table had bucked her off twice already, would she try a third time? A good disaster dog would.

She did. She performed it with care, landing and sitting as I had trained her to do. With a sigh of relief, we finished the test with thirty seconds to spare.

Once again, I played with her, letting her relax as the evaluators set up the rubble pile portion of our test. I pulled out the cheater card they had given us months before on what questions to ask before searching a pile.

I ran through them in my head; what time did the collapse happen, type of structure or occupancy, how many do they believe are inside, has it been searched before, and if so, by whom? Checked by a structural engineer, and if so, what were their findings? Any HazMat present? What about utilities such as gas, electric, and water? Is there heavy rescue available? Medical and veterinary care?

I was ready; until the evaluator approached and started the interview. I felt very unsure again. What was wrong with my brain? Nothing that a few hours of sleep wouldn't have cured.

I finally got myself going and only missed one question, and that is if there were veterinarians on scene. But it was acceptable apparently, as they led me to the disaster scene. It had grown since I had been there last. There even more pallets.

My hands were shaking as I pulled Jael's collar off. I had my borrowed hard hat, my leather gloves, and heavy construction boots. My dog would enter the pile naked; Nothing to protect her.

I watched as she sailed around the perimeter of the downed 'structure' and saw her hit odor. Within minutes, she had it narrowed down, but she hesitated. The only access point was covered in pallets. As if hit by inspiration, she raced around and, according to the observers on top of the pile, leaped like a gazelle onto the side of the pile that had mainly old furniture. Her only mistake was that she landed on what looked solid but was in reality a large sheet of Styrofoam. It snapped in pieces and she dropped a clear foot before coming to rest on the top of a stove.

One shake and she was off across the pile, navigating clearly and well; until she reached the pallets again and hesitated. I waited, remembering at the training class that I was told I talked to my dog way too much. I stayed silent; and prayed.

Jael, realizing the only way to the odor was to cross the pallets, moved, taking careful steps, slipping as she went. Finally reaching her point, she poked her head down and started to bark, except she looked at me to do the bark. I didn't care, I called the find. The hider, from somewhere deep in the pile, poked her tennis ball up and Jael, happy as a clam, took it and skittered off to play with her toy.

We finished searching without another find, which scared me. I remembered there was to be two hiders on the pile. We had only found one. Still, I reported my single find and waited for the ax to fall.

"No other alerts you want to recheck on the pile?"

I shook my head in the negative. It was scary, standing there waiting as they checked their paperwork.

"Alright then, let's proceed to checking the minimally damaged home over there." She pointed at Patty's home nearby. It was then it hit me. Like the bark, I missed something in the information and rules. As a rule-obeyer by nature, it came as a shock that I kept missing small pieces of critical information.

"Can you please refresh my memory about this part of the test?" It was said meekly. They didn't have to tell me anything, it was my job to read and understand the rules.

As if taking pity on my tired brain and body, they consented, and explained that there were up to two hides, they could be both in the pile, or both in the house, or one in each place. They would not tell me what it was, however. I could have missed one in the pile.

Starting at the door, I let my dog loose to free search while I walked slowly behind. A rambler style home, no basement, it appeared to have five main rooms, living, dining and kitchen combination, bedroom, bathroom, and laundry. Jael rocketed through the house and in less than three minutes, she was barking up a storm in the bathroom. Entering, I could see nothing at all but a shower stall that could hide a person, but my dog was doing a solid focused bark at the floor.

"I call this as a find, although, I can't tell you for sure where the person is, but I believe they are under this floor somehow."

"Next bark at the floor, throw that toy in to her." I did, throwing it in fast and hard. As soon as my dog had her ball, they pulled a carpet away to reveal a small framed door in the floor which led to a crawl space under the bathroom. My dog had made her finds.

I completed a report for the test, and we were given our piece of paper, our certificate. I was so proud of my dog at that moment. She had done her job.

"Rebekkah, when you were here last, I'll be honest, I didn't think you'd do this. You've got a good dog, but in reality, this was all you, and your training. You had to have worked like crazy to achieve this. Good job."

I drove home in a state of euphoria. We had certified for disaster. This wasn't an easy accomplishment, it had taken time and training. I had no idea if we'd ever have to use the training, but for now, I was incredibly happy.

I was also incredibly tired. Arriving home, I overslept and woke to find my mom had taken the truck to go to church.

Making myself coffee and an egg sandwich for breakfast, I found I was still floating on air.

When mom got home from church, I had a nice lunch on the table for us, and we had a relaxing afternoon. I hadn't had one in quite a long time and felt almost as good as passing our disaster testing.

My cell went off, and I wondered if I should even answer it, but duty drove me to pick it up. It was Al, who wanted to know if I had heard what happened at the bridge.

"It was on the internet; seems they found this truck by the river, and everyone assumed it was a jumper. Ended up, the sucker was out of gas and yesterday they finally figured it out when the owner showed up, only to find they had towed it. He was alive and well, and pretty upset about it all."

"No wonder they didn't have a clue where they wanted me to search. Oh well, I'll send my report in anyway."

"By the way, congrats on the disaster certification. Good job! Don't take this the wrong way, but I hope you don't have to use it anytime soon."

"Thanks, and I agree with you. Have a great night, Al," I hung up and was glad the dog had been right, no one had been in the water by the bridge.

# Chapter 18

*Even the night shall be light around me.*

rriving at McCaffrey on Monday, I realized that while I was gone for the search and my certification, a few things were missed in our normal routine. Calling in Agnes, Connie, Bella, and The Sisters into the kitchen, I asked them if they had an opinion on hiring someone to help, even on a part-time basis.

"It would help, Rebekkah, especially on those days you're gone." One of the things that had been missed was returning a phone call for a reservation, which we ended up losing.

"What would you want the person to help with?" Martha asked the pertinent question, and to be honest, I wasn't sure. I withheld my own comments, to see what the others thought.

"Laundry and the bathrooms, if you ask me," Bella was doing them nearly alone now, and I could see her point.

"I'd say office, as no one else seems to want to do that part," Connie's input, which was seconded by an emphatic nod from Agnes.

"If we hire someone to help in the office, would that mean someone else would help with the laundry and bathrooms?" Bella, still concerned about being left to manage all of the manual labor tasks, wasn't going to let it die that easily.

"Yes, it would. Is this what we want to do?" I asked, wondering if it was really what I wanted to do or not.

"I'd say yes. If it would help us," Margaret spoke this time, and with nods all around, I promised to put an ad in the local paper for the coming week.

Martha had one final question, "Rebekkah, can we afford it?"

"Yes, I think we can, and we can't afford to lose reservations by not having the staffing."

It didn't take long for the applications to start coming in for the position. With Connie's help, we carefully began weeding through them, sorting those who had experience with those that didn't, but were trainable, and those that had none at all.

A few weeks later, I was training a new person to assist me; as I once trained in Megan a few short years ago. It felt distinctly odd, but Elizabeth, or Betsy for short, seemed to pick up on the office tasks quickly. Our goal was that she would assist Bella when I was at McCaffrey, and when I was away, she'd handle the office. It was a bit of relief, knowing she'd be there.

As summer turned back into fall, I was starting to get my normal test jitters with Jael's re-certification coming up. Our job was harder this time, as we were testing under a new organization that required off-leash obedience first.

Unlike the disaster obedience, this version was precision, something we'd never tried to attain in SAR. If my dog walked beside me without yanking me off my feet, I was happy. I didn't care if her rear swung out wide, or when she came to me that she sat perfectly square to my left leg. If I could get my leash on her without having to grab at her, it worked for me.

I quickly discovered through research that I was in trouble. While my dog could find source and give me a picture perfect sit at source, she wasn't quite so pretty when just doing obedience.

Unable to train my dog to tug for disaster work was a blow to my training ego. I questioned if I could tackle precision obedience on my own. With some trepidation, I started my training plan.

Day one, I merely worked on getting her to walk beside me without straying ahead, behind or to the right. Jael, having never had to worry about being exactly at my leg, became as frustrated as I was with it.

Day two, three, and four, I was ready to give up and walk away from the whole thing, when I had an inspiration. I'm sure it wasn't in the training book, or if it was, I hadn't seen it, but I decided, on day five, to try it.

Walking out, I, with great drama, showed Jael that I, her owner, master, and caregiver, had a tennis ball. Her eyes widened and I had her complete focus. Showing her the ball, I let her watch as I tucked it into my left armpit. Within seconds, she bounced next to my left side, hoping to dislodge the toy.

"No. Jael, heel," and I started walking. Jael, as I had once said, would do cartwheels and headstands to get her ball, fell into step beside me, her head in perfect line as she stared up at my arm. After five paces, I let the ball slide down into my hand and gave her a release command of, "Okay!" and gave her the ball.

We played fetch and chase, while Ari stood by and watched our craziness. Calling Jael back over, I took the ball back, now slimy wet, and tucked it back under my arm. With a strong heel command, I splayed out the fingers of my left hand by my hip and started walking.

Jael, for all the teasing I had done over the course of her life on her intelligence quotient, or if she had any, did learn. She saw my hand open, ready to catch the ball, and learned to pace close to me as I walked, anticipation in her every step.

It worked and Jael was suddenly heeling in perfect precision beside me; or at least, close to perfect. She was a touch too far back, and tended to look up, but it was working.

We slowly added distance to our heeling, and as Jael got used to the idea, the ball made fewer and fewer appearances. Our playtime after each session was huge and fun, and I was feeling a bit better about our obedience expectations.

That is, until I decided that this time, I wasn't going to miss anything in the rules; so I reread them. To my dismay, I discovered that I had missed some critical facts, such as that at some point, I'd have to stop my dog while I continued to walk.

I had just spent a lot of energy teaching my dog to stay by my side in the promised hope that she'd receive the ball I carried under my arm. I had slowly stopped carrying the ball there, but she had become so conditioned to believe it was there, I wondered if I could get her to stop while the ball – me – kept walking away.

Day in and day out, we worked on the different steps of the obedience test, while still fitting in odor detection training, and of course my full-time job. I was feeling very much like I was stretched far too thin.

Still, I took a week of vacation to attend the workshop, and I was truly feeling ready for the test. As I prepared to leave, I had notes stuck all over the office at McCaffrey House, an agreement with Dr. Gary to keep an eye on my mom, and Dr. Dan on call in case Ari had another medical crisis.

Packing my truck to live for a week at another place with a dog was interesting, and my only consolation was that we wouldn't be in the wilderness, but near places I could shop if needed.

We arrived at the campgrounds and I had a flashback to the first training I had ever attended with Ari so many years before. There had been a storm, tornados actually, ripping through the state of Iowa when I arrived. In a torrential downpour, I had fallen and basically smashed my face on a graveled surface. I still had the scars from the stitches received in the middle of the night in the emergency room. I spent several days eating, or really drinking, only liquids, and dealing with throbbing headaches. It was an unusual start to a person's life in search and rescue.

Thankfully, there were no storms, no tornados, and no accidents this time. I checked in and met some of the other handlers, which was always interesting and often fun; especially when one met their dogs, which could be just as diverse as their handlers.

Years before, German Shepherds were part of the normal scenery in Search and Rescue. The classic black and tan dogs, sometimes weighing in at a hundred pounds, were expected.

Within a year or two, I was finding myself as the sole Shepherd handler as more and more people were choosing Labradors, Goldens, and other types of Retrievers. The big reason was good German Shepherds were getting harder to find. Either they had massive physical issues, or they were neurotic. Or both. Breeders, in trying to make a better looking dog, lost some of what made the breed a working animal.

It hurt to see, because I loved the German Shepherd breed. Thankfully, over the past several years, it was becoming easier to find solid Shepherds again, and they were making a resurgent comeback into Search and Rescue.

It amazed me, however, how many breeds were being represented that I had never considered for SAR work, or heard of, for that matter. Such as a small Schipperke who appeared to be a touch overweight as well. I couldn't imagine the dog being able to work in the Boundary Waters, where we responded, but as I talked to her handler, I realized she only did urban search work.

The first day of the workshop started, of course, with our obedience testing. As the trainers pointed out, there was no point on continuing with the odor detection if the dogs couldn't obey us.

As soon as they said it, my stomach clenched, and I felt the familiar test nerves kick in. I watched the first dog, and once again, questioned why I was there. I had a great dog; I knew I did, but I was also unsure if she'd remember everything I had been cramming into her wee little head over the past few weeks.

A small Border Terrier, a breed I'd never imagine obeying anyone, did a perfect obedience run, and instead of impressing me, only made me depressed.

"Go get your dog, you're on deck," The owner of the Cocker Spaniel waved at me.

Grabbing my leash, I unloaded my dog and encouraged her to take care of business, and was not happy when she didn't do anything; nothing at all; except jump on me all the way to the testing area.

"Whenever you're ready, bring her on over here. Start with a heel, I'll tell you when to turn and how to turn." With a deep breath, I looked down at my dog and placed my right hand under my left arm for a moment. Releasing her leash, I gave the command to heel.

I dropped my left hand, spreading my fingers out as I had been doing, and set off with my left foot. I couldn't walk while constantly watching my dog, so I put my head up and kept walking. I could, however feel her ears periodically brush my hand as we walked. At the left command, I waved my hand to the left and turned, Jael turning in perfect unison with me. A right turn, and then it came.

"Stop your dog while you continue walking." I put my hand into a fist and said as firmly as I could, "JAEL, STOP," and kept walking.

I couldn't help it, I glanced back to see my dog hesitate and then stop, and not only stop, but sit. I was shook to the core. She had done it.

"Heel your dog back up," the trainer called out, and I, in turn, called to my dog, "JAEL, HEEL UP," while I continued walking. I almost forgot, but at the last second remembered, and released my left hand from the fist, meaning stop, to the open palm, meaning heel with me here. And she did, nearly perfectly.

From there, it went well with only one flaw; the trainers disliked the fact my dog didn't sit square beside my leg, she sat cock-eyed next to me.

It was truly a real sigh of relief as we passed the obedience. I was still stumped that my dog had done so well. I had to admit it wasn't perfect, but it was better than expected.

Tuesday brought the start of the odor detection testing, which wasn't what I was worried about; I knew my dog knew her job. What I forgot was - I stressed out. All the time, I stressed out.

I stared at the six vehicles that were lined up, waiting for us to take our dogs around them, sniffing for the elusive odor of human remains. I knew that according to the standards, two of the vehicles would have an odor source, one on the outside, one on the inside. We had to identify which ones.

I couldn't watch the first dogs because of course, if they got it right, I'd know where it was. Instead, I sat by my truck and chewed on my fingernails. Something I had given up doing years before.

When my turn arrived, I walked Jael over to the evaluators to get our briefing. It was simple. Tell them which vehicles held the source. I could not open a vehicle until I asked first.

"On leash or off?" I wasn't sure why I asked, but it was likely because I wasn't sure what I wanted to do myself.

"Either way, whatever you are used to doing is fine. Same with where you want to start."

Nodding, I tested the wind, and then went to the furthest vehicle, and started my search. I made the decision to start her on leash, and within minutes realized it was a mistake. I was getting in her way; she was tripping me. I stepped away, unleashed her and suddenly, our flow happened. It just fell into place, that rhythm we had when working together.

"Good dog," I watched as her focus changed, and every change of behavior I knew to watch for happened. Jael, ignoring my nerves and inadequacies, stuffed her nose into the crack between the passenger door and the car's frame and pulled in a nose full of air. With no hesitation, she sat. Not only sat, but barked.

It was at that moment I failed my dog. I equivocated. Was she right? Did she really find the first source? This test only allowed one incorrect response, so if I called this and it was wrong, I couldn't get anything else wrong the rest of the week. And there was still eleven other sources to find.

I moved her on to the next vehicle, only to have my dog race back and actually paw at the door, sit and bark. I called her one more time, when I heard a snort behind me. It was one of the evaluators. Realizing what had just happened. I finally, timidly, raised my hand to indicate a find by my dog.

242

"And it's about time – that dog was ready to bite you. Next time, trust your dog," He shook his head and I sent Jael back to work. The next source she once again gave a solid final trained response. I was better about calling the find quicker, and was told to put my dog in the vehicle to locate the source.

Jael happily jumped into the cab of the small sport utility vehicle. I watched from the driver's door as she checked the cab and then hopped into the second seat. I heard it; I didn't see it. She huffed. It was a classic sign she had found her source.

I glanced into the back and there was my dog, ears standing straight up, peeking over the back seat. She was sitting, I could tell. Feeling stressed once again, I finally said, softly, "Touch it girl."

Jael's head disappeared and then popped up again. How close was she? Was she close enough to pass? What to do; ask her again?

Finally, I sucked it up and called out "My dog has given her final trained response in the back section of this SUV." I was pleased with myself; I was trusting my dog.

"Where in the back, eh?"

"I can't see her well, but it appears she's indicating a spot in the corner of the passenger side, far back section."

"Reward your dog; and good job this time."

During our lunch break, we all chatted about the testing, and I learned two of the handlers had called incorrect finds by their dogs. Exactly what I worried about constantly and I knew could happen to me.

The afternoon testing was the wilderness area, and thankfully I had no problems with trusting my dog as we were both in our element.

That night, both dog and I slept like rocks. I didn't think I'd sleep at all with my nerves but apparently those very nerves had worn me out.

With morning came another area I felt comfortable in; burials. Jael had exhibited a flair for burials since she was young, I wasn't worried at all. Until my dog slammed her little behind to the ground and I called it; and was told it was incorrect.

I wanted to cry. I muttered under my breath about doing as they told me to, trusting my dog. Apparently, my evaluators weren't deaf, as their response was, "Trust your dog until I tell you not to!" This made no sense to me, so I left it.

The reality was I had no mistakes left to make. If my dog missed a source, or I called one incorrectly again, the test was over. Struggling to understand what happened, I sent Jael back to work. I had not rewarded that sit, and so she went back and sat again. Frustrated and actually shaking, I spit out "LEAVE IT" to my dog. I saw her confusion and wished I hadn't yelled.

She went back to work, and after ignoring several more attempts to give me that same spot, she finally gave me some of her behaviors before sitting at another mound of dirt. I had no idea what to do, we had checked the area over three times, and I never saw what I normally would have seen from my dog. I finally raised my hand as my dog started to bark at me.

It was wrong. The evaluators simply shook their head. I was done. My dog was no longer certified. I had this happen before, but I just couldn't accept it this time. The last time, I had another dog I could work. Now I had none. I didn't understand what happened. My dog was always solid on burials.

I wasn't completely able to hide the tears, and I was suddenly very happy I didn't know anyone well, as I would have lost it completely with friends.

Putting Jael back into my truck, I overheard a couple of the handlers who tested ahead of me that they, too, had failed. They were as upset as I was, because they, too, were usually solid on burials.

After the last dog ran, the evaluators called us all together, and let us know that, for whatever reason, the burials had gone wrong for just about everyone. They were not sure what was wrong, but they had the authority to reset the test for a different day, if everyone was agreeable.

For my part, I was happy to be given a second chance. I couldn't believe that it was happening, but I grabbed at it as soon as it was offered.

That afternoon we worked the water portion of the test, and I was incredibly happy with my dog as she nailed the problems, one from a boat, and another along the shoreline.

Joining several of the other handlers for dinner, I learned that only the first two dogs had passed the burial, and after that, everyone either failed completely or only got one correct.

"What happened between the first two dogs and the rest of us?" It was the handler of another sable German Shepherd, only his dog was a solid thirty pounds heavier than my dog. Still, he was a beauty and aced all the other stations before the burial.

"Someone said one of the handlers probed the holes but forgot to clean it between probes." We all looked down the table at the person who spoke, and realized it was the handler that went first, and could have watched what happened.

Probing the earth was a common enough thing to do when searching for burials. Probes, which could be any long, slender object, were used to pierce and enter the ground, which allowed odor to filter to the surface faster. Generally they are used on burials of any significant age, or in soil that was compressed, like clay, to help aerate it.

For myself, I wouldn't probe a burial that was only twelve to twenty four hours old. Our test burials were less than twenty four, and listening to the other handlers, it sounded as if they felt the same.

"Well, if that's what happened, and a probe was put through a source by accident and then stuck in the ground all over out there, it sure explains quite a bit. The dogs would have the odor of human remains all over the field!"

Either way, I was happy for the opportunity to try again and show what my dog could really do. The next morning, we started again in a new area for the burials. After what happened the day before, however, my confidence was shot.

To make it worse, I was up first this time. Walking up to the search area, I kept telling myself to chill out, to calm down, and to not stress. It wasn't a particularly successful method. The only thing on my side at that point was my dog. She was ready to go, and when I released her leash, I could only pray we would be alright.

Within minutes I saw what I wanted to see. Jael had dropped her nose and was detailing along a small natural groove in the ground, reaching a certain point, I could actually hear her snort into the ground. Her whole body went still, she pawed once, sniffed one more time and I saw her tail begin that steady swish-swish. I had my hand up before her rear hit the ground.

"YES – reward the pretty little dog of yours!" Relief flooded through me, and the next find was as solid as the first. I couldn't help it, as we left the field I was whooping it up with my dog.

Returning back to the truck, I was flooded with nearly as much exaltation as I felt after passing the disaster testing. It lasted for a good hour as I watched the other handlers and their dogs. It was as I was watching the last dog team that I remembered this wasn't the climax of the testing. There were still two stations left to go; building and rubble.

Thankfully the rubble was a breeze for Jael, who had just passed a similar test, although then she was finding living people.

The last day, we finished with the building test and the fear settled in my gut once again. No more errors. That is the mantra that went through my head as I got my dog ready. It didn't help my confidence when two more handlers failed ahead of me.

Entering the building, I stood at the door and let Jael adjust to the odors in the room before letting her go. It was dark in the rooms, and I worried I had forgotten my flashlight. Tapping my pockets, I finally found it and pulled it out, just as the evaluator asked why I wasn't using one.

Shining it into the room, I could see my dog moving fast, and zip past me to head for the next room. The evaluator, suddenly behind me, snapped, "Did she search that whole room?"

"She didn't need to, if there was source in there, she'd still be there," I responded back as confidently as I could. I only hoped I was right.

A moment later, I heard that distinctive huff. She was in odor, and I was hanging back answering the evaluator.

"Excuse me, my dog is in odor," I slipped past him and found my dog scratching at a closed door. "Can I open this door?"

"Yes, you can, your search warrant covers this room."

I don't know if he saw me roll my eyes in the dark, but I hoped not. I slid the door open a crack and watched my dog's head, letting her breathe in. Then I opened it to give her full access. It was like a skunk in the room, as I had heard one trainer say some years ago. The whole room smelled of cadaver. I very nearly backed out it was so strong. But my dog was working, so I remained at the door.

It was soon obvious that the odor was overpowering her as well. She was struggling to locate the source, and was bouncing from one side to another, sniffing up a wall and over a desk.

"I'd like to take my dog out of the room for a moment and let her clear her nose, then we'll go back in." He nodded and I took my dog outside into the air. She sneezed twice and gave a complete body shake, something I'd never seen her do before, but heard other handlers say their dogs did. It was like they were shaking the entire odor off of themselves.

I took her back in, and the second time was the charm. She immediately dove for a filing cabinet and snorted at the second drawer. Calling the find, I was happy to see them nod at me. One source left to find, and if we failed it, we would still pass. We didn't fail it however, as Jael located the source in the drawer of a desk a few rooms down.

Walking out, the evaluator had one parting comment for me, however. "Learn to use that flashlight properly. Don't shine it right at the dog, shine it on the walls above her, it helps illuminate

248

the room without blinding everyone." I nodded and thanked them, happy for the advice, but happier we had passed yet another certification.

Returning home, I called the unit to let them know all was well. As I was speaking, I heard my dog whining in the back. A moment later I could smell it. She had pottied in her crate. Stopping the truck, I discovered my little heroine had not only pottied, she had diarrhea, and it was all over the back of my truck.

Staring at my poor dog, all I could do was shake my head and remind myself that into every life a little rain must fall. I had my moment in the sun when Jael passed her test. Now I needed to get back to earth and clean up the mess.

Dr. Mikkelson quickly diagnosed the problem; it was the water from the campground. I had only let her drink it twice, but it was enough. In a few days, she was fine and back to her crazy self, which included banging into poor Ari as he was moving slower now.

She needed a puppy to play with was my diagnosis on her behavior. Ari no longer played with her, he was becoming more and more cautious of being knocked into, or even patted too hard. Watching him age was difficult, and yet, it was a normal part of life. It didn't mean I had to like it.

# Chapter 19

### *The darkness doesn't hide me from you;*

G etting back to work at McCaffrey, I found Betsy had done a good job with keeping things up in the office, but I heard there was a slight clash between Bella and Betsy. Agnes filled me in as I checked the registrations for the upcoming week.

"I have no idea what she was thinking, but Betsy sort of got the idea that she's Bella's boss. You might need to smooth some ruffled feathers."

"What exactly happened, do you know?" I printed out a report, checked the totals, and then looked up at her.

"It seems that Betsy was giving Bella direction on how to do her job, and Bella was, well, telling Betsy to mind her own business. It didn't go well after that."

I nodded and figured cleaning up my truck after Jael's little incident was far more appealing than dealing with yet more personalities.

I called them into the office area and sat them both down, deciding that at this point, I had to be the boss and not the friend.

"First, let me say that Betsy, things in the office look pretty good. There are just one or two things I'll go over with you later on. Secondly, the reason you're both here, however, is I've heard of some dissension. Bella, can you tell me what the issue is?"

Bella, who had been with me from the start at McCaffrey, had always been a quiet, low-maintenance employee. She came, she worked, she did an excellent job at her tasks, rarely complained, and yet I knew she could have a sharp tongue. It was rarely felt, but it was there.

251

"I've worked here a long time, Rebekkah. Ya, sure, she's young and learned to do the office stuff, but I don't want her telling me how to change and make up a bed. I can't take the time to deal with that nonsense."

"It isn't nonsense, Bella. I'm offering suggestions on making your job easier, not harder."

"Telling me to bundle each room as I go along, but no clue how to tote those bundles is stupid." She was set in her ways, that's for sure.

"Okay, ladies, stop for a moment." I wanted to walk out; I was just tired of it. Who was right, who was wrong. I wasn't a counselor to tell people what to do with their lives, or how to change their lives, or who they should love or date.

Thankfully, they did quiet down. I waited, taking a few deep breaths to let myself calm down. I'm not sure why this conversation was grating so hard on my nerves, but it was.

"Here's my proposal. Betsy, please write down your ideas that you think would help McCaffrey function better. Be clear, and don't offer a suggestion without backing up how it will be accomplished. If you think this bundling idea would help, consider how the bundles would be handled; alright?"

She nodded, looking as if she had won the argument, that is, until I turned to Bella.

"Bella, you have worked here since we opened. You know what you deal with in your daily chores. I'd like you to consider some ideas for change, realistic changes that could help you. For example, would it be beneficial to have a laundry chute added to the House? Where would you put it?"

As both women started to talk, I held up my hand, "No, I want it all in writing. Until you have submitted the ideas, I want you to function based on the current system." Seeing Bella's eyes widen, I just shook my head.

"You both will submit your ideas in writing within the next two weeks. If one of you doesn't, I'll assume you're willing to adopt the other person's ideas wholeheartedly. Agreed?"

There was a nod from both, and at that point, I relented just a little. I was just feeling tired of trying to walk through the minefield of personality conflicts.

"Please, both of you, consider that every time you have a conflict of interest, you are disturbing the peace of this house and our guests. Please don't do that."

With that, I stood up and watched them leave. I had no idea what I'd do with their ideas, but it gave me a two week hiatus.

Bella stopped at the doorway of the office and looked back. I could see she wanted to, as we used to say, make nice in the sandbox.

"Rebekkah, I'm sorry. I just didn't think about it and how it would affect others."

I nodded and accepted her apology, hoping if Bella could move past it, things would settle down. After she left, I sat back in the chair and felt drained. I didn't anticipate or want my next visitor.

"Hey, you busy?"

"Go away, I'm busy." I sat where he found me, slouched in the office chair; my head tipped back, my eyes closed. I had a resounding headache, which in turn made my stomach queasy.

"Yes, I guessed as much. Well, I won't take up too much of your time, as I can see you are quite busy today."

"Go away, Benjamin." I repeated myself. I did not want to play word games with him just now, but I knew he wouldn't leave. I finally squinted at him, only to find he had that devilish grin he was so good at. On top of which, he had a sugar cookie in his hand.

"Fine, but don't take any longer than it takes me to wolf that cookie down," I took the offered bribe and waited. I hoped putting some food in my stomach would help.

"I just wanted you to know that we may have a break in the case, and wondering if you and Chris would be available on Saturday."

Brushing the cookie crumbs into the wastebasket, I pulled the calendar closer and slipped on my reading glasses. As I leaned over the book, a shadow fell over it and I looked up to find he was leaning over me, trying to see it as well.

"Here, Benjamin, you check it. I believe I'm scheduled to work, but I could possibly switch with someone. I'm sure your young eyes will find it faster."

I shoved the calendar over to him, frustrated that I actually couldn't read the words on the page.

"I doubt my eyes are any younger than yours. If I'm not mistaken, they are actually older. I just wear contacts."

"So do I; and I still need to use reading glasses," He didn't respond, which was likely a good thing.

"Can you switch? I would like you there." He was serious; I could hear it in his voice. I nodded, and standing up, I very nearly passed out. One moment I was tired and cranky, the next I had Benjamin helping me into my chair.

"What's going on Rebekkah? Should I call Dr. Sheffield?"

"I don't know, just felt light-headed all of a sudden. Actually, I don't feel good at all." And with that, I embarrassed myself further by throwing up into the wastebasket that held my cookie crumbs. Now it held the cookie too.

He held me as I violently vomited again, keeping my long ponytail out of the way, and yelling for Agnes at the same time. It wasn't Agnes who came, it was Martha. I could tell by the efficiency with which his requests were accomplished.

"Call Dr. Sheffield, and can you get a cold wet rag?" I sometimes forgot Benjamin had been a paramedic, and still was as far as I knew. While I was humiliated beyond belief, I was very glad for his training at that moment. He was strong enough to keep me from falling into the wastebasket, and at the same time kept the damp cloth on the back of my neck.

I really didn't care much about what happened after that. I was simply sick and wanted to die. Somehow, they got me to the clinic, where I continued with dry heaves, which are incredibly painful and exhausting at the same time. Through the fog of feeling horrible, I heard them talking about me, and I wondered, somewhere deep inside, if I really was dying.

I ended up in the hospital, and this time, it was my mom who came to see me. I hadn't been so miserable in so long, it was hard to deal with. One moment I was hoping I wouldn't die, the next, wishing I would.

I knew there had been visitors, but my memory wasn't keeping track of them. Eventually, I started to improve; but moving was hard, my body was so incredibly worn out. I was

255

glad I didn't remember most of it, but it felt so very uncomfortable knowing that everyone I knew had to have seen me at my worst.

They told me it was four days before I sat up one morning and informed the nurse I felt filthy and wanted to get cleaned up. While I remember asking for a shower, I didn't know then it had been four full days of being ill.

They finally determined that, like my dog, I had eaten or drunk something at the seminar that had done me in. It dawned on me as I slowly recuperated that although I had drunk only bottled water, I had used the tap water to brush my teeth.

A shower never felt so good that I could recall. The nurse helped me wash up, and even went so far as to help me wash my hair, which, in my opinion, needed it the most. The rest of me they had kept fairly tidy. I didn't have the strength to put my hair up in a ponytail and the nurse really felt I should leave it down until I informed her I'd look like a pot scrubber if it wasn't combed smooth and tied up in some way.

Clean, but completely drained from it, she found someone else to come and assist getting me back into my bed. I was hooked to an intravenous line which we had towed along as we went from bed to bathroom and back to bed again. I smiled up at the good old fashioned lactated Ringers; just like my dog had received when he nearly died.

"They put something in there to cheer you up?" Looking up, I saw Benjamin and the very beautiful, what was her name again? Something that matched her perfectly, but I couldn't come up with it. He carried a bud vase with a single, perfect peach colored rose. I sniffed it and was pleased he had gotten a flower with a strong spicy aroma.

"I was thinking how they used the same stuff to make my dog better too." I nodded up at the bag of Ringers. He smiled and touched it, turning it slightly as if to read it, but I knew he knew exactly what it was.

"So, you're feeling better I see. And it's about time. We had you scheduled for a search yesterday, in case you had forgotten."

"Yes, I guess I had. I had a previous engagement here, as you can see. Can I ask what happened?" I glanced over at, what was her name? I wasn't sure if she could hear what he might say.

"Oh, Priscilla is back in town for the weekend. We postponed it just so we could have you there. The search, I mean." He smiled engagingly, but I had a feeling more was going on than I was aware.

"How are you doing, Rebekkah? I hear it was touch and go there for a bit?" Priscilla's voice was as I remembered; melodious and low.

"It was? I know I wanted to die there for a bit, but I didn't realize it was that bad. Was it, Benjamin?" I saw a shadow cross his face, and instantly I knew she was right. It was a scary thought, knowing I might have died.

"Well, I guess you're stuck with me for a little longer. How is my mom holding up? And the dogs? She hasn't given them away yet, has she?"

He laughed, and it sounded rather shaky. Looking up at him, I finally asked, "Are you alright? It wasn't catchy, was it?"

"No, it was all yours. Your mom struggled a bit, so I went and stayed at your place with the dogs so she could stay close to the hospital. They are pretty incredible. I've never realized how obnoxious Jael can be."

257

I laughed, feeling sorry for anyone who had to live with my dogs without any type of warning, "Well, thank you for being willing to sacrifice yourself for my dogs."

I felt his hand touch where the tubes were feeding into me, and again, I had a feeling he was using it more as a means to cover something else. What, I had no idea. Had someone else died while I was sick?

"Benjamin, is Ari okay?" He looked up, rather startled.

"Yeah, he's terrific, why?"

"You are scaring me a bit, you're very subdued. I know you can be quiet, but never subdued." He gave me a rueful smile and was saved by my mom coming in. He gave her a hug, and putting his hand on Priscilla's back, they left with a small wave to me.

"Hi mom, I hear you had a rough time of it. I'm so sorry!" We had a good hug, which with my mom, was something unusual.

"I'm really tired, but tell me what happened while I was laying here, being sick and feeling sorry for myself," I put my head back, and as my mom filled me in on the world outside of my hospital room, I fell asleep.

Now that I was on the mend, I had more visitors, more flowers, more plants and cards. I couldn't wait to go home, see my dogs, and try to regain the strength I had lost. I had also lost several more pounds, which wasn't exactly the way to do it, but I was secretly glad.

Adam and Amy helped move me back home, with Adam doing all the driving. No one was convinced that I wouldn't fall asleep at the wheel. I had developed the habit of falling asleep at odd moments, but of course, I wasn't entirely aware I was doing it.

My dogs were beyond reason as I walked with slow steps into the house. Jael, in typical Jael fashion, was jumping all over me and around me. Ari, trying to avoid his sister, sidled up and leaned against my leg, content to have me press him closer to me with my hand.

My mom made up the couch in the family room for me to sleep on so I wouldn't have to walk up the stairs to my own room, or, more worrisome, down again. Gary informed us it would take more than a couple of days to rebound, but I pushed myself anyway. I wanted to get out and work my dogs.

To my amazement, however, Benjamin still came every day and took Jael for a run with him to burn her energy off. He left Ari with me, knowing he couldn't keep up with them. When he got back, he'd take Ari out on his own and play with him, leaving the monster child, now tired, with me.

My mom informed me that without him, she wasn't sure what she would have done. No one else had the time to do what he had done. She asked if it would be alright with me if she invited him to Thanksgiving dinner with us. It was only a few short weeks away, and he usually went to McCaffrey House or the church's free meal. I agreed, thinking it wasn't much considering how much he had done.

What mom didn't tell me was he would bring Priscilla. While her presence stumped the entire community, I had begun to like her, in spite of her perfect looks and the fact she appeared to be living with Benjamin without the benefit of a marriage license.

I had been raised, and still believed, to honor the sanctity of marriage. Living together just didn't mesh with my Biblical

259

beliefs. Still, as they walked into the house, I had to acknowledge what a handsome couple they really were.

Agnes arrived next, followed by Connie and Dave. Mom had made a spectacular turkey dinner with all the trimmings, and she didn't scrimp on anything. Thankfully, my body was still only allowing small portions, or I might have indulged far more than I should.

After the meal, my mom and the guys went into the family room to watch the Minnesota Vikings play the Dallas Cowboys, while Agnes, Connie, and Priscilla helped me clean up.

Priscilla, I learned, was on a music scholarship, and hoped to become a concert pianist someday. As we got to know her, I realized what a sweet young lady she was as well, and she seemed to have done wonders with slowing Benjamin down as no other woman had been able to do yet. I wondered, I couldn't help it, how such a sweet girl got involved with Elk Ridge's most notorious confirmed bachelor.

She didn't talk about him or their relationship however, and somehow, we all knew not to bring it up. I had to admit a very deep curiosity about it though, such as how they met, if it was truly serious, and if Benjamin's question that day about being gullible was about her.

Saying goodnight as everyone left, I was startled when Benjamin gave me a strong hug, and whispered in my ear, "I'm so glad you are here Rebekkah."

Looking back at my mom, she shrugged. Neither of us knew what had brought on that sudden show of emotion. It was nice, however, to get a hug like that. He ruined it, as usual, by finishing with, "By the way, I wanted to tell you, you are the first person I've met who can throw up really lady-like."

260

I was back to work fulltime by the week after Thanksgiving, and upon my return, I discovered that not only had Betsy and Bella made up, they had made the improvements Betsy had suggested and also ones that Bella had come up with to help them both.

The rest of the ownership had agreed to them, and with minimal work, a laundry chute was nestled into a back wall of the top floor which dropped the clothes directly into the laundry room in the garage. It saved Bella time and back pain. In addition, a small laundry cart was ordered which helped them with moving both clean and dirty bedding.

Connie, settling herself into the full routine of McCaffrey, was starting to test her own recipes on our guests, and the best compliment she could receive was from The Sisters who informed me she was getting her own requests for her recipes from our guests.

As McCaffrey prepared for another Christmas, my own excitement was to receive another Christmas card from Arturo and his family. We had set up a mapping system, where they let me know where he was, and what he was picking, such as grapes in Colorado in September. We had become rather like a distant family with them, and the map on my office wall helped remind me of a life so very different from my own.

I celebrated Christmas with my whole family for the first time in many years. It didn't take a rocket scientist to figure out my mom had made sure they knew they had nearly lost their sister, and with the help of Betsy, had arranged for rooms for all of them at McCaffrey without telling me.

It was wonderful to see everyone. I think we all realized how brief life can be and that one should never neglect their family. As we went to the Christmas Eve service together, I found my arm linked with my sister and sharing giggles on childhood memories.

"Remember how dad used to stick his false teeth out at bad drivers?" We laughed gaily, the recollection of my father's sense of humor still feeling fresh, even today. My brother caught up and reminded us how dad used to pump the gas pedal in whatever vehicle we had back then to the beat of the radio. Thankfully, he did it only on the back roads, but we children loved it.

Childhood reminisces made way for memories about growing up in a family that moved as often as the military required my dad to move. And after the military, his own chosen profession of being a pastor continued our frequent moves. That is, until the last few years before he died at the age of fifty; far too young.

On that sadder note, we entered the church and found a place to sit as a family. In fact, a few neighbors stood up and moved just so we could stay together.

As the service progressed, Pastor Dave and Father Michael asked for a moment because one of our community members wanted to share a blessing.

Amy and Adam, along with Grace Pearson, went to the front, and I was amazed how little Charlene had grown already. I was so used to dogs that shot up quickly and then stopped; it seemed odd to see almost a small child already.

"Thank you, we won't take much time, but we wanted to share this with all of you, the community and family of Elk Ridge. All of you know Grace Pearson, Megan and Tommie's mom. This past week, Grace has made the decision to allow us, Amy and me, to formally adopt Charlene as our own daughter." There was a moment of complete silence, and then the "amens" began, like a small rolling river, across the congregation.

"This decision was difficult for her, so I want to say this in front of all of you, as a testimony for Grace," Adam turned and faced Grace, taking her hands in his as he spoke, "Grace, you and George are a part of this community, and this family we call Elk Ridge. Just as if you had raised us as your children, we promise that Charlene Rae will be raised to love, honor, and respect you and George as her grandparents. You will be welcome in her life, and we pray she will be welcomed always in yours."

There wasn't a dry eye in the place, and I watched as Grace was enveloped in the love of the Drahota family, and indeed, the family of Elk Ridge. I don't know why, but something drew my attention to a few pews away from mine, and I saw Benjamin, sitting with Priscilla, and he, too, was crying. I don't think I had ever seen him cry before.

The service ended and as people made their way into the basement for treats, I felt a hand on my arm.

"Rebekkah, can you stay up here for a minute?" Benjamin waited as others passed us and disappeared, and we were suddenly alone.

"I hope you don't mind, but I really wanted to talk to you, if I could, about Priscilla."

It wasn't hard to see just speaking the words was difficult for him. I simply nodded, not knowing what else to do.

"Rebekkah, a lot of years ago, I was a very different person than I am now. I didn't understand things about life and love and people I guess. When I was a young man, I lived for myself, and I wasn't the nicest guy in the world." He paused as he looked around, and I waited, still not sure why he wanted to tell me about his girlfriend, or his past, which he'd never talked about before.

"I had a girlfriend, nice girl, a Catholic, as it happens. I, well, she got pregnant. I paid her to get an abortion. I didn't want to be tied down by a baby, a wife, and that picket fence thing," his words had speeded up, as if he wanted them out of his mouth as fast as they entered his brain.

"What I didn't understand, was what it would mean to a woman, no, a girl, raised in the Catholic Church. She took the money; I left, and forgot all about it until just over a year ago."

He paused again, and I could see he was trying to formulate how or what he was going to say next. It was at that moment, I knew, and before he could continue, I simply said it, without stopping to consider it wasn't my news to tell, "She's your daughter, isn't she?"

If had shot him, I don't think he'd have been more surprised. He just nodded, looking down at his hands, which were clenched in his lap. Finally drawing a deep breath, he continued, "Priscilla found me. You know the story, her mom died of cancer, and she found all about me in her mom's things. It took a few months to track me down, and she contacted me. I had no idea what to think, I had assumed…"

"Let me guess, her parents sent her away to have the baby, assuming she'd give it up. Instead, she had the baby and raised Priscilla on her own."

"Yeah, how did you figure that one out?"

"She sounds like she was a pretty strong woman."

He smiled, and said, more to himself than me, "I guess so, although I never knew it at the time,"

I thought about how I had thought they made a handsome couple. It made sense that they would. She had similar features, although I hadn't put the pieces together until now.

"I've never told that to anyone except Pastor Dave. I'm ashamed of it. I'd basically forgotten it you know, buried the memory of it. Priscilla opened up that time in my life again, and I'm having a hard time dealing with who I was back then."

As we sat there, I realized Pastor Dave had come back upstairs, bringing the woman in question with him.

"I see he finally told you, Rebekkah." Glancing up, I wondered if I was the last to know, or perhaps the last to figure it out.

"No, she guessed it. I don't know how, but she did. I hate to admit what a coward I've been about this Dave. Rebekkah, I'd like to introduce you to my daughter. I was afraid to tell anyone, and even asked Priscilla to not say anything. It was incredibly childish of me. "

I don't know what came over me, but I wrapped my arms around her and felt her suddenly begin to cry. I had no idea why he was so afraid, but perhaps it was more the memory of what he had been that caused the fear.

Looking over her shoulder, I could see he was looking away, trying to hide his own emotions. Reaching over, I touched his arm, and he turned back toward us, tears coursing down his cheeks. I squeezed his arm in my hand before returning it to hold onto Priscilla.

"Welcome to the family of Elk Ridge, Priscilla. We had two new children added tonight," I whispered in her ear. She nodded against my shoulder, and I knew that they hadn't been sure of her welcome.

"Am I the only who didn't know?" I offered Priscilla a few tissues from the box at the end of the pew, and took a few for me as well.

"Actually, only Pastor Dave, Adam, and Amy know. Amy found out from Priscilla at the Christmas Tea last week. She just couldn't stand the deception anymore," He looked at her with the same look I remember Grace had on her face when she looked at Charlene. Half joy, half sadness for what was lost. It was a humbling look.

"I couldn't figure out how to just tell people. It sounds so simple in concept, not so easy in reality. I don't even know for sure what I was worried about. It isn't like I have a sterling reputation as it is."

"Well, I think we should go downstairs, snack on some goodies, and now is as good a time as any to step up and be a man. People will understand." Dave smiled as he spoke, holding his arm out to Priscilla to take.

Entering the room behind them, I could hear him introducing her, properly, as he should. Scraps of conversations came to me as I joined my mom.

"She was raised Catholic you know, actually attended a Catholic school."

"She's a pianist; she's going to school for it on a scholarship."

"Her mom did a marvelous job raising her."

As we left the church, I felt a hand on my arm, and turned to find Pastor Dave this time.

"Thank you for being so good about that tonight. He's been more worried about you than anyone else."

"Seriously? Why was he so worried? She's a beautiful young woman, looks to have a bright future. Her mom raised her to be strong and independent. That's a good thing. He should be proud of her."

"Except that he had nothing to do with who she is or how she turned out. He was there for one thing, and nothing else, and in reality, he feels guilty. He's still not sure how to cope with it."

"I guess I can understand that. How does she feel, do you know?" I could see Benjamin helping Priscilla into his truck, and wondered, again, how we could have missed all the fatherly signs that now looked like they were made in neon.

"Unsure, she hasn't talked to me that much. Maybe you and Amy could talk to her a bit. She has to head back to the city, back to school soon."

I slapped my head, literally. Yet another puzzle piece fell into place. Benjamin dressed to the nines, going into the Guthrie Theater. Of course, to escort his daughter to something she would be interested in.

Dave just looked at me, knowing me well enough that if it was something he needed to know, I'd tell him. It really wasn't; it was gossip, and now unimportant gossip at that. I was just glad I hadn't spread it around.

Amy is the one who made the arrangements for us to take Priscilla out for an afternoon. With Christmas in full swing, we decided to do a shopping stroll through the small shops in Elk Ridge, ending at a new coffee place that had opened just before Thanksgiving.

As we walked through the snow and tinsel and red bows, we learned more about Priscilla and her mother. It was clear her mom was her guiding star, the person who raised her to think for herself, but not turn a blind eye to others.

"What did she do, your mom?" I opened the door to the little "Minnesota Made" shop. The first thing that I noticed was a small white birch basket, full of wild rice, loose, with a scoop, a scale, and bags. Rather like a self-serve market.

"When I was young, she cleaned houses for people. Most didn't mind she had a small child, as long as I was quiet and good. Which, I wasn't always. She tells me often that if there was a piano in the house, she couldn't let me see it, or I would start banging on it." We all laughed, and I could see her, small, delicate, and yet banging on a piano.

"Oh look at this ornament!" Priscilla held it up so we could see. It was a grand piano, with a moose at the keyboard. It was very kitschy, yet the moose was adorable, and I had to admit, it made us laugh.

We continued on, weaving our way through the shop, and Priscilla went back to telling us about her mom.

"She was amazing, really. I'm not sure exactly when, but she and another lady decided to join forces, and soon, they hired another lady, and by the time I was in high school, they owned a very busy cleaning service. They had expanded and did not just homes, but businesses."

"I'm impressed, I barely find time to do laundry for us, let alone start a business." Amy bought some spiced walnuts for us all to share.

"She was an amazing woman. When she couldn't keep me away from the pianos, she managed to scrape enough money together so I could have lessons. She was so proud when I won the scholarship," Tears filled her eyes as she spoke, and I slid my fingers through hers, clasping them together. They were strong fingers, I could feel the strength.

"Priscilla, didn't she ever say anything about your dad?" Amy was the first one brave enough to ask. I still struggled with the thought of Benjamin as a dad.

"No, only that God allows us to make decisions, even bad ones. That the thing to remember is, He'll always redeem the mistake if we let him. She said I was hers."

"I'm sorry, we shouldn't pry like that." Amy gave her a squeeze and we went on to the next storefront. This store was new as well, and had trendy clothes and accessories. Interestingly, we didn't stay as long, although I could see they were busy.

"You aren't. Well, maybe a little. I am a stranger who showed up and claimed to be family to a man you all like and respect. I understand. To be honest, when I found his name among my mom's things, I had no idea who he was. It was paper clipped to the outside of a small envelope, and inside, I found five hundred dollars."

I felt startled. Her mother had not even used the cash he had given her. Had she considered it rather like blood money? Glancing at Priscilla, I wondered if she knew all about that part of her life yet; if they had even talked about it.

We ended up at the coffee shop, and after indulging in a number of treats at nearly every store, some purposely put out for sampling, and some we simply bought in order to try, I knew I couldn't put anything more in my stomach than some coffee.

Priscilla and Amy, however, split a chocolate croissant. I wished I could ask straight out questions, but it wouldn't be right,

I knew. I had no idea how much she knew about her father, or that he had tried to pay for her to be killed.

"How did you figure out he was your father?" It seemed an innocuous way to delve deeper.

"I asked my grandparents. Momma had made up with them when I was in junior high. I brought them the envelope, the money, and the note and just asked. They told me, I suspect, hoping to stop me from digging further into it."

"What did they tell you that would make you want to stop?" Amy sounded innocent, and I suddenly wondered if she didn't know about the abortion money. At Priscilla's answer, it was obvious she didn't.

"Grandpa said the man on the paper had given my momma the money to have an abortion, to terminate my life. But my momma wouldn't do it." She paused, and we could see tears sparkle in her eyes as she finally went on, "They didn't tell me until later, in a heated argument, that while they didn't want an abortion, they didn't want me either, at least not back then."

"Oh, Priscilla, I'm so sorry," Amy, too had tears, and of course I was hard upon their heels with mine.

"I'm not sure yet how I feel about it all. I wanted to meet my father, but I had no idea what to expect. Would he want to know about me or not? Wish my momma had gone through with the abortion? Or would he want to meet me, see his daughter?"

"May I ask; how did he react?" I had to know, as much as it seemed an intrusion into Benjamin's personal life.

She smiled, and said, "He started to cry, and you know what he said? He said it was if God had redeemed time for him."

"Benjamin said THAT?" Amy sounded as stunned as I felt. Benjamin, who only spent time in a church was when there was free food or to escort his new daughter? Thanking God for redemption?

"Well, it was something like that. It made me think of my momma."

The coffee gone, the croissant a distant memory, we started the walk back to my Suburban in the waning light. I had just one more question I wanted to ask, and wasn't sure how to ask it.

As if reading my mind, Priscilla touched my hand and said, so softly I almost didn't hear her, "Rebekkah, I have found I can forgive him for what he wanted to do back then. He appears to be a very different man now. I rather like him."

"We do too," I responded.

# Chapter 20

*But the night shines as the day;*
*the darkness and the light are both alike to You.*

The week after New Year's, Benjamin called me. I wasn't surprised when he asked if we could come back for the Derek Nieland search.

"Yes, you had a break in the case, if I remember correctly."

"Well, yes, we did have a break, but that one fell through, actually. The case is sort of, well, can you and Chris come back tomorrow? Our Law Enforcement Center this time, we're back in our home county."

We arrived as scheduled, the ambient air temperatures hovering right around ten below. While my dogs were used to working in the cold from training, we also kept the sessions shorter. I wasn't sure what to expect today.

The briefing was fascinating, at least from a cadaver dog handler's perspective. Their person of interest, the reason they couldn't access the property all that time, had died. Not just died, but died by electrocution in a freak accident. In the home they wanted us to search.

"How long was he in there, before they found him?"

"We're not completely sure, but the coroner believes about ten days. You see, it has been so cold, it really delayed decomposition."

I know my eyes widened. Glancing over at Chris, I could see she, too, was wide-eyed. They wanted us to search an area where a man was known to have lay dead for ten days, but they wanted us to find a possible murder scene from how long ago now; if there even was one?

"Okay, I know it adds a bit to the challenge, but we know where his body was found, and that helps by eliminating that spot," Benjamin was trying to convince us it wasn't as bad as it sounded.

"Only if he didn't die on the spot of the possible murder," Chris bravely piped up.

"All that aside, the family has been notified of our interest in the buildings and the curtilage. They are very supportive, and it sort of sounds like they harbored no great love for him. In fact, they hadn't spoken to him in several years. They inherited only because he died intestate."

No will would mean his nearest living relative took control of the creepy place. I actually felt sorry for them. Arriving on scene, I not only felt sorry for them, I bumped it up to a complete misfortune on their part.

The driveway wasn't really a driveway; it was a rutted track that led to the cabin that likely had never seen better days. All around the place trash, refuse, broken things were thrown about as if the man periodically threw a temper tantrum. The outbuildings were even worse, if possible, than the main cabin.

Taking a deep breath, we decided to draw straws as to who attempted the search first. I won, which meant Chris unloaded Onyx while I sat on the bumper of my truck, facing the other way. I had sudden recollection of the old neighbor, and wondered if he was shocked that the druggies were back, even with his weird neighbor dead.

I sat alone, except for my dog who was sleeping. I would have liked to say I was thinking deep thoughts, but in reality, I was just cold. Just as I decided to climb in the cab and warm it up, Benjamin showed up at my side and indicated I needed to get my dog out.

Pulling her out, I slipped on her search vest and pushed the tennis ball thrower into the small of my back. I added a second ball to my pocket for back up. We had been known to lose one or two on searches before.

Chris walked past me with a solid poker face, nothing to tell me anything. That was good; I didn't want to know anything.

I decided to start with an exterior search of the buildings, and within minutes, my dog had flown over to the second building to the north of the house. Checking with Benjamin first, I opened the door a notch, and let my dog take a sniff. Then I slid it open further.

It was a pit; no, it was worse than a pit. I wasn't even sure if my dog could get into the building, it was so crammed with junk. Stacks of magazines taller than I was; rolled up tarps, and broken furniture. Jael, making several huffing noises, tried to push and shove her way into the pile of debris. And she wouldn't give up.

I finally grabbed her collar and pulled her back, giving her a sit and stay command.

"Benjamin, can we move any of this?" I watched as he hesitated. His hand went toward his phone, and I made a counter offer, "You ask the question, I'll work her around the other buildings."

With that agreement, we left, although my dog was not happy. To finally appease her, I handed her the tennis ball as she sat at the entrance of the over-crowded and likely dangerous shed.

We did a modified tug game, and she only held on because she wanted the ball that badly. I wondered briefly if I finally find a way to train the tug finally.

I started her again, and as we worked closer and closer to the cabin, her intensity increased. It was then I remembered, the cabin is where the body we knew about had been for the ten days.

Still, I let her work it as we had no idea for sure if there wasn't another place in the cabin that might trigger a response from the dogs.

We entered the cabin and in just a few minutes, my dog was sniffing up the walls and staring at the ceiling. I glanced up and saw that there was a loft above us.

"Yep, that's where he was, the dog is right. We'd like you to check that crawl space too, however." He popped open a small square hole in the floor and I looked down at the shaky ladder.

"How do I get the dog down there?" I looked again. I didn't have a harness with me to lower her down, and I didn't trust that ladder to hold me, let alone me and my dog.

"You go down, I'll lower the dog to you." The DEA agent who stood by the hole sounded so sure of himself. I remembered the last time we attempted something like this. I still had the scar on my shoulder from Jael digging her claws deep into my flesh, trying to avoid it.

"Sure, okay, we'll try it." I put a leash on Jael and handed it to the officer. I started down the ladder and watched as my dog peeked down at me. If I was a betting person, I would have put all my life savings, which wasn't much; that my dog was waiting to watch me search the crawlspace on my own.

"Hand her down if you dare." I called up, my arms waiting to catch her, my winter coat zipped up so she couldn't catch me again with a claw.

A moment later, my dog was in my arms and squirming to get out and to work. I was stumped. I had never seen her so complacent about being lowered into a dark hole. Maybe she finally was learning.

I turned her loose, and too late, realized her search vest was catching on every single floor joist. Calling her back over, I pulled it off and sent her back around. I had my flashlight on, but taking a tip from my training instructors, I had it shining upwards, which actually gave the whole area an eerie effect as my dog looked like a gray-green shadow flitting around me.

I have to admit, I was very happy she never huffed once. There was no odor in the crawlspace. I started to lift her out when she saw the nearly vertical ladder. Every ladder she had been trained to climb was set a forty-five degree angle. I didn't move fast enough to stop her, and she started to try and climb up on her own.

I shook my head and simply helped lift her body rung to rung, giving her the illusion of climbing, but in reality, to get her paws to the next rung on her own, she would have fallen backwards and gotten hurt.

We arrived to the outer world in time to see Benjamin come in with news. Permission was granted to move as much junk as we wanted. Now, I just needed to identify the junk I wanted moved.

We returned to the shed, and I watched as the officers donned protective gloves and awaited my command. I had no intention of moving stacks of magazines, although they likely would fall anyway once we started moving things. No, we needed to move the bigger things in order to gain access.

It was Chris who came up with the brilliant idea of having my dog sniff items as they came out. It was an interesting concept, but I wondered if my dog would be patient enough to stand still. It was worth a shot, however.

First out was a decrepit wood rocker with a broken runner, followed closely by a box of tools. None of the items truly made sense; it simply looked as if someone pushed more stuff in until it was too full to add more. Part of me wondered if, by taking the stuff out, the roof and walls would collapse in.

Twenty minutes later, I was getting more restive than my dog, when she suddenly lunged, pulling the leash completely out of my hand. Every behavior went on parade as she tried to shove past the men to get back into the shed.

I couldn't see inside, so simply asked the man at the doorway, who was still holding the end of a roll of tarp, to tell me what he could see.

"She's sniffing really hard at the tarp below the one we just picked up. She checked this one first, but moved to the next one. She's scratching at it. What does she do when she finds human remains?" He asked suddenly.

"She sits, why?"

"You mean, like that?" He backed out, pulling the other officer with him so I could see. There was my dog, sitting on top of a pile of tarps. As soon as we made eye contact, she slashed her head downward, her nose grazing the top tarp and then she barked.

"Good girl, that's my girl."

"Can we take that one next? I'd like to have it put away from everything else you pulled out of the shed." I praised my dog and got her moved away so they could pull the next tarp out. I needed to verify if it was that tarp, or the one below, or something else in the shed. Odor, especially odor that had been there for some time, could permeate everything in the shed.

After they moved the tarp, the guys waited as I had my dog recheck everything that had already come out of the shed. While I saw her sniffing and showing some behaviors, she didn't show them all. As I watched, I remembered where I had seen that before. It was at our testing last fall.

It was when we had failed the burial station because a previous handler had inadvertently spread cadaver odor all over the field. It wasn't enough odor to get full behaviors from the dogs, but enough to throw confusion at their handlers.

As I walked her toward the tarp in question, Jael's tail bannered out and wagged gaily. She huffed and pawed, and sat on the tarp again.

"Good job, Jael. I believe you, awesome girl. Now come with me," and we walked back to the shed. Letting her enter ahead of me, I watched her muzzle.

It immediately turned toward where the tarp had been, but was no longer. And then it switched directions. It was an incredible moment for me as I watched my dog navigate through a myriad of smells and sights and slowly but surely hone into one area. I think we could have blindfolded her and it wouldn't have mattered.

She moved across the floor, stepping on things, stepping into holes in the floor boards, and then began to scale some broken wood slats. As she reached up, she pushed her head under what

279

looked like a small mattress, like for a crib. I decided that the slats were likely what was left of the crib itself, and allowed myself a moment of wandering thoughts instead of focusing on my dog.

She had located something, and she was bound and determined to get at it, although the mattress was already wedged at the top of the ceiling. Without pulling her head out from between the mattress and the slats, she began barking, and barking.

"Guys, she has located something by the mattress. I'm going

to pull her out again, let you get the mattress out of the way if you can."

I played ball with my dog over away from all the detritus that had come out of the shed. If we had to do another run by it, I didn't want her throwing sits just to get a ball.

It ended up I didn't have to run my dog again. Benjamin waived me back over and pointed at the mattress. At first my brain didn't understand what my eyes were seeing, but my dog didn't need her eyes, she had found cadaver odor, and she knew it. She sat once again and barked at me, doing that swishy thing with her head toward the mattress where it was darkly stained.

I tossed her the ball and walked her away, down toward a small unused trail where I threw ball after ball for my dog. As I walked away, I heard Benjamin tell Chris she could let Onyx approach so she could reward Onyx who had also given a final trained response on that shed. His only admonition was not to touch anything.

The dogs had located at least part of the place where Derek Nieland had lost his life. The forensics crew, who detailed the balance of the items in the shed as well as the building itself, confirmed what the dogs had already told them.

It was believed that Derek was shot while unconscious and lying on the mattress. Further analysis identified one of the tarps as having been used to transport the body, as fibers from the tarp were on the body, and vice versa.

The ending of the Nieland search was at once a relief and depressing. We had known he was dead, and likely murdered. The real problem was a question of what good did it do? To have helped find the proof, but not have anyone to prosecute seemed a slap in the face of everyone who worked so hard on it.

The family, angry with it as well, blamed law enforcement for not doing enough. Attorneys were called, the media reported, and Chris and I just hunkered down, hoping not to be dragged into it. I watched as Benjamin and the other officers in his department took hits from all sides, and it only made things worse for us emotionally.

Thankfully, the media attention died down fairly quickly as it always does, and the family went home to mourn. Elk Ridge Search and Rescue went back to our normal lives, and I, wondering why I had wanted a cadaver dog, started wondering about getting a new puppy again. This time, I wanted a live find puppy, one who found living, breathing people who needed to be rescued and not recovered.

Ari, the regal and dignified dog that he was, still looked amazing for his age. He had served as my live-find dog for so many years, I wondered if another dog would ever measure up to him. Watching him with his head held high as he walked around the yard, I also worried about bringing in a puppy to agitate and irritate him in his twilight years. Would it make him age that much faster?

He wasn't playing with Jael anymore except for a periodic play growl. In fact, he avoided contact as much as he could, other than a snuggle every now and then with me. The seizures, while still not horrible, were still hard to watch. It was a hard decision, whether to start a puppy search or not, but in the end, I decided to at least put out feelers. Then, I left it in the Lord's hands; or tried anyway.

# Chapter 21

*For you have possessed my inward parts;*
*you have covered me in my mother's womb.*

It was in February that Connie approached me, and I wondered what she had going on this time. The mystery only lasted only a short time as she slowly held out her left hand. A tiny diamond sparkled there, and I felt that momentary jealousy. Squashing it as fast as I could, I hugged her instead and told her how happy I was for her.

Margaret and Martha, having decided to take Connie under their wing as a chef, now went a step further and decided to play mother to her for all her bridal festivities. I had to admit noticing a change in Connie ever since she started dating Pastor Dave. It was quiet, the changes, but they slowly built on each other, and as I looked at her, I knew that she had truly come to accept herself, forgive herself, and was in a position to move on in her life.

I had to admit to myself that when I saw everyone around me growing, and changing, and learning to navigate to new lives, I felt stuck.

Perhaps it was midlife crisis, I wasn't sure. I looked at Arturo's map, and wondered about the life he led. Did he feel stuck? Traveling year after year, picking the same crops in the same places, or planting the trees over and over?

I was actually looking forward to the arrival of the planters again. It was something to look forward to anyway. I knew Connie's wedding would be as well, but that was months away yet. The planters, they would be here soon. We had planned another potluck to welcome them back, and the Vegas family had let me know that Arturo's son had joined him this year.

Pushing myself back to work, I opened the mail, and discovered a small card addressed to me. Opening it, I found a thank you note from Priscilla, and a smile, unbidden, came back to my face.

Before she had left, I had purchased the little moose at the piano ornament for her. I had anonymously left the gift wrapped box at the greeters table at the church on Christmas Eve. She must have figured it out.

It was with that card we started an old fashioned hand-written correspondence, and it served as another window on the world for me, to hear from her and the world she lived in. I felt free to tell this young girl about my feeling stuck, she felt free to tell me about being discouraged with her studies.

I shared with her the joy of watching Connie plan for her wedding, she shared with me about reconnecting with her grandparents, and how happy it had made her.

The week the planters came in, Elk Ridge welcomed them with another potluck, and I learned that several families had sort of adopted some of the planters, as Arturo and I had adopted each other. This year, we gave hugs and I watched as he carefully greeted my regal Ari. I could tell that this man cared about my aging partner, and would weep when I lost him as much as I would.

Arturo's son was taller than he was, and I was amazed at how old he looked, before realizing that Arturo himself wasn't younger than I was, but older. Oscar was a handsome young man, and spoke fluent English, which was handy for us.

Sending them home with the leftovers, we hugged and I promised to stop out later in the week to see them and take some photos for their families.

The week, however, got away from me. McCaffrey House suffered a major breakdown when the entire walk-in refrigerator in the kitchen died. It was old, we knew that, but it was still unexpected. The repairmen came, the repairmen went, and still no fridge. Finally an estimate was given for the repair. It was enough to stop us cold, no pun intended.

The request for quotes went out to replace it, and the bids came back in. The least expensive option was nearly six thousand dollars, and that didn't include installation; or removal of the old fridge. We were stuck, we had to do something.

An emergency meeting of the owners and advisory board was convened, numbers were crunched, and finally, a decision was made. We had to replace it.

I was midway through the process when I got an email from the Vegas family in California, wondering how their father and husband were doing. Feeling guilty about forgetting, I promised to go out the next day.

What I didn't anticipate was that I would be going out the next day for a very different purpose. The call came at about ten in the morning, and was simply to put us on standby, as there was a missing man in the Boundary Waters. I emailed Arturo's family to explain that, once again, my visit would have to be delayed, and why.

They were very understanding, and said they would pray for the missing man. Another call came in at five in the afternoon, asking us to round up our resources, as many as we could. The area was large and dense. They weren't sure of a point last seen, and could only tell us the person spoke limited English.

My heart stilled. There were several tree planters all over out there, what were the odds it could be Arturo's group? Slim, unlikely, but possible.

We pulled in K-9 teams from all over, knowing this one was way too large for us. We were first on scene simply because we were closest, but eventually, other teams would trickle in, some from as far away as six or eight hours drive.

Getting out of my truck, I felt a sense of horror as I recognized the young man standing by the incident command post. It was Arturo's son, Oscar.

I lifted a hand in greeting, but went straight to the area designated for check in. Most of Elk Ridge SAR arrived at the same time, and we received our briefing together.

"We have one missing man at this time. What we've been able to understand is, one of the planting crew was not feeling well and was going to return to their base camp. Their crew chief offered to go with him, leaving another man in charge. This sounds smart in theory, however our understanding is the man who was ill wanted to go off trail to take a nature break, and got lost. It is assumed the chief went in after him. The first man, the one who was ill, made it back to the trail. However the crew chief is still missing. We have a good interpreter; the problem is, he is the son of the missing man, so we have to go carefully here."

I blurted it out before I could stop myself, "Arturo is missing?"

"Do you know him?" The incident commander wasn't someone I knew, and I hoped he was good at his job.

"Our whole community knows this group of planters. Well, many of them, but some of them change year to year. Arturo, however, has been back for three years now."

Those around me were nodding, and I was glad we were here to help. We needed to find him.

"Good, then he'll hopefully be aware of things to do to stay safe," He paused, pointed at the map, and began an overview of areas that needed to be checked.

"What has been done so far to try and find him?"

"We have some sound attractants out there, stationary that blast every twenty minutes. We have several teams running trails, but the terrain out here, as you know, is rugged. We are requesting permission to move in mechanized equipment, such as ATV's, but we have to wait for the Forestry Department."

I saw Oscar raise his hand, and knew he was worried and intimidated and afraid all at once.

"This is Oscar Vegas. He can serve as an interpreter. What do you have, Oscar?"

"Sir, the crew, they've made some signs that if you think it would help, maybe we could get them hung up," Oscar held up a simple cardboard sign which had the words, 'Arturo - sigue las señales para estar seguro!'

"What does it mean?" Amos spoke up, wondering, as we all were, what it meant.

"It is my father's name, Arturo, and it means, basically, 'this way to safety', so we would like to put them on the trails and point the direction he should go if he comes out on one of them."

"That is a great idea, help him self-rescue if he can. Alright, unless there is anything else, let's get some areas split up."

I had signed in with my cadaver dog, not expecting to be utilized, but I was immediately paired with a young Forestry

287

agent and sent out to search. One by one, our unit members took their assignments, checked their radios, their maps, their GPS, their packs, and their water before deploying. Spare batteries for the GPS and flashlights were put in handier front pockets instead of the pack in the back.

I set out with Jael understanding that there was a chance my friend was already dead. I didn't want to think about that, however, and instead, focused on just working my dog as I normally would, without thought.

The day wore into night and we came in covered in black fly and mosquito bites. I couldn't believe the pests were out this early, but they were actually swarming us.

After a short rest and food, we restocked our water, and of course dug out the bug spray. We then went on to our next assignment. As we walked out, I heard the helicopter coming in. FLIR, or forward looking infra-red, could pick up on the heat signature of any human, or animal for that matter, out there.

My dog wasn't used to working at night. Most cadaver dogs are run during the day, mainly because dead men haven't been known to walk away, and would still be there in the morning. However, we still wanted to cover ground. I only hoped if Arturo was in our section and still alive, my dog would respond in some way that I would recognize.

By morning, we were bone tired. More searchers and dogs had been arriving all through the night, and were being deployed as we rested. I climbed in the back of my truck and stripped off my pants only to find three tiny ticks on me. I wondered how many were on my dog, ready to jump ship and land on me.

I also found our trip through a slash field, where they pile up all the trees that are cleared off, had taken its toll not only on my legs, but on my dog. She had a long abrasion up one leg. Thankfully it wasn't deep or concerning. I washed it off, put some antibiotic on it and let it alone. My own legs were banged up, but no skin was broken.

I slept fitfully for several hours before waking up and getting my next assignment. I saw they had gotten permission to bring in the ATV's, which was a blessing as they used one to transport us two miles away to my new area.

Within a short time, I had my answer if I could tell if my dog had found a living person. She had gone out of my sight when I heard her bell change from a steady ding-ding, to the rapid sound of a dog in full sprint. She hit me with her front paws, grabbed my pocket, ripping it, and raced back into the woods. I followed, but not fast enough for my dog, as I received two more hits like the first. As we came around a clump of heavy buckthorn, there stood a group of searchers.

"Way to go Jael, I'm so very proud of you, you found people. Awesome." I tossed her the tennis ball, before hooking up her leash. I apologized to the other searchers, and left with my dog. It wasn't until I was far enough away and too tired to walk back that I realized they were in our search area. I wondered if it was assigned to them, or if they were lost themselves. Or if I was so tired, I was the one that was lost.

By the end of the third day, I was starting to crack. The knee that had been the bane of my existence for so many years was now stiff and swollen, and I knew I'd have to stop at some point.

I had been praying hard the entire time, praying that God would direct searchers to Arturo. That he would walk out on his own. I didn't care who found him, only that he would be found. He had become part of our family.

As I came in from yet another search area with nothing to show for it but more bruises, bug bites, and ticks, I saw one of the cardboard signs they had made, this way to safety. By now, the paths were so well traveled, if he just stepped out and stood, he'd be found. But so far, he hadn't.

As I debriefed, I was informed that I was to stand down for twenty four hours to rest and recuperate. If I wanted to stay in town, they had arranged for a place at the local high school where the dogs could stay with us. The Red Cross had been providing meals on scene, but he was happy to report that the Salvation Army was providing meals at the school. He finished with the coup de grâce; there were showers at the school.

I took him up on his suggestion, and arrived at the school where I was able to set up Jael's crate by a cot in a small room, and take a shower for the first time in days. I found ticks residing in my hair and a few other places.

At that point, I went over my sable colored dog with finger tips and eyes closed. I had discovered years ago, with my longer-furred dogs, that I could feel the tiny ticks better if I wasn't focused on using my eyes. After twenty five ticks, I gave up counting. I just dropped them into an empty plastic water bottle that I could cap and throw away when I was done.

Given that I was in a room with ten other handlers, both male and female, I was surprised I slept. Being a control freak, it is hard to relax in strange places. But sleep I did.

I was sound asleep when they found Arturo. Someone shaking my shoulder and my dog barking at them woke me up. Looking up, I saw Amos and Marge standing over me.

"What, is it time to go again?"

"Rebekkah – they found him! They used the life flight helicopter with their night vision goggles. Apparently he managed to find a place that got cell phone reception and texted his son – they had him turn on his phone and hold it up – and they could see him from like, a mile away!" Marge, standing behind Amos, was nodding madly.

"Seriously? I can't believe it. Where was he?"

"Not sure, but get up and we'll go find out. Come on!"

With no time to reload my crate, I left it and just loaded Jael loose in the truck. Marge got in with me, and we drove out to the Incident Command post, and as I drove, I questioned our intelligence. They wouldn't want us there; they would be shutting down and sending everyone home.

We arrived and Oscar was the first person I saw. He grabbed me and swung me around, literally dancing with joy.

"Oscar, do you know where they found him?" I held out the map I had been using for the past several days.

"I think so, way up here, by this river here." If Oscar was correct, Arturo had traveled nearly six miles through some of the worst country in the area.

It ended up he was accurate in his father's location. Arturo, chewed up by insects, dehydrated, and a little feverish, was, however, alive and well.

He spent only a day in the hospital getting checked over, and was soon out again planting with his crew. I wondered if I was getting too old for SAR, that a man older than I was could travel that far in those conditions, while I was bruised, battered, and exhausted just trying to find him.

It helped my attitude when Chris dumped our GPS tracks and informed us that on average, we all put in some seventeen miles each on the search. Maybe I wasn't so old after all.

I met up with Arturo and his crew a few days later, and took the promised pictures for his family. Looking at him as he worked, I sensed this would be the last year we would see him. The woods had taken something out of him, and I was sorry to recognize it. He had faced dying alone out there, and he would never look at the woods the same. Instead of a place of work and beauty, it was a scary place to him now.

# Chapter 22

*I will praise you; for I am fearfully and wonderfully made.*
*Marvelous are your works and my soul knows it well.*

I returned to McCaffrey House and to my computer, trying not to scratch the many insect bites I had sustained. I was happy to see that Betsy had kept things going, and I didn't have much catch-up to do. Going into the kitchen, I found The Sisters were not only planning dinner, but Connie's reception dinner at the same time.

Shaking my head, I went to the library where I found a cushy chair and simply sat. I had fallen back into the familiar, if boring, path of my life in Elk Ridge. A short spurt of excitement that ended well, and here I was again.

I didn't hear the door as it opened, so I nearly jumped out of my skin when a hand dropped on my shoulder.

"Crying out loud, are you trying to give an old lady a heart attack?" Benjamin, that devilish grin on his face, dropped in the chair across from me.

"Old lady or not, I'm wondering if you would do me a big huge favor." I studied him for a moment. What kind of big huge favor could he possibly want from me? Safe answers were well-rehearsed in my life.

"Depends on the favor," I responded.

"Priscilla has let me know she has her first big recital and, well, I know you have that terrific fancy dress you rarely get to wear, and I have a tux I rarely get to wear, not even sure I remember why I bought it," He paused as I continued to watch him. It must have made him nervous, because he finally said in a much less gay tone, "And I don't want to go by myself."

"There are only two problems with your idea. First, while I do have a lovely dress, that last search wreaked havoc on my legs. I am not only covered in bug bites, but huge bruises which nylons would never cover. Second, Priscilla invited me too, and how do you know I haven't asked someone else?"

I had him, and it surprised me. Normally he would have had a sassy comeback. Nothing. I suddenly felt a bit guilty.

"Okay, so I don't have a date either. I'll be your mercy date if you'll be mine. Not sure about the dress yet, but we'll see."

He picked me up in his truck and I had to admit a moment of perfect silence in appreciation for what our sheriff could look like when he put his mind to it. Of course, a tuxedo helps almost any man look well. I only hope I measured up. The bites had cleared up, and with Connie's help, we masked the worst of the bruises with makeup before putting on the stockings.

It was a wonderful recital, with talented musicians giving their first real performance to an audience of more than their peers and parents. As we stood up at the end, I saw a couple near us who, when turning toward us, stop cold and stare.

I slid my hand onto Benjamin's arm and nodded toward them, asking softly, "Are they Priscilla's grandparents?"

The muscles in his arm went instantly taut. The answer was yes, although he didn't respond. Instead, he walked slowly toward them, with me still attached to him with my hand through his arm.

"Mr. and Mrs. Strong?" He said it in a tone that engendered forgiveness, if there was any to give. I studied them as we waited for a response. Mr. Strong was a solid American of no noticeable ancestry, but his wife was, if my guess was correct, Korean and as beautiful as her granddaughter.

"Mr. Rafael. I never thought to see you again."

"Yes sir and I'm sorry to intrude. I would like to tell you first, I'm very sorry for what happened so many years ago. I was wrong, and I hope that you will find it in your hearts to someday forgive me."

Mrs. Strong, her hand clenched on her husband's arm slowly loosened. She leaned forward and simply said, "I did, many years ago, when we first saw our granddaughter."

"Thank you. May I introduce a friend of Priscilla's and mine, Rebekkah James."

"Mrs. Strong, your granddaughter is quite as beautiful as you are. I am very pleased to meet you both. She talks of you so often."

"To be honest, we are still trying to make sense of why she should ever want to associate with any of you." When he finally spoke, I heard the pain more than the words.

"I don't know why myself," Benjamin turned and his face changed; I saw that look again of love, joy, pain and even guilt cross his face. Priscilla had joined us.

Invitations were extended to go to coffee, but the Strong's declined, and with only a brief moment for a hug and a few words of praise for his daughter's performance, they swept Priscilla away from us. Or more accurately, her grandfather did.

"Can I interest you in a cup of coffee, Ms. James?"

"Always, Mr. Rafael," I responded. He held out his arm, and I took it, our actions almost comically overdone. He needed some humor to ease the pain of watching her walk away. I don't know what possessed me, but I slid my hand from his arm and put it around his waist instead, giving him a squeeze of reassurance.

He dropped an arm around my shoulder and we left the concert hall into the cool night air.

I came home to find my dog had decided to make her own late-night snack. I found a small dark brown waxy paper shredded on the floor, along with an empty peanut butter jar. I finally realized the paper was the kind they put crackers in to keep them fresh. Peanut butter and crackers, well, it could have been a lot worse.

I was informed it was, of course, my fault as I left the peanut butter jar too close to the counter's edge, and my counter-surfing dog didn't need much encouragement.

"Really, Rebekkah, you've taught that dog some amazing things, why is it you can't teach her not to steal food off the counter?"

I had no idea. As we argued, I discovered my dog was whining, and glancing down at her, I had a moment of confusion. Was I imagining it, or did my dog look pregnant?

The second thought, hard upon the heels of the first, was that my dog was bloating. Rushing her to the clinic, Dr. Dan stabilized her while trying to figure out what happened. The peanut butter and crackers couldn't have caused the bloat, there were only a few crackers left in the wrapper and the jar was almost empty to begin with.

With no clear idea of what she had eaten, we were hesitant to give her something to heave it all back up, and instead, went to medication to help her digestive tract relax, and not fight the contractions trying to clear it.

The night was spent walking her, just as we used to do with horses when they got colicky. By morning, she was starving hungry again.

It was a day later that my mom discovered what Jael had gotten into. Opening the spare room we rarely used except for storage, she found wrappers of six different types of power and granola bars, a chewed up package of instant oatmeal, and, ground into the neutral ivory carpet, dark brown stains, which, upon damping to clean it up, smelled exactly like powdered cappuccino mix. The nearly empty container was found hiding under the bed. Jael had located and raided the stash of snacks Elk Ridge SAR kept for meetings and events. It's a wonder she hadn't died.

Ari, of course, hadn't partaken. He was likely telling her the whole time not to do it, and then left her to own devices. Not like he hadn't done mischief himself at times, but those times were long ago, and only half-remembered. Come to think of it, he never had done anything quite that stupid in his life.

I took the dogs to work with me, mainly to give my mom a break. There were times I wondered how I had managed all these years to have kept her good graces about my dogs. The thought of inviting yet another puppy into our home was something I hadn't brought up yet.

Ari had taken to simply lying in the office with me, and while he normally would follow me around the House, I had noticed there were days when he stayed on his big thick bed and waited for me.

The seizures occurred on a more regular basis, sometimes just a minute twitching of eyes and ears, sometimes they were worse and his legs would start to crumble beneath him. Thankfully, he'd never truly fallen, as often he would seek me out to support him when he felt it coming on.

I was holding him up during one of his stronger episodes when Connie peeked into the office. She saw what was happening, and just quietly waited until the moment had passed and Ari, with tail wagging, walked over to greet her. I was never sure if he understood something had happened, but I did know that he maintained his dignity throughout.

"Hey, hate to interrupt, but I'm hand delivering these. I know proper protocol says I should have mailed them, but oh well. Here you go!" She handed me a heavy cream-colored envelope and I knew it was her wedding invitation.

I stood and gave her a hug, realizing again how much of a transformation had happened in her over the past two years. Her relationship with Pastor Dave had been blossoming like the flowers in our garden. Slowly, petal by petal, their love had been opening up for others to see and enjoy in its beauty.

I thought of Margaret and Jack, in the twilight years of their lives, and yet they held hands and got silly as much as any young couple did. I had always hoped to have something like that, someone that would be happy to age with me, and love me even when I was old and gray.

The wedding was perfect, with perfect weather, and perfect flowers, and a perfect reception. She was a June bride, and Charlene, being carried by Adam, was their not-quite ready for the spotlight flower girl. As she approached the front of the church, she turned, looked at all the people and started to cry, her little arms wrapped around Adam's neck.

Even that, however, was perfect as Connie took a small pink rose from her bouquet and was able to entice a smile out of the tears.

Connie's children, whom I hadn't seen in years, arrived and stayed at McCaffrey along with her parents. Pastor Dave's large family took up the rest of the rooms which were all booked for the event. His mom, tears in her own eyes, whispered to me that she had, at one time, held out hopes he'd marry me, but she could see that Connie was going to be a wonderful daughter-in-law.

I sat with my mom, and she cried with the best of them, which amazed me. When I glanced over at her, all she said was, "the redemptive power of love," and left it at that.

That night, as I walked my dogs through the woods behind our home, I allowed myself a small pity-party. I had sat with the single old ladies at the reception. Most were, of course, widowed, but it had sent a small bolt of fear through me.

As I walked, I asked God to help me to accept my singleness and use that time for Him instead of a husband or children. While it eased my heart pains, I knew that I'd still wonder, after all these years, why some of us, like Martha and me, were like we were.

Shrugging it off, I instead started planning my marketing strategy to my mom on how we needed a new puppy. So deep was I into my scheming, I nearly jumped when my cell phone went off.

"Elk Ridge Search and Rescue, how can we help?" I promised myself yet again, that I'd get one of those ugly bugs that hang out of your ear so I wouldn't have to keep digging for my phone and nearly missing calls, or worse, hang up on people by accident.

"Rebekkah? We have a toddler missing over on Hope Road; can you guys come?" Benjamin sounded concerned, a missing child always tended to escalate things.

"I can, but is it ok if I bring both dogs? Ari could use the boost to think he's still needed."

"Sure, I don't mind. I'll be at base and can watch him."

The unit responded quickly, as the area was close to most of us. The only one who couldn't make it was Amos, which bothered me. We could have used that big tracking bloodhound.

Arriving at the Incident Command post, better known as base to most of us, we signed in and Benjamin grabbed my arm and pulled me aside.

"We have a perfect point last seen, Rebekkah. Two tracks and then nothing as he went onto the tar road. Is there any way – any way at all – you could try the track with Ari? I know he's retired, I know you didn't recertify him, but the next tracking dog is four hours away."

"I'll ask the unit. He still trains, but he gets tired so fast, Benjamin, I can't promise anything."

The unit members, with an additional phone call to Amos, gave me the nod. I was petrified, to be honest. I knew my dog could track, but if it ever got out that I used an uncertified dog on a real search; I didn't want to think about it.

But I also saw Bobbie's parents standing nearby, hope in their eyes, fear in their hearts. I pulled my harness and long line out of the truck and carefully helped Ari onto the ground.

He gave a mighty shake that nearly took him off his feet, and with his head up, started to whine. He was as ready as I ever saw him. Putting on his harness, I took him for a walk around the area, and then up to the scent article, a tiny baseball cap, that was lying on the ground.

"Ari, scent," with barely a movement, his head dipped fractionally over the cap, "Ari – TRACK." I gave the command, hearing behind me, the parents questioning if my dog really got the odor.

He had, and as I slowly let out line to him, he cast in a circle around me. I knew he hit the trail by the sudden pull. It wasn't nearly as strong as it had been a few years ago, but it was sure.

He had located the two small prints in the mud, then another mark on the tar with a bit of mud on it, and then he was moving fast. Or at least he was going faster than he had been. He had never been a speedy dog, just a steady one.

Fifteen minutes into the trail, he began slowing. I knew he was tiring. His heart didn't work as well as it used to, nor did his lungs. But he was still on task, so I just let him slow to a pace he could handle. It was easier on me as well.

The odd thing was he was circling back toward the family's home. As we came back into the yard, I waved Benjamin over.

"Come up empty?" He sounded discouraged, knowing he'd have to tell the parents.

"No, he's still working. Benjamin, did you do a hasty search around and through the house?"

"Yep, all the way, twice, why?" I pointed at my dog, who was moving straight toward a deck attached to the side of the home. A moment later, his tail went into that steady swishing, and with a strong whine, he pushed his nose into the lattice work that surrounded the deck. It gave the deck a nice, finished look that enclosed it to the ground.

"Bobbie? Are you under there? My doggie would love to say hello." I waited, and a moment later, I heard a tiny giggle.

"His name is Ari and he loves kids, can you come out so he can say hi to you?"

A moment later, a tiny little boy came crawling out from under the deck, pushing aside the lattice on one corner. He stood up and toddled straight to my dog, who promptly gave him a big lick on his face.

The parents came rushing over, and Ari, terrified of being knocked down, stumbled over himself to get away. Still crouching down, I wrapped my arms around him and whispered he was fine; I'd take care of him. As I held him, I felt the muscles begin their horrible twitching, and I knew the trail and excitement had been too much for him. If I hadn't been supporting him, he would have collapsed.

"Benjamin, I need to get him home, can I go?" He turned from watching the family to look at my dog and saw what I saw often; my dog in the throes of a seizure.

"What happened? Oh my gosh, yes, of course, is he okay?" He reached down and put his hand my Ari's head, and almost instantly, the seizure was over. My dog sagged into my arms and I felt my throat constrict. Sliding my hand over his rib cage, I let out a sigh and could swallow again. That steady old heart, with the murmur he had since puppyhood, was still beating.

Benjamin simply scooped him up and carried him to my truck, letting Al explain the dog was all right, just older and the trail had worn him out.

Ari slept for longer than I'd ever known him to sleep. All day I had several calls for interviews, which I referred to the Law Enforcement Center. I had calls from friends who wanted to know if Ari was okay. I was happy to say he was; he was just tired.

I spent the rest of the week at home with him. I was proud of my dog; he had once more earned his supper, as we had jokingly said after searches over the years.

What I didn't expect was a letter a few weeks later, letting me know he was going to be given an award. Thinking it was related to the search, I contacted Benjamin, who claimed innocence. He hinted, however, that perhaps I should talk to my vet.

Calling Dr. Dan, I learned he had, indeed, submitted Ari for the award months before. It was a big deal, held at the Hilton in Minneapolis, with hundreds of people there to see it.

I recalled my own thoughts not too long ago about how my life's path never changed. Pastor Dave had given a sermon the previous Sunday, and with the coming of this letter, it suddenly made sense. I hadn't understood until now.

His reference was Psalms 139:1-6. It was a scripture I knew well; after all, my father was a pastor. Dave's focus was on verse three, and I read it in my favorite King James Bible, *"Thou compassest my path and my lying down, and art acquainted with all my ways."*

I loved the ancient and poetic King Jim, but it had fallen so out of use. As I studied it, I wondered what he meant by "compassest". A compass? My mind was wandering at the time, so what Pastor Dave said next went into my head, but wasn't truly heard until this very moment, days later.

"Some of you may see the word 'compassest', or 'perceive', or even 'chart' in your Bibles. I want to tell you, however, that the Hebrew word in that verse is the word 'zarah' – which means to winnow, or broadcast, or disperse. Sort of confusing if you say, the Lord disperses your path."

"Well, I want you to think about what winnowing is, what it does. To winnow grain means to sift it – to remove the dust, debris, and the things that don't belong."

There was silence in church at that moment; I remembered that because it brought me back from my own scattered thoughts.

"So, the scripture really is saying, that God sifts our path, our way of going, to help remove the debris and the things that don't belong."

As I stared at the letter in my hand, I realized that God had placed me in this path of Search and Rescue. He had cleared away things that He knew I didn't need. I just hadn't ever quite accepted it. I had wanted some of that other stuff in my life. But God, in His wisdom, was helping guard and clear my way to serve.

The day of the award ceremony, as I stood on the stage with my dog to receive the Professional Animal of the Year award, I knew this was God's reminder that He had blessed my life with some amazing dogs that had served their master well. I prayed that I, too, was serving my Master well.

Retaking my seat next to my mom, she leaned toward me and whispered how proud she was of us both. With a sly smile, I simply whispered back, "Proud enough to consider helping me pick out my next puppy?" With a shake of her head, she looked away.

A moment later, she leaned back and whispered, "Does it have to be another German Shedder? Your last two have ruined our vacuum cleaner." I smiled, knowing God had not only been working on my path, but on my mom's as well.

# *Reviews of Sharolyn's books*

## K-9 SEARCH: One Handler's Journey

*"Fun to read, it's hard to believe at times that this is a work of fiction."*

*"I enjoyed reading this book and hated it to end."*

*"Rebekkah's story makes you feel like you are there sharing in the tears of making the all too rare find and the heartache and joys of struggling to balance SAR with a "normal" life."*

## K-9 SEARCH: Journey Through the Storm

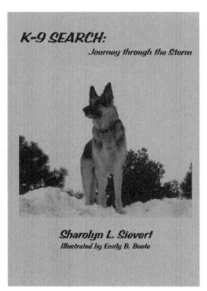

*"Where have you been hiding? A super book and hopefully just the first of many."*

*"Oh what fun! I thoroughly enjoyed reading about a handler and her dogs in Search And Rescue adventures!"*

*"Sharolyn wrote with so much love that you could feel it coming through the pages."*

## Available online at:

## *www.K9SearchBooks.com*

# About the Author

Sharolyn Sievert, an engineering coordinator by trade, has been active in search and rescue since 2003. She lives near Garfield, MN with her mother and her German Shepherd search dogs Ariel and Jael.

**Author with K-9 Ariel – age 10**

Sharolyn is an Air Force brat, her father having spent 20 years serving in the U.S. military. She was born on Mother's Day in Tachikawa, Japan. Her dad was an avid outdoorsman and hunter, however Sharolyn ended up going into hunting of a different type – using her K-9 partners to help find missing people.

Search and rescue gives her the ability to be outdoors, work with dogs and give something back to her community. Sharolyn over the years has trained and certified 3 search and rescue dogs in several different disciplines. She also has served as an instructor at national seminars, as an evaluator for K-9 teams and maintains certification in a number of areas related to SAR beyond the K-9 work she loves.

K-9 Search: Navigating the Journey is her third novel.

Printed in the United States of America

28514420R00179

Made in the USA
Charleston, SC
14 April 2014